THE BARRICADE

STEPHANIE ELLIS

LVP
PUBLICATIONS

Lycan Valley Press Publications
1002 N Meridian STE 100-153
Puyallup, Washington 98371 United States of America

Printed in the United States of America

First Edition

ISBN-13: 978-1-64562-022-8

"Stephanie Ellis worms her way under your skin with The Barricade, a monstrously grim dystopian tale exposing the human condition with all its frailties. Uncovering themes of abandonment, trauma, and mental health The Barricade examines exactly how far we might be prepared to go to survive the impossible, both as individuals and as a species. Provocative and compelling." —Lee Murray, five-time Bram Stoker Award-winning author of Grotesque: Monster Stories

"In The Barricade, Ellis presents the worst kind of dystopia: one which is all too believable, especially in the actions of the few who remain. With a diverse cast, and a compellingly underrepresented choice of protagonist, the author's unique voice and perspective bring this post-apocalyptic world to chilling life." —Kev Harrison, author of Shadow of the Hidden.

"With The Barricade, Stephanie Ellis has created a story where the strength of older women is celebrated. Topics usually shied away from, such as menopause, are part of the story just as they are part of everyday life for many of us. Her heroines are human, and it's the limitations they overcome that make them special. A riveting story that doesn't flinch from the worst in us and, in spite of this, somehow left me feeling stronger. An empowering narrative that will lodge in your thoughts for a long while." —Angela Yuriko Smith, 2x Bram Stoker Award® Winner

THE BARRICADE

THE BARRICADE

CHAPTER ONE

THE SCREAMING had stopped and the door remained closed. Faith continued to watch her only remaining neighbour's house for another minute before turning away. Linda was fine. Every other house in their cul-de-sac remained silent, as did those in the streets beyond. Those windows stayed dark. It was the same every morning.

She returned to the kitchen to find her daughter gazing out into the garden. Josie preferred this view, with its possibilities of nature's return. It worked provided you ignored the shadowy backdrop of the city's tower blocks.

Faith slipped her arm around Josie's shoulder and gave her a light squeeze.

"Regular as clockwork," said Josie, as she leaned back against her mother, continuing to stare into the early morning gloom.

"The worm turning," said Faith, thinking on

Linda's latest fixation.

It's in me, Linda had said, *It's in all of us. Can't you feel it crawling inside you?* Nothing anybody could say or do would dissuade her from the idea her body was playing host to an all-consuming creature, a slithering snake devouring her from the inside. They would stay with her, watch her poke and prod her stomach, occasionally prevent her from cutting herself open. She wanted to show them, she said. She wanted them to *see.* Their few remaining doctors had given up on her and her mania continued to progress. Only Josie seemed to take her seriously, paid closer attention. That worried Faith.

It was nearly eight o'clock and the sky was still dark but there was a shimmer of grey in the distance announcing day was about to break. Faith took it as a good sign, coming an hour earlier than on previous days.

"I'll go and sit with her when you leave," said Josie. "Two mad women together." Her laugh was humourless.

Faith pulled her daughter tighter. "No," she said. "Not mad, just troubled. Like everyone else in this godforsaken place." Sanity wore its colours lightly.

"You've put up with a lot because of me, Mum," said Josie, turning to face her. "I'm sorry, so sorry. You do know that, don't you? I mean, I'm not a kid any more. I'm not *that* kid."

At thirty-two, Josie was a grown woman but when Faith looked into her eyes, all she saw was the traumatised twelve-year-old from twenty years ago. There were many such fragile minds in their abandoned community, left to survive, left to witness the expected end of the world. How could anyone remain unmarked by that? They were all damaged, even Faith. She however, had a daughter to protect, could not afford to show weakness and learned to fight.

Increasingly, she noted snide comments about Josie's apparent inability to be a useful member of their society, her lack of contribution. Faith answered these accusations by regularly doubling her own workload. Not begrudged when Josie was a child, it was hard as she became an adult; harder still to suppress the resentment on those occasions when exhaustion claimed her. Even harder to deal with the guilt triggered by such feelings.

They found their own answer as Josie began to care for those even more vulnerable than herself—souls like Linda who could barely step outside their door. A hidden role but of no lesser importance. Nobody else wanted to look after these damaged men and women, would mutter about them as they did about Josie, looking at the Barricade as they did so. *There* was a contribution they would be happy to support, their eyes seemed to say. That monstrous beast always needed feeding.

Occasionally, this wish would be granted and a body found on the Barricade. Those deaths were a double-edged sword. Guilty relief at the lightening of their workload, sadness at the loss.

"Hey, I'm your mum," said Faith. "Goes with the territory."

"You're Callum's mum as well," said Josie.

The mention of her son's name plunged them back into silence. She had not seen him for twenty years.

"Do you ever think about him? What he'd look like?" asked Josie.

"You know I do," said Faith. "Every day." The only image she held in her head was of a fourteen-year-old walking away from her and the doors closing behind him. That particular pain had never lessened, despite the intervening years. Thinking of him as a man was impossible. Every time she did so her husband's, her *ex-husband's*, face became superimposed over Callum's youthful features. It was an image she didn't want to see, knowing it coloured her thoughts against him.

"And Dad?"

"Him. Not so much. It still makes me angry. You know that. What's brought this on? You know we said we wouldn't dwell on the past."

Easier said than done, thought Faith as she considered the focal point of their community. The Barricade. The permanent reminder they'd constructed to focus their minds on survival.

"Yeah. But it's been so long."

"Please, love." Faith didn't want her thinking about the missing half of their family, it was guaranteed to send her into a depression, black moods which could last for weeks.

Josie suddenly hugged her. "Don't worry, Mum. It's safe to leave me. I'm not going to do anything daft when I've got Linda to look after, am I? I'm a lot stronger these days."

The look on her daughter's face surprised her. There was a lightness of mood evident she hadn't seen since Josie was a child. Could she really have come to terms with what happened after all this time? Most minds shattered by those long-ago events remained broken.

"I'd better go," said Faith, sighing as she contemplated the day ahead. It was her turn to patrol the outer edges of their zone, ensuring no strangers gathered on their borders. She could never be certain which was the more depressing, patrolling the city or up on the Barricade. Both were reminders of their downfall. At least it kept her away from everyone for a while, spared her the complaints of the estate's residents when their limited power supplies failed yet again or when the aeroponics plant which she'd designed and got running failed to yield as much food as they wanted.

That was the trouble when you were one of the few with specific skills; from being one of their saviours in rebuilding a functioning community, you soon bore the brunt of their dissatisfaction. Gratitude had flown out the window a long time ago.

"Do you expect to see anyone?" asked Josie.

"No. I reckon it'll be fairly quiet," said Faith. "There's barely anyone left now. Our comms pick up fewer and fewer responses. As far as I'm aware, it's only us and those with the farmers. Other countries are pretty much the same."

"An empty planet at last," said Josie. "Those environmental protestors would be so happy. If only they could see it now."

"Yeah," said Faith, opening the door and looking beyond. "They'd say it served us right."

"You'll be careful, Mum?"

"Course," said Faith. "Aren't I always?" She hugged her daughter. "And check Linda's supplies when you go over. Let me know if she needs anything."

"Okay."

Faith let herself out through the gate. It groaned in protest as she pushed it open. Most people would oil the hinges but Faith kept both front and back gates like this. The noise served as an additional alarm against intruders.

"Mum!"

Faith turned around.

"Perhaps… perhaps next time, I can come with you?"

Faith stared at her daughter, Josie was certainly full of surprises that morning. "Perhaps," she called back. "We'll talk about it when I get back this evening."

Faith continued to walk past the neglected gardens of the surrounding houses. Straggly weeds and stunted or dead shrubs and hedges poked through broken walls. Cracked pavements were coated with a sheen of moss and slime. Linda was at her window as Faith made her way out of the crescent and gave a small wave. Part of Faith wanted to stop and pop in, make sure she really was okay but she knew once in there, she could be held up for ages. Instead she returned Linda's wave and continued on, Josie would be with Linda soon. There was nothing to worry about.

On cue, a familiar rush of heat stormed across her body. Sighing, she undid her coat and flapped her layers of clothing to allow her skin to cool down. Actions no doubt she'd be repeating all day. The thought was depressing, accompanied as it was by her lack of energy. She'd tossed and turned half the night as her internal combustion engine erupted whenever she drifted off, making unbroken nights a thing of the past. Sadly, the human condition, particularly that of the female, was one of the few things that didn't change when society imploded.

It was much lighter now, almost reaching that shade of grey which would remain to cloak the sky for the rest of the day. Occasionally, she'd wonder if this was the same sky the rest of the world saw but she stopped herself dwelling on that for too long. It only reinforced how precarious their existence was.

A chill washed over her. The sudden burst of heat had dissipated and she swiftly refastened her coat.

"Oy! Oy! Oy!"

The cries brought her back to her surroundings with a jolt. They came from a nearby multi-storey car park. Long since empty of cars, it served as a shelter for the many homeless before they killed themselves or each other. These days most steered clear of its confines. When the wind howled through its levels, it was as if the ghosts of those lost souls had returned to haunt the place.

There was a rumble to accompany the cry and shouts of laughter. A movement flashed above and then the rumble grew louder. Faith relaxed as she saw the figure come closer, followed by others hard on his heels. Skateboarders. A group of youths had escaped the confines of the compound and were enjoying a rare burst of freedom. Their expressions dropped when they saw her, knowing they shouldn't be there. Faith shrugged her shoulders and smiled. Relieved, they waved back, continued racing down to the basement level. Their noise was a comfort, a reminder of happier times gone by. Everyone deserved a break, a chance to be normal. Then there was silence.

The shouts and whoops had stopped. There was no echoing laughter or teasing banter floating up to her ears as expected. Faith was immediately on alert, retracing her path. The grey light followed her down to the basement level where she found the group of youngsters stood in a circle around a heap of old blankets. Their faces were deathly pale, all earlier good humour gone. Moving between them, she saw the mass was a body. Not anyone she recognised, although there wasn't much left for a person to recognise from the apparent damage done to them.

"Fuck," said one of the lads.

"Yeah," said another, whilst a third could contain themselves no longer and was retching loudly in a corner.

"Come on," said Faith. "Think you'd better get back now, don't you?"

"You want us to send anyone?"

"No," she said. "I'll call it in myself. Don't want to draw you lot into this do I?"

Grateful looks greeted her reply. It meant they would not be getting into any trouble with parents or the Council.

Once they'd gone, Faith squatted down to take a closer look. The smell was overpowering yet she'd become acclimatised, desensitised almost, over the years. She picked up a nearby metal pipe to lift up the blankets from the hidden part of the body. It revealed a torso ripped open, the abdomen split apart and its contents torn out. Where the organs had gone, she did not know. They certainly weren't anywhere nearby. She dropped the blanket again and returned outside, taking a minute to breathe in the relatively clean air.

It was the third body to be found in this manner. Nothing to worry about really, so Howard said. Rats were vicious monsters, known to make quick work of anyone unwise enough to fall asleep in an unprotected area. You couldn't blame a rat for trying to survive, now could you? *Howard and the rat*, thought Faith. *Kindred spirits*.

Although this one… Faith took another look at the abdominal rupture. Pulled and torn, it still somehow appeared as if it had first been cut open. She shook herself. No. She would not start seeing puzzles where none existed. She had no brain power, no energy for anything else.

She pulled the radio from her belt and called in. Someone else could deal with this. She had other streets to walk.

As she made her way along the route Howard marked out for her, she listened to the back and forth of voices on her radio. It was a comforting noise, reminding her she wasn't completely alone, that in nearby streets, others also walked their paths to ensure the safety of the community.

The shops, looted of anything worthwhile at the time of the abandonment, remained empty. She didn't always need to go in. Simply by standing at the door and listening, tuning in to her surroundings, she could tell whether the building was empty or not. Faith called it her sense of absence.

The further she was from the compound and the mountain of the Barricade, the freer she felt. Maybe next time she came out here, she *would* bring Josie, talk over the possibility of moving away from the zone, a hypothetical discussion they'd had more than once in recent times.

"Faith!"

Looking up, she saw Malik at the other end of the street where their routes overlapped. She waved and made her way over.

"Heard you call in," he said.

"Yeah, rats got to him," she said. "Nothing I could do so no point staying. You?"

"Nothing," he said. "Streets are quieter than ever. Really can't understand why Howard keeps sending us out."

"It's as if he's hoping we'll find something."

"Yeah, but what? All we've collected lately are dead bodies."

"And he doesn't seem unduly worried about those," said Faith. "I think he just wants us out of the way."

She didn't mind being away from Howard and the compound. Recent times had nurtured a healthy dislike for the man. Once upon a time, when they'd worked in the same research labs and he'd been a mere technician on her team, she'd regarded him as capable but lacking imagination. A follower, rather than a leader, when it came to coming up with the novel approaches society was demanding.

Faith's lab at FutureProof specialised in biotechnology and its application in agriculture, whilst the other labs under the company's umbrella focussed more on the treatment of disease and eradication of disability by gene manipulation. Howard, she recalled, flitted between departments, never settling in any one lab for very long. She'd puzzled it briefly, then dismissed him from her thoughts. Now, she had the nagging suspicion she should've paid more attention.

Malik laughed. They'd had this conversation before. "Still pushing the conspiracy theory?"

"He's up to something. I'm sure of it."

"Well, I doubt he's behind the bodies. Can you imagine him as some kind of serial killer?"

The idea made them both laugh. Dumpy, sweaty and middle-aged, Howard was the last person you would envisage summoning up the energy to rip someone apart. They continued laughing as they headed back to the compound, the first part of their patrol finished.

"Do you want to check in on them?" Malik was nodding his head in the direction of her home as they passed the turning into the crescent.

"No, they're fine," said Faith. "Josie's really been picking up lately. She'll be okay with Linda. Let's just get to the Barricade and get the rest of our shift finished."

CHAPTER TWO

A CLATTER drew Faith's eye back to the rusting metal scrap heap looming over her. She had already done one circuit of its lower perimeter and groaned at the thought of having to go up to its battlements. Its circumference took a good hour to walk and she didn't want to have to do another lap. Malik had been summoned by Howard and she'd been left to continue part two of their morning routine alone. He'd be back soon, he promised. Howard would keep him back however, push her that bit harder. Like always.

Those who lived in its outer shadow called it the Barricade—not to prevent anyone getting in, but to stop those it encircled from getting out. Not that you could see them, they lived in comfort far below the earth's surface, unlike Faith and her companions stranded above. The Barricade was the physical embodiment of the betrayal of those who, like

Faith, had been abandoned. The remnants of their society had built it, added to it, almost worshipped it in the absence of any meaningful structure to their lives. It had become the glue which held them together. It generated the anger which drove them to survive. It was the darkness at their heart.

She hugged herself and stamped her feet on the hard concrete, trying to get her circulation going. The light remained dim despite the morning's promise and the temperature had dropped back to freezing. She shouldn't have got her hopes up. How she longed for one of those inconvenient hot flashes to warm her up, they kept her awake half the bloody night after all. Why couldn't they appear when she needed them? Her internal thermostat had evolved into a contrary creature, preferring to play silly buggers rather than help a middle-aged woman out.

She stifled a yawn and peered again at the structure. It was still early, too early for anyone to be out and about, except for those whose turn it was to patrol its periphery—or those who sought some respite from the strictures of community life, like the youths in the multi-storey. The general consensus was, why get up when you had nothing to get up for?

The crashing grew louder and Faith made her way up the steps welded to the side of the heap, feeling every vibration as she did so. The railings were coated with flaking metal, rough to the touch.

Even through her gloves she could feel the gritty texture, the slivers trying to work their way in through the material, the Barricade attempting to infiltrate her body as well as her mind. One hundred steps. What had seemed a good idea at the time now seemed bloody stupid. All they'd done was make life even harder for themselves. She was gasping for breath by the time she reached the top. Faith clambered onto the corroded walkway at the summit and was able to see the person responsible for the noise. Crap. The woman had finally snapped.

"Jenny!" Faith's voice sounded feeble in the vastness of the Barricade. If she shouted louder though, she risked triggering the eruption of unnerving echoes, vocal distortions which were flung back at their originator in a frenzied chorus. Some claimed the echoes weren't theirs, that they belonged to the Burrowers living within the Barricade. Ghosts, mutations, nightmares. All had their theory about the Burrowers' origins. No one dared brave the interior of the structure to confirm it.

Jenny took no notice but continued to hurl steel, distorted coils of wire and old bits of wood over the side to add more to the monstrosity on which they stood. Faith understood what she was doing, had her own catharsis years ago when she'd destroyed and dragged the remnants of her marriage bed to the Barricade and fed it to the monster. A process repeated by so many of the community.

She raised her voice a notch. "Jenny!"

Still, she was ignored. Faith moved closer, observed the woman's shrunken body struggle to lift even the lightest items over the token railing, heard her sobs and chokes as she did so. The effort appeared almost too much which begged the question as to how she'd got the scrap up there in the first place. Muttering and cursing, Jenny paid no attention to her, shrugged off the hand Faith placed on her arm.

"Do you want me to help you?" Faith could smell her now, the mix of unwashed body and cloying sickness which clung to so many these days. She refrained from pulling her back, although Jenny appeared ready to tumble over the side together with the items she was attempting to hurl over its rim.

Jenny didn't reply but nor did she stop Faith from picking up a cracked mirror.

"Seven years bad luck," she said. "Reckon we've had that already and some."

The fragments reflected little, they were no more than shadows themselves at that height and Faith resisted using her torch. She did not want to see the woman she was becoming thrown back at her, the reminder of so much time passed, years which had vanished in a blink. Jenny was of an age with her. Was that what had triggered this late realisation of the truth of her situation?

Faith leant over the flimsy barrier and tossed the mirror into the depths of the darkness. She watched its trajectory as it fell, down, down, ricocheting off projecting edges, wondered if anyone below heard the noise being generated at this early hour. Even when its journey ended, she continued to stare, reassessing the path it had followed as she noticed another shape. One more rounded, curved, clothed. A body. Shit. There was only one person it could be. Explained why Jenny was up here at last. She pulled out her torch and shone it on the corpse. She hoped it was a corpse. An instant death wasn't always guaranteed.

Harry. Understanding dawned as she stared into his sightless eyes. Harry helped his mother carry the remnants of their lives to the top of the Barricade before taking his final step. One allowed, condoned, desired even by the community. It wasn't just wood and metal which fed the Barricade.

"Jenny?" Faith's voice was a whisper. "Jenny. I'm so sorry. I thought Harry was getting better. We all did. He seemed so much brighter the last time I saw him."

The woman threw the last piece of broken furniture over the edge and gripped the railing tightly, stared down at her son's body.

"He said he'd come back for us. He'd find a way." The pain and anger of her words, so clearly evident, cut through Faith. Jenny was not talking about Harry.

Of all those left behind, Jenny Linton had been the one who continued to believe nobody, no *husband*, could—would—be so cruel as to leave their wife and unborn child behind. For twenty years she repeated this belief to herself, to her son, to anyone who would listen. The survivors had long ago given up trying to persuade her such faith was misplaced. Her son certainly never believed her. Faith realised it was only because of Harry she'd been able to remain in denial. The breaking of this link, her last to her husband, had finally destroyed her.

"He lied," Jenny hissed, shaking the railing, triggering a further clattering of metal as loosely-packed pieces were dislodged and sent tumbling deeper into the edifice.

"He fucking lied," she screamed into the hollow at the centre of the Barricade, shaking the railing even harder in anger. "How could he do that?" Tears streamed down her face.

Her cries echoed around them, no doubt disturbing those trying to sleep nearby. No one would come looking though. They knew what the distress represented, knew there were patrollers on duty to help the sufferer if needed. They would simply roll over and go back to sleep, maybe grumble a little when they eventually rose. Ask about the culprit, gossip a little and then get on with their day. It was simply a part of the fabric of their life. Like the Barricade.

Faith moved to comfort her but Jenny was too

quick, climbed over the railings to balance precariously on the other side.

"Jenny. No!"

The woman shook her head at Faith, a warning to keep back. The light lifted a little more and Faith turned off her torch. She didn't want to see the defeat in the woman's eyes, see her jump. It was forbidden to forcibly stop someone. Another unwritten rule of the Barricade.

"It's Harry's birthday, today," she said. "Did you know? He'd have been twenty."

"Oh, Jenny. I'm so sorry," said Faith. "Why today though? Why didn't you come to me, we'd have tried to help." She was hoping to keep Jenny talking whilst she sought desperately to think of some way to get her to change her mind.

"Because it's his birthday. Because he couldn't bear seeing the Barricade grow with him, knowing they shared the same day of creation. I shouldn't have told him but I did. Remember how the day I went into labour everyone started building this thing. It used to be so small, like my son. When he was little, we would walk around it and he would say how one day he would be taller than the thing. That he would climb over and bang on the door for his daddy and that once he saw us on the other side, he'd open the door and we'd be together. I shouldn't have done it, you were alright. All I did by denying it to myself and to my son in those early days was build up an impossible hope. It's why he went off the rails in his teens…"

Jenny's voice trailed off as she gazed down at the corpse. Faith remembered the teenaged Harry, seeking comfort in whatever illicit drug could be synthesised to numb his feelings. It did nothing to cure the anger and resentment barely concealed below the surface or the depression which sent him spiralling into long black moods from which no one could pull him.

"He told me he couldn't bear being inside his own head," continued Jenny. "Felt he was about to explode and if he did that he was certain he would hurt somebody. He didn't blame me though, even though I've blamed myself. No. He blamed his dad. That's why we're here. He told me what he wanted to do and asked me to be with him. The doc couldn't help him and Harry wanted an end to his suffering and he wanted his father to see what he'd done to him, what he'd caused."

She had stopped crying, her eyes were dry. Faith recognised the emptiness there. It was a hollow she felt inside herself—but she had Josie. That fact alone prevented her from clambering over the side and joining Jenny. It was a dangerous condition to be in. At that point, you knew there was nothing you could do to change their mind, all you could do was stand aside and let them go.

Many had jumped from the Barricade as it increased in height, ending their lives impaled on the jagged shards and spikes beneath. Some had been slow, agonising deaths but they'd not begrudged their pain. Such deaths were expected to be recorded by the surveillance cameras of those below. Faith however, doubted they watched, would not want to be reminded of the consequences of their actions. There were fewer now. If people went over, it was in the dark, alone. A quiet end.

She quickly scanned the perimeter, hoping to see patrollers who could come and help. Those on the other side of the doors in the small squat building over and around which the Barricade now towered, certainly wouldn't come. They would stay below, waiting until all the disasters affecting the world had passed by. The great and the good had run away to hide under the guise of saving humanity. They were cowards.

CHAPTER THREE

Faith's memories of that time were hazy, continued to give her nightmares where she saw bodies, so many bodies hidden away in the dark, ghosts which smelt of sulphur. Demons and darkness. A mind could play so many tricks as it tried to make sense of events. None of it had been real, how could it? Her memories, like a computer's files had become corrupted, unbelievable.

"Jenny!" As her thoughts drifted, she failed to notice Jenny had moved a little further forward, was letting go of the railing. She risked scanning the perimeter again. Nobody. There should be other patrollers out and about. Not just her. She would have to bring it up at the next Council meeting. Already she was moving into the future, putting the now in the past.

"No," said Jenny. "With Harry gone, there's no

point. *You* understand, don't you? Will you say the words for me, for Harry?" Her voice shook, even though her face was set, had become a rigid mask.

It would be foolish to think of this as a window of opportunity. It didn't matter how determined you were to end it, everybody felt the same fear. Faith nodded and stepped back, despite her reluctance. The choice was Jenny's. It was her right. A community rule and yes, she understood, and it was a path which beckoned to her more as Josie became a grown woman, no longer a little girl. What would hold her back if she went into a similar downward spiral like Jenny?

Josie. She was finally adapting, considering a future. Her daughter would continue to anchor her to the remnants of the world they lived in. Josie and the change she sensed coming, the lift in the air around them. Nothing too tangible at present but enough to be cause for optimism. Shoots were reappearing, promises of a better life.

Her thoughts drifted to Callum. He'd turned his back on them because of such a promise. How had it worked out for him? Despite the circumstances of their parting, she desperately hoped he'd survived and thrived below regardless of the words they spoke on the Barricade.

The railing behind Jenny, so flimsy in its construction in order to facilitate rather than prevent the jumpers, creaked and groaned as she peered down at her son. Faith could only watch, pray it would be a swift end to the woman's suffering.

Then Jenny let go, looking nowhere but at Harry, sending her body plunging towards his. Mother and son reunited again. How could she feel sad about that? They'd both suffered for so long. They deserved their own peace, regardless of how they took it.

Apart from the crash as the woman's body hit the barrier, there was no other sound, no scream. Faith waited a few minutes and then peered over the railings, into the depths. It was easy to see Jenny's body, impaled on a spike, the tip protruding through her chest, blood seeping through her clothes. Fate had been merciful and given her a quick death. It made it easier for Faith to speak the words recited as tradition demanded:

> "Let the world reclaim these bodies of
> a woman and a man
> Let their blood and bones seep into
> the earth below
> Let their ghosts haunt those who hide
> Let them gift them Hell
> Amen"

The words were their condemnation of those who'd abandoned them. It gave those aboveground the illusion of revenge, filled the gap caused by their impotent rage. Inhuman. That was how they regarded those below and the term became the name by which they were called. Faith could imagine them, after all these years, well-fed and living in comfort, free from disease and fear whilst thousands had been left to fight to stay alive. Such thoughts stoked the flames of her anger, of the community's fury. How could they?

Sometimes she imagined herself on the other side of the equation, one of those who'd been chosen at the start. She prided herself on thinking she'd not have been so arbitrary in her choices of who was saved, who was left to survive on their own wits. It was a false dream. She knew she would've allowed her own prejudices to colour her choices. She was no better than anyone below. It was a human failing. This personal revelation, she kept to herself. Nobody would ever admit to being just like those who'd left them behind. And she protected the memory of her son from this anger. He'd not been responsible for his actions, not all of them anyway.

When the world is ending, you have to build an ark, they said. The pandemic of pneumonic plague had certainly reached biblical proportions leaving populations unable to support themselves. Steps, harsh steps, cruel steps, had to be taken for the future of humanity. People would understand, wouldn't they? Then they chose the intended survivors, the best of the human race—apparently —who would return and reclaim its surface when the time was right.

Faith's husband had been regarded as one of the

best, although not by her. A mutual feeling, she realised when the doors opened to admit him and he chose to take his secretary rather than her, took their son and left behind their daughter. That the best could include a corrupt politician, an unfaithful husband, an uncaring father was something she had never been able to grasp. In fairness, it hadn't only been husbands and fathers who'd walked away, wives and mothers had also left.

A cold wind drifted across the walkway. Faith shivered and pulled up her collar. The light was dim, blocked out by the never-ending grey clouds. The whole world had been grey for so long, the splash of colour afforded by Jenny's blood was almost a welcome relief. The Barricade stood high enough now to allow an unimpeded view across the old industrial estate at the edge of the city, to the houses and flats beyond, the deserted office blocks and empty churches.

When it was clear the government was serious in its proposal to go underground, many had gone into the countryside expecting to find the elusive ark there. They'd been fooled. Faith had marvelled at the sheer gall of their remote rulers when it was discovered they'd constructed the complex right on the city's doorstep—or at least an entrance to it. A nondescript unit on an industrial estate no one would look at twice, near to the docks which had become a monument to the collapse. Talk about hiding in plain sight.

The docks were a vast industrial wasteland. A landscape containing mountains of containers stacked on top of each other, vast multi-coloured brick towers, huge cranes throwing their arms across them like broken limbs, warped and twisted steel skeletons. Adjacent to this maze of metal lay the estate with its huge parking lots and warehouses. Bleak and empty, the estate soon filled with a bizarre collection of caravans and portacabins as well as co-opting the containers and warehouses into additional accommodation. A community grew up around the Barricade, one of the few remnants of the British population to survive the last attack of disease and civil war, the disintegration of society, all flocking together for the illusion of security. There was also the unspoken hope buried deep within many that the doors would be opened and they too, would eventually be invited in.

How many inhabited this ragtag community of rejects? About a thousand, initially, from what Faith could remember, but her memory of those early days was hazy, filled with bizarre imagery and frightening blanks. PTSD, she'd been told. The number dwindled over the years. Death was the main collector, others simply got up and left, certain of a better place in the countryside, forgetting they had to cross another divide. Rural and urban communities polarised in those dying days. Countryfolk had grown tired of the demands and lectures of those from the city, people who shied from the reality of muck and mud and blood. The farmers refused to let anyone cross *their* border. Death too, awaited them there where the barricades had been built from the blades of the plough and the harrow.

"Faith!"

It was her turn to be summoned. A figure on the far curve of the Barricade was waving at her. It looked like Malik. Howard had finally released him. About time.

"Coming," she yelled back, her voice a drop in the emptiness. It reminded her of how small she was, they were. A pinpoint, a mere atom, on the earth's surface. She quickly fixed tape to show their location and headed towards him, leaving Jenny and Harry behind. She would record their names in the site's log book when she completed her morning's work.

"What did Howard want?" she asked.

"Nothing much," said Malik. "Wanted to go over some figures, that's all." He stamped his feet on the walkway, causing the dead metal beneath to groan again that morning. "It's bloody freezing up here, I was hoping we could make this quick."

He was keeping something back. Faith bit her tongue, it could wait. She would get it out of him eventually.

"Sorry," said Faith. "I found a jumper." She looked across the hollow to where she had been standing. The light was so bad, even for that time of day, the two new additions to the Barricade could not be made out. "It was Jenny. She and Harry——"

"Christ," said Malik. "After all this time. Got someone here as well. Must be the morning for it. We're racking them up today."

Faith gave a grim smile. She didn't need to ask where Malik's latest find was, the smell signposted the direction. That was unusual.

"Someone's not doing their job," she said.

"Huh?"

"If they smell like that, it means they've not been spotted before. Recorded. Section marked for a remembrance."

"I've noticed one or two patrollers skipping duty lately," said Malik. "We'll raise it at Council."

It was a rule of the community to patrol the Barricade. Everybody had to take a turn. It was meant to reinforce their anger, their determination that should the day ever come and the doors opened again, those who had hidden would NOT be allowed out. They dug their own hole and they could bloody well remain in it.

"Down there," said Malik, pulling out a small torch and shining a beam into a gap in the safety barrier which appeared to have been deliberately forced and pushed aside.

That was strange as most, like Jenny, simply stepped over. The so-called safety barrier was anything but. Faith tracked the light down to the body wedged several feet below. She recognised the old man. Donald Luthgow. Once a doctor, then a drunk when he found he could no longer save his patients, like Harry.

"Got too much for him in the end," said Malik.

There was sympathy in his voice. Living could be too much at times for many of them, despite the gradual improvement in the air, the soil recovering enough to start feeding them soon—according to their last contact with the farmers. Despite mutual suspicion, rural and urban communities had carried on a limited trade. Of necessity, the fight for survival overrode any dislike.

The knowledge they'd been regarded as not good enough, were deficient in some way, was hard to live with. It warped their sense of self-worth, gave rise to humans capable of unspeakable things. The blame, it was agreed, lay with those safely cocooned in the bunkers below.

"We'll have to close off this bit, create a diversionary path around it," said Faith, scanning the width of the barrier. "There's enough of a surface up here."

"Smell might keep them away," said Malik.

"Give them masks," said Faith. "We can't let anyone have an excuse *not* to walk here. If they skip one day, they'll skip another and then another. Start to forget what was done to them, us. Seeing Donald should reinforce this unjust punishment."

"Better say the Last Words," said Malik, continuing to stamp his feet and rub his hands together. "Do you want to do the honours?"

The cold had begun to lessen its grip on Faith as her internal heating system swung into action in its latest erratic fashion, finally giving her the warmth she craved. It wouldn't last long but she allowed herself to enjoy it for a little while. The moment would come all too soon when it would prove too much and she'd have to cast off her outer layers in order to prevent any spontaneous combustion. Being menopausal in an apocalyptic world was not easy. She welcomed it though, carrying as it did, the promise of freedom at the end. She wanted done with everything which imprisoned her as a woman. The chains of biology could be a miserable tyranny.

Faith took the torch from Malik, shone its light full on the dead man. Buried deeper than Harry or Jenny, he was harder to pick out. The beam revealed metal spikes piercing his body and a sheet of corrugated iron slicing into his torso. Carved open, he'd become the food pouch a human really was, providing sustenance for the rats and whatever other shadowy creatures moved in the gaps they knew existed beneath their feet.

As the Barricade had grown in width and height, human-shaped shadows were glimpsed moving about within its walls. They had been dubbed Burrowers but were never seriously regarded as a threat to anyone and no one wanted to look too closely into their legend. Somehow it was understood the Barricade and the Burrowers were co-dependent and it was left at that. That the disappearance of the corpses might not have been simply due to the rats was rarely discussed.

Those who chose to take their own lives in the same manner as Donald, Jenny and Harry, were always left to rot down where they landed. It was hoped their death and decay would be captured on surveillance cameras and transmitted beneath. The intention, of both the dead and the living, was to make the inhuman mass underground feel guilty. Faith however, doubted they would feel anything. When you turn your back on millions of living, what was one person's death worth?

She continually allowed the bitterness of her hatred to flavour her words. She nursed the flame of anger with her daily walks of the Barricade, her pause at the doors through which she had seen her husband and son walk without so much as a backward glance.

Twenty years ago, they had thought the world was ending because the computers told them so. Projections foretold the pandemic, the meltdown of reactors, the increase in hostilities between nations. The computers predicted Armageddon and world leaders and global business had believed them and run away to hide.

With the best scientists taken away, when the pneumonic plague bacterium mutated and became more aggressive in its form, leaping from species to species, there was no one to work on an answer and so the pandemic became true.

When people died from disease, claiming specialists in engineering and technology, the power industries went into literal meltdown.

When power-hungry generals realised their bosses were no longer there to contain their ambitions, they went to war.

Yet despite all this, somehow there were pockets of survival. The remaining population did not mutate or become flesh-eating zombies, at least as far as Faith was aware. The people in her community had come together, built shelters and scavenged for food, helped each other as best they could, gradually learning skills that allowed them to envisage a future of sorts. Of course, there were those who sought to rule, to fill the power vacuum and lead through fear but those who attempted to claim Faith's people in this manner, quickly disappeared. It was rumoured the Burrowers had taken care of them, a return for the Barricade and those who died there.

The people above ground had been left to die and they had not died. She looked down at Luthgow and spoke.

> "Let the world reclaim this body of a
>   man
> Let his blood and bone seep into the
>   earth below
> Let his ghost haunt those who hide

Let him gift them Hell
Amen"

There was no reference to God or His Mercy. The one thing that had died and remained dead in all this time was God.

There was a skittering beneath her feet, and Faith imagined the presence of the Burrowers. They always seemed to wait until the Last Words were spoken. She regarded it as a sign of respect. Perhaps Donald wouldn't be there as long as they thought.

"That's three down there in the past week," said Malik. "Aren't you worried?"

"No," said Faith. "Have you noticed how it's usually the old folk, the ones near their end or the ones we can do nothing for? This is their way of contributing, reinforcing the reminder we need."

Malik was quiet for a minute. "Would you do that? *Contribute.*"

"Thought I already did," said Faith, laughing. "But if I became a burden, then yes, I would. And you?"

"Perhaps. Though I would personally like to strap a bomb to my chest and walk up to those doors and blow them apart. Take some of the bastards out. But I won't do that," he said, catching Faith's glance. "I know it would allow them to get out and that is the Unbreakable Law."

"They chose to go in. They can never come out," said Faith, reciting the simple premise, the phrase repeated at the start of every gathering, every discussion.

Malik was quiet for a moment. "What about those who were taken though," he eventually asked. "Like Callum. He didn't choose."

A silence stretched out as she remembered her son turning his back on her. Callum had been fourteen when he went with his father. She had wanted him to go so he would live, as any mother would want for her child, but it meant he had also turned his back on her and the pain of that final parting was still as fresh today as it was then.

"I made him go," said Faith, eventually. "He had a choice. Although—although it's hard to understand why he did what he did to his sister. Graham gave him that choice too."

Her husband said it was up to Callum whether Josie would form part of their new underground family. And her son looked at his sister, smirked in that irritating way of his and said no. Then they walked away. Leaving Faith and Josie in stunned silence.

That had been something else she had never forgotten. The gathering space for those who'd been chosen had been packed, filled with men and women expecting to be accepted with their partners, children expecting to go with their parents. It had been so dark, the power had often gone out in that time. The strange orange glow and smell of gas had cast an otherworldly feel to that chamber and it still infiltrated her dreams now. When she allowed herself to think about those specific moments, she would usually come to the conclusion they had been gassed to allow the chosen to make a safer getaway.

The initial hubbub had descended into stunned silence as the doors opened and they were abandoned. That silence had gone on and on. The crowd just stood looking at the gateway in disbelief and then gradually they'd found their voices and screamed and shouted at their treatment. Many had rushed forward thinking it easy to storm the doors as they had apparently been left unguarded. The doors had held and the rejected could do nothing but turn and stumble into the darkness beyond. The message couldn't have been clearer. Nobody else would get in, their lives were not valued. That had been when the first suicides had taken place and the bodies piled up at the door.

"How's Josie doing?" Malik's tone was careful, as if aware he was stepping on shaky ground.

Josie had been twelve when left to stare at her brother's retreating back. The psychological problems she'd suffered for the past twenty years had more to do with her brother's betrayal than the collapse of everything else around her. She'd never fully recovered from Callum's actions, suffering breakdowns on a depressingly regular basis. Faith had had to fight for her daughter when others questioned why she should receive the same rations, the same treatment as the rest of them. Whenever rationing got tight, there was always talk about getting rid of the 'dead wood'. Not only had Faith worried about what Josie might do, she also harboured concerns someone else might harm her, and others like her, in order to relieve the strain on their resources.

"Much better," said Faith. "I can't get over how upbeat she was this morning."

"Do you think she knew about the doc? She spent a lot of time talking with Donald."

"It's possible," said Faith, a new worry now beginning to form as she considered how that topic might have gone. Had her daughter's mood been a front, a move to put Faith off her scent. "You don't think…" She looked back at the area they'd taped off.

"No," said Malik.

But she could hear the doubt in his voice. If Josie and Donald made a pact, it would be her daughter's body found in the Barricade next. She needed to get home, make sure. They quickly descended the ladder and taped off access at the bottom, then moved along the structure to the next ladder which would take a person up to the point the other side of Donald's body and taped that off as well. Then they made their way to the small guard hut across the waste-ground.

No more than a garden shed in reality, its main function was to provide shelter for those on duty and to hold records of those who'd perished. A place for people to go to when someone went missing. The other two who were patrolling that morning had yet to show their faces. More and more, those who should be doing the rounds of both upper and lower perimeters simply stayed inside the hut for their allotted time.

CHAPTER FOUR

HOWARD LOOKED up as they entered whilst Declan kept his eyes focussed on the chess board. It was obvious he'd lost but still he sought a way out. A feeling Faith understood only too well.

"Well?" asked Howard.

"Donald Luthgow, Jenny and Harry," said Faith, waving away the offered drink. She wanted this over with as quickly as possible.

"Makes thirteen now," said Howard.

"Thirteen? I thought it was three," said Faith.

"Three this week, ten others from the start of the month." He nodded at a gallery of photos on the wall.

Faith walked over and studied them. She had not been in the hut since that first one was taken and heard nothing beyond recent events. Usually names reached her ears as gossip spread but the grapevine had been silent. Her long held assumption that those who jumped were at least at the end of their lives faded. Their ages were a shock.

"Why wasn't I told about this?" She caught a look between the men. "You told them not to tell me," she accused Malik.

He shifted uncomfortably. "You were having a difficult time with Josie. Remember? She was having one of her... episodes."

Faith remembered. Josie had been particularly depressed at the start of the month, a stark contrast to today. It was the sort which terrified her with their intensity, her daughter's determination to harm not just herself, but those around her, including Faith. It had taken a while to work itself out.

"You could have told me afterwards," she said.

"I was going to," said Malik, "wanted to give you a breather first."

Faith pushed down her irritation, she still needed to see her daughter, make sure she was alright. The morning's events had shaken her more than she cared to admit. "I'd better get back. I don't want to leave Josie too long."

Another look between the men.

"Isn't it time you eased up a little. Allowed Josie to earn her keep?" said Declan.

"I do enough for both of us," snapped Faith. "You know that."

"You do more than enough," said Howard, his

voice soothing, irritating. "And you're not getting any younger…"

"I am exactly the same age as you," said Faith, feeling the betraying heat rise up in her again, the feeling of being unable to breathe, bringing the anger with it. "So what's age got to do with it?"

"We just think…"

"We? *We?* Who exactly is *we?*" Faith had the feeling something had been discussed without her, an idea mooted. Malik kept his eyes averted. Not a good sign.

"Go home, check on Josie then come to Council," said Howard. "You remember there's a meeting tonight?"

Shit. She'd forgotten. Hopefully, Linda would keep Josie company. When she missed Council meetings, there was a tendency for actions to be voted through which she would have resisted. There'd been murmurings lately about the falling population, the birth rate needing a boost. Some of the ideas to solve the latter were disquieting to say the least. A wave of tiredness washed over her and she shook herself. It wasn't just exhaustion born of broken nights, crippling bouts of insomnia also gripped her. Her eyes stung from the lack of sleep.

Howard grinned. "Looks like someone could do with a nap."

He knew she'd done a double shift but still he made her sound as though she was old and feeble. Again, Malik kept quiet. He used to jump to her defence.

"Malik, I'll leave you to fill Howard in on the remaining details," said Faith, biting her tongue. "This old lady needs to go home." She laughed to show she could take a joke but her smile faded as soon as she stepped outside. She was halfway down the street when she heard feet running behind her.

"That was quick," she said, when Malik caught up. He was breathing heavily. Part of her felt some satisfaction she was fitter than her partner even though he was ten years younger but what was evident and what was perceived appeared to be totally different things in Council.

"Not much to say was there? ID, where to work on the barrier. That's it."

"Not even speaking to friends, family about why?"

"We know why," said Malik. "There's no need for that."

"There's always a need for that," said Faith. "If we don't ask, we might start missing things."

"Well you can ask, then," said Malik. "I don't have time."

"Don't have time? You've got all the time in the world? No family, no..." She stopped herself.

"No friends, you were going to say," said Malik, unable to keep the bitterness from his voice.

"You don't count me?"

"Okay, one then," he said.

"Do you know what they're planning?" asked

Faith. "There seems to be something going on and you seem to know what it is."

"Oh, it's just a stupid idea. Some of the men talking."

The men talking. That did not sound good. When only 'the men' got talking the subject was usually the women. And stupid ideas had a tendency to become reality if you weren't paying attention. She sighed. Despite her protestations earlier, she was feeling her age but only in the sense she was currently navigating a menopausal minefield, a topic not to be raised amongst 'the men' as it was seen as a weakness. If they were the ones suffering, she considered, they'd be taking time off and commiserating left, right and centre. But no, it was another weapon to use against women in this age-old battle of the sexes. The workings of the female body, so vital in the survival of the human race, was something too often derided.

It was as if the ground was shifting beneath her. Not just her body betraying her, but all the old relative certainties seemed to be vanishing. From all of them in it together, now people were trying to claim power. Any further down that path and they would be reverting to the type of society which had turned its back on them. Couldn't they see that? She wondered as to the cause of this change. Was it just the distance wrought by time or had something else triggered it?

"Tell me."

"No," said Malik. "If I do, you'll take it out on me. I'd rather you found out from the others."

There was no use pushing him. When his voice took on that tone, he became immovable.

"I'll be there," said Faith and turned off the street towards her own house. She could feel his eyes on her back as she walked away from him. Usually she invited him to join them for their evening meal. He was one of the few people Josie tolerated. There was no invitation tonight.

Faith thought of her cul-de-sac, the empty houses either side, preferring to keep herself and her daughter separate to the main settlement, although still within the Community Zone. Not many chose to live in traditional housing, most were in the motley collection of adapted containers and warehouses on the industrial site, drawing comfort from the nearness of others. Faith had never felt that a security, only danger. Safety was being on your own and not relying on anyone else. She had to remain part of the community however, in case something should happen to her, because otherwise, who would look after Josie? This morning though had begun to open up other vistas. If Josie had really turned a corner then they could leave all this behind them. She made a mental note to put subtle feelers out when she next took a trip to the farmers' barricades. A life in the re-emergent countryside, away from the Barricade at last seemed possible. If the farmers allowed them in.

In the meantime, she needed to know what Howard planned. If it was something which could affect Josie, she needed to fight it.

"Josie! Josie, I'm home," she called as she opened the door. A small light glowed in the hallway, a testament to her determination to bring some semblance of civilisation back to their lives all those years ago. A solar power panel rigged up to a generator and a lot of trial and error and you could almost pretend everything was normal. Provided the sun chose to shine to charge the panel in the first place.

The house was quiet, and cold. A lamp was on in the front room, curtains drawn. The old fireplace still held wood and paper, ready to start a fire. Choosing an older house with a chimney had been deliberate to allow for this old school, but effective, method of heating their home. So many evenings— when not her turn to patrol—had been passed curled up on a sofa watching the flames dance, allowing them to hypnotise her. So much pretence in trying to hold on to those old feelings of domesticity.

She should have accepted the changes back in those early days, moved in to the same blocks as the others, not isolated herself. They would've got used to Josie, helped look after her. She checked the kitchen but that was dark. The back door was locked and there was no one in the small garden beyond.

Faith stood at the bottom of the stairs and looked up into the darkness. Nothing moved. Already she knew the house was empty, Josie wasn't there. She needed to check though before running out in a panic and coming back with a search party, only to find her daughter asleep in her bed. Slowly she mounted the riser. One step at a time, pausing all the while as her ears strained to pick up any sound, any feeling she was not alone.

The doors along the short corridor all stood open. The first left, hers, empty, the first right, the guest room, empty. The next left, the bathroom, empty, the next right, Josie's room, empty. She stepped inside and flipped on the small lamp by the bed, held it up to scan the room. There was nothing there. Her bed was unslept in. The book she was reading, closed on the bedside table. Dressing table and shelves were all bare, no traces of feminine clutter in here. Heart pounding, Faith went to the chest and pulled the top drawer open. It still held her clothes, as did the wardrobe. Only then did she admit to herself how frightened she'd been Josie would one day run away, a threat she frequently made when depressed.

Faith thought back to the morning. Linda. She was probably still there. Why hadn't she thought of that in the first place instead of allowing her imagination to run riot? Because of years of conditioning, that was why. She ran out of the house and across the road to her friend's bungalow and banged on the door. There was no reply. Faith flipped up the letterbox and called inside.

"Linda! You there? Josie?" There were no lights on but that meant nothing. The woman often sat in darkness, terrified of phantoms running down the streets threatening to drag her away. Even with Josie and herself there, she would often insist on this and they humoured her.

"I hear them," she'd say. "Don't you? They whisper vile things, shout obscenities. What they would do to me, to your Josie…"

"You don't tell Josie this, I hope?" Faith had asked once, worried Linda was falling apart after all this time on her own, would pull Josie deeper into her madness.

"No, no. Course not," she said. "Wouldn't want that poor girl to suffer any more than she is doing already. This other Eden," she laughed. "No garden is it? But there is a serpent in our midst. Haven't you sensed it wriggling around you yet?"

Her laughter had become more hysterical, making Faith recoil, begin to worry about the time Josie spent with the woman.

"Linda!" she called again, pounding her fist on the door, feeling it give way easily beneath her assault, swing open to reveal the darkness within.

She sensed immediately something was wrong. She tried the light switch but it didn't work. And then she listened. There was no tell-tale hum of the small generator she'd rigged up for her neighbour.

Faith pulled out a pocket torch and flipped it on, its narrow white beam a string, threading its way through the gloom. She walked quietly, peering into the lounge, the kitchen, the dining room. Empty. Then through to the back, two bedrooms. One was empty. In the other, a shape lay on the bed.

"Linda," whispered Faith, not wanting to frighten the woman if she was asleep. "Linda." She reached out and put a hand gently on her shoulder, shook her lightly. Linda rolled on to her back. Faith turned away and grabbed the door frame to steady herself. She swallowed hard. Focussed on her breathing. She'd seen worse things before, only that morning she had seen the body in the carpark, Jenny and Harry, Donald. Bodies torn apart and corrupted but this seemed different. This was murder.

Linda lay there, eyes rolled up in her head, blood soaking into the mattress beneath. Her throat had been cut, her stomach carved open. Even in the dark, the exposed organs glistened, almost seemed to move.

Josie was missing. Linda was dead. She knew what they would say. Josie had made it clear what she would do one day and the last meltdown had been bad. They wouldn't care that she felt Josie had changed, that was no sort of evidence. She would talk to Malik first before she told anyone else.

Faith backed out of the house, scanning her surroundings as she did so, feeling for the first time as if she was being watched. A feeling which grew as she walked swiftly down the street heading for Malik's room in the compound, making her increase her pace, jog, run.

"Alright, Faith?" asked the guard at the outer fence. "You look upset."

He glanced down and noticed the blood on Faith's sleeve. "Accident?"

She shook her head. "I need to see Malik, urgently. Work business," she said.

The guard let her through. "It would be a lot simpler if you just came and lived in the compound like everybody else," he said.

She nodded. "You know, I'm actually beginning to think you might be right."

She didn't see the surprised expression on the guard's face as she left him behind but she knew it was there. The compound had grown in a haphazard fashion, homes constructed within warehouses and old containers on the industrial estate at the edge of the city. It was depressing. Another reason she'd chosen not to stay there was because it reeked of failure, not just hers, but of mankind's as a whole. All those years of progress and they were reduced to this, inhabiting empty tin cans, hiding from a world which had appeared to turn on them but which in truth was their own creation.

Hundreds lived there but just as many left and were never heard from again. Some tried for the country but they would have been rebuffed. Faith sometimes took part in trade negotiations with the farmers and endured their never-ending diatribe. *Don't like it so much now, do you? Lecturing us about everything from breeding cattle to planting the wrong type of crop—you're paying now.* At least they'd agreed to trade, that was something, and that was how they became aware of an oh, so slow, return to normality in the cycle of the seasons, the return of growth in some crops. There was still a long way to go, but the shoots of recovery were there. Nobody had expected that.

Malik lived in a container at the end of an artificial alley, the inside partitioned into four sleeping areas with a tiny communal space. Cooking and washing facilities were elsewhere. It was primitive, but for those unattached, or unencumbered as Malik preferred to term it, it was adequate.

She stepped into the container and made her way down to his cubicle, tapped lightly on its flimsy door frame. "Malik." No answer. She pulled the curtain aside and looked in. Empty. She knocked at the next cubicle.

"Gary, you seen Malik?"

"There just a minute ago. Said he had a Council meeting to go to."

"Meeting? But that's not for another hour."

"Moved forward apparently. You should've heard him swear when Howard sent one of his cronies to tell him. Shouldn't you be there?"

Crap. Faith didn't know what to do. Go to the meeting and tell them about Josie and hear their usual responses or continue her search and through her absence allow some ever-more restrictive law— or voluntary code as they preferred to call it—come into being. Or go to the meeting and tell Malik about Josie and Linda afterwards. Guilt and indecision ripped at her.

Still unsure, she found her feet deciding for her, heading towards a portacabin which doubled as a meeting place. She glanced down at her sleeve and rolled it up, hiding the blood. Awkward questions would start at some point but she needed to find out what Howard was up to first.

As she approached, she heard raised voices, a woman speaking out, protesting. Others shouting at her. She pushed open the door and immediately the room fell quiet.

"Ah, Faith. Glad to see you made it."

"Seems I wasn't informed of the change in time," she said, glaring at Howard who'd taken the seat at the top of the table, again. The position of Chair was supposed to revolve on every occasion.

"No? Please accept my apologies for the... oversight." Howard surveyed her for a moment and then turned back to those at the table.

"And I suppose it's an oversight that I have no place here?" She noticed her usual position was occupied by a man she did not recognise. In fact, most of those at the table were men. Only two women, Faith and the one who'd been speaking, were present.

"Where are the other women?" she asked.

"That's what I was asking," said Helen. "Seems they weren't informed about the new time either."

"Well, I'm here now and if that fool sat in my seat allows me to take my place, then *he* can go and round up the others." She glared at the young man in her chair, kept her eye fixed on him until he yielded in embarrassment. "Now be a good boy and fetch the other members of the Council, you know who they are."

"But…" he turned his face towards Howard.

"Oh, Howard is perfectly happy for you to go and run this errand. I'm sure he doesn't want to be seen as undemocratic. Do you, Howard?" Faith smiled sweetly at the man and he glared at her. "Now perhaps one of these other gentlemen wouldn't mind making me a cup of coffee or whatever substitute we're using at the moment. It's been a long day and it's getting late."

She smiled at the man opposite. He was sitting in Ruth's chair. As before, she kept her smile fixed on him until he too, eventually did as he was bid. Unlike the previous male, she knew this one, a known idler in the compound, shirking the most unpleasant tasks whenever he could. It annoyed her that her work carried people like him.

CHAPTER FIVE

HOWARD STARTED to speak again. Faith interrupted.

"Sorry, Howard. I'm sure your young man won't be long. I really think it best we wait."

He tried again. His pudgy face glistening with annoyance.

"Ah, ah, ah." She was speaking to him like a naughty boy although they were of the same age and he looked as though he was about to explode. Faith couldn't resist riling him. It distracted her from thinking about Josie and Linda. The sight of Linda's mutilated body floated across her vision, triggered another wave of nausea which she found hard to suppress. Where was her daughter? She pushed the thought to the back of her mind. Preferred to remember the positive light in her daughter's eyes that morning. It was possible she'd not been anywhere near Linda at the time the woman had been killed, but if not, then where was she?

A movement drew her back to her surroundings. She'd known Howard since her days at FutureProof, before the world went south. A man of limited ideas and intelligence—or so she once thought. Now she was not so sure. He certainly enjoyed bossing her about when he could, a reversal of their old roles.

Pudgy. The description didn't just fit his face. How could he be so obviously overweight on their current rations? Metabolism, he'd said, hormonal imbalance and everybody appeared to accept it. Those who didn't? Well, not a few bruises were being sported in the community at large. Faith knew he and his bully boys were behind this but she'd yet to catch him out, no matter how hard she tried to remain alert.

They waited in silence. Occasionally she'd try and catch Malik's eye but he steadfastly refused to look in her direction. She knew then he'd deliberately avoided getting a message to her when he'd been informed of the time change. So much for friendship. She felt she was being wrong-footed at every turn.

The door burst open at last and the six other female members of the Council entered. All looked furious.

"Howard," said Faith.

Howard nodded at the men who were occupying

their unelected seats and they rose, with some reluctance, and left. The women sat down.

"Care to tell us what this is about?" asked Ruth, one of the new arrivals. "Why didn't you keep us informed?"

"We knew the women would be busy," said Paul, at Howard's right hand. "Feeding the children, looking after their parents..." He smirked as he said it.

"Or fixing circuitry or carrying out a Barricade patrol," snapped Faith, rising to the bait. "And I believe there are plenty of men taking on the same domestic role. Domestic or otherwise, we are all making a valuable contribution to this community, unlike some of those specimens we just unseated. They do have too much time on their hands but I'm sure I can find them something to do, perhaps Ruth might find them a job in the sewage plant. I'm sure they'd feel right at home there."

Howard's face reddened further. She was pushing all his buttons but she couldn't help herself. Malik shot her a warning glance but she ignored it. She did not feel she could trust old allegiances any more.

"Hear, hear," said Ruth, stepping in. "Now I suggest you get us up to speed with whatever little scheme you've been cooking up."

Silence.

"Well come on, speak up," said Helen. "Or shall I share your disgusting little plan. Any of you? I mean you were *all* for it."

Faith realised she was including Malik in her statement; he was complicit in whatever they were hatching. Silence continued.

"Then I'll go first," said Helen. "These *men*—and I use the term loosely—have been concerned with the composition of our population. Too many elderly, although that seems to be being dealt with, considering the increase in *suicides* on the Barricade."

Howard flashed her an angry glare but remained quiet.

"They are also concerned there are not enough children, that women are not doing what nature intended and breeding."

"Well, that's true enough," said Paul. "Without children, the human race will die out."

"Can't fault you on your logic there," said Helen. "But it's how you propose to deal with the issue that's barbaric. Forced motherhood."

There was a gasp from the women, a shocked look shared between them.

"That sounds horribly like the Nazi Lebensborn programme," said Ruth, with obvious distaste.

"You make it sound worse than it is," said Howard. "We're simply offering the women of child-bearing age an opportunity to serve the community in a completely productive manner. Nor am I proposing women should have to engage in sex with a stranger or unwanted partner..."

"God forbid you should permit rape," said Helen.

"Artificial insemination," said Malik, suddenly speaking up for the first time. "The women who agree to this are allowed to be free of all other duties…"

"Which means people like us pick up the slack even more," growled Ruth.

"And the community gets the children it needs."

Two of the women were actually nodding their heads.

"You don't agree with this, do you?" asked Faith, incredulous.

"Why not? If the women want it and there's no physical coercion?"

"Then think about the birth itself," said Helen. "We have very few doctors now. We have limited drugs and medicines. The last woman to have a baby died."

"The baby survived," said Howard. The men around the table nodded.

Faith couldn't believe they were even contemplating this.

"You would all allow your wives or daughters to go through this?"

The men looked uncomfortable at that and it dawned on her. "But *your* women will be excused from this, won't they? It's for others to risk death on your behalf. Just like always."

"We need to rebuild society," said Paul. "We've

got to do something. When the others return…" He suddenly flushed and shut his mouth.

The whole room went quiet.

"What do you mean when the others return?" asked Faith.

"He means nothing," said Howard. "We know the law. I suggest we adjourn this meeting until tomorrow. Give you women time to think it over."

He got up and left the room quickly, the remaining men of the Council following him.

"Malik." Faith tried to catch his sleeve as he walked past but he shrugged her off. There was an anger in his eyes which surprised her.

"Seems Howard has been busy building himself quite the little empire whilst we've all been out, slogging our guts, for their benefit," said Helen. "Things are changing and I don't like it."

"I don't either," said Faith. "And Josie's gone missing."

The women looked at her.

"And Linda's dead."

The younger women who had appeared to be giving thought to Howard's plans backed towards the door. Faith noticed how quick they were to give in to Howard's requests, were susceptible to his suggestions. She wasn't sorry when they left.

"His little pets," said Ruth, nodding after them. "Probably running after him to tell him now."

"No, I don't think so," said Helen. "They don't like trouble. They'll just keep their heads down. Plus

I provide some of their little 'extras'. They won't want to forego that."

"Come on," said Ruth, taking charge. "You'd best show us."

Faith could have cried. She hadn't expected this support from the women having kept herself so separate but she welcomed it and something told her she could trust them implicitly. Perhaps it was because they were all of a similar age, faced similar struggles, refused to pander to Howard and his cronies.

"Ladies night out?" joked the guard letting them out of the compound.

"Party at my place," grinned Faith.

Helen and Ruth shared a little more banter with the man before they headed off into the night. It would allay any suspicions.

"You know, I haven't done anything, but I feel as guilty as hell," said Faith.

"We're all getting a little jumpy lately. Things have been changing, just little things yet slowly and surely we're being contained, directed," said Ruth.

"You've felt that too?" asked Faith.

"Yes," said Ruth. "It's like some of the worst features of our old society are slowly coming back to life. Impositions made on the basis of age or sex. Rules changed. It's as though now we can finally see the light in terms of survival, the possibility of a return to the norms of the past, we have to bring back all its baggage. As if we've learned nothing."

As they walked, they appeared to be the only ones out on the deserted streets, but all were aware the shadows hid many secrets. Once a month, the patrols would do a full sweep of the buildings within their Community Zone, attics and basements, alleyways and sewers, all were inspected and marked off as safe. Faith never had much faith in these checks, believing those who lurked in these places simply slunk away, just beyond their search perimeter, to watch and wait until it was safe to return.

Occasionally she glimpsed them, those who chose to live a solitary existence, those who preferred to operate in the small gangs which replaced their severed families. Sometimes she spotted children. It was an existence Josie had hankered after, the freedom to wander and roam at will, freedom from rules and regulations. Society doesn't flourish under those conditions she'd told her daughter. Society hadn't flourished under law and order, retorted Josie.

"Never could understand why you would want to live out here," said Ruth, breaking into her thoughts. "I mean doesn't it keep the past too much in the present, hold you back?"

"And you're so isolated," said Helen, glancing around. Despite her words, she sounded unafraid. All of them were used to patrolling such areas at night when necessity demanded. They carried guns, had used them, had learned to fight.

"That's why," said Faith. "I prefer to be able to escape from work. Too many people present all the time. And remember when I tried it that short while, right back at the beginning. I'd go from a day fixing circuits and drafting plans for construction work to finding people knocking on my door to fix watches, rig lighting."

"I hear you," laughed Ruth. "God knows the issues I have with people and their bloody plumbing. Our taps won't turn. Our cisterns won't flush. Our pipes are blocked. Don't want to get their own hands dirty do they. They're lucky they've got any of these little luxuries."

"Never thought the end of the world would still have running water *and* electricity," said Faith. "I think we can be proud of ourselves for that."

Helen, who'd been scouting a little way ahead, raised her hand and the two women immediately fell quiet.

"Thought I saw something," she whispered. "Up near Linda's house."

They were almost at the bungalow. Its white walls giving off a faint glow. The other houses running along either side of their approach were only visible by vague outlines. Linda told her she would occasionally have neighbours but Faith had never seen them, assuming they were figments of her friend's imagination and in the daylight, she discovered each building was as empty and neglected as always. Stark contrast to Linda's neat garden where she somehow nurtured scrappy plants into being, keeping them pruned and tended as if they were prize blooms. The grass, sparse in most parts of the city, also seemed to be struggling to come back.

Was it like that in the countryside? Faith would love to have known but the farmers kept up the borders at the city edge, refused to let them see beyond those first wasted fields. Land where the fires raged in hot summers with no one to put them out. The countryside's first line of defence against urban marauders.

The women allowed Helen to approach first. A trained soldier from Her Majesty's armed services, her skills had been as valuable as Faith's and Ruth's. She saw her friend slip into the garden, disappear from their sight as she moved round the back, reappear from inside. She waved a small torch beam at them to indicate the all clear.

"Nothing," she said.

"Nothing?"

"No," said Helen. "Must've been just a trick of the dark."

"And Linda?" Faith swallowed as she remembered the last sight of her friend.

"Isn't there," said Helen.

"What?" Faith pushed past her into the hallway, rushed down to Linda's room. Helen was right. The bed was empty. The body gone. "But she was lying here. Her throat was cut. There was blood everywhere."

Ruth and Helen came in behind her, Helen flipping on the small lamp on the table. The bed had been made, sheets pristine in the lantern's soft glow. The floor spotless.

"I don't understand," said Faith. "I'm not making this up." She pulled back the sheets, hoping they were simply hiding the evidence which would have seeped into the mattress. It too was clean. Replaced?

Helen ducked down to scan the frame, the floorboards. "I can't see anything but I can smell something. Ruth?"

Ruth joined Helen, peered and sniffed. "Flurzine," she said. "It's a disinfectant we use in our more *extreme* situations. It's one of those chemicals which can also absorb smell."

"Perhaps you should consider using it a bit more in the compound," said Helen. "It'd make life so much more bearable."

Ruth laughed. "Sorry. We don't have that much of it. We can only make small amounts at the moment, and we've pretty much scavenged all we can."

Faith left her friends behind, went back into the other rooms, retraced her earlier steps. Imagined herself walking in to Linda's room, retreating to the doorway, turning and grabbing the frame. She rolled down her sleeve. The stain had deepened to brown, but it was still there and on the frame where she had placed her hand, was a similar marking, faint, but there. There had been blood.

"Helen, Ruth. Come here," she said. She directed their gaze to the mark, to her sleeve. "Linda's dead," she repeated. "I did not imagine it."

"We believe you," said Ruth. "You've never been one to make things up or exaggerate. Plus Linda never left this house did she? Couldn't go very far on her own. Wasn't she a bit agoraphobic?"

"Yes," said Faith. "That's why I would usually bring Josie over here when I couldn't leave her on her own and Linda would look after her. And other times, if Josie was okay, I would get her to look after Linda."

Josie.

"Ahead of you," said Helen, vanishing from the house and making her way to Faith's small dwelling.

By the time they caught up with her, she'd turned on every light in the house, making it a beacon in the darkness. It did not, however, reveal her daughter. Josie was still missing.

"Thoughts?" asked Ruth, putting her arm around her shoulder and pulling Faith into a hug. Faith clung to her stocky form tightly for a moment, pushing down her tears and distress. When she felt she'd regained her self-control, Faith pulled back.

"The Barricade," she said. "We found Donald there earlier. All that time she spent talking to the doc and then finding him there. I just have a horrible feeling."

"Right," said Helen. "Then that's where we go next."

"Should we let people know Josie's missing?" asked Ruth.

"No, not yet," said Faith. "I don't know why but I've got a feeling it's better to keep it quiet just a little longer. Besides, I know exactly the response I'd get." *Good riddance, you're well shot of her, she was a drain on your energy, what sort of a daughter leaves it to her mother to do all the work...* On and on they would go. And there would be relief in their eyes. Despite their protestations, they were scared of people like Josie, feared becoming like her, hopeless, empty, could see themselves already part way to that desolate isolation.

None of them said anything but Faith knew they were thinking about Linda and Josie, considered whatever had happened earlier was related. It worried her that possibly Josie had seen something and been taken because of it. Or had she seen something and run, disappeared into the abandoned section of the city like she'd threatened to do so on so many previous occasions. Or she might simply have got wind of this plan to increase the birth rate and saw some danger to herself? Unlike Faith, she was still of an age to carry children.

They headed back to the Barricade, its location just beyond the compound, which they skirted without drawing attention to themselves.

"If anyone asks," said Helen, "we say we're here to pay our respects to poor old Donald and you were showing us where he fell. I know there's tape but we're *friends* supporting each other. They should get that."

The darkness was fading and Faith felt the old familiar exhaustion seeping through her body whilst her mind sent frantic thoughts whirling round her head. The three women clambered up the steps bound with the tape denoting death, stepping carefully over rusted projections which occasionally crept out as the construction shifted beneath them. Sometimes it felt as if she was walking on the largest scrapheap in the world because that was all the barricade really was, a scrapheap of the discarded —just like their community.

"Here we are," said Faith. She shone her torch down to where Donald rested but its beam was weak. It was sufficient however to find the shape of him, the parts remaining.

"Burrowers been busy," said Helen. It was a matter-of-fact statement, a truth.

Donald's head remained in outline, his eyes had gone, so too his nose, lips. *They went for the soft parts first.* His stomach seemed to have sagged and that was because its contents had also been claimed. His body had slipped further down, the lessening of its mass allowing the flesh to be pulled away by the spikes which pierced him, like a banana being peeled. Soon he would slip between the cracks below and vanish. Not even a day had passed.

Faith wondered when the moment of death had come. Had he taken something before he jumped? Was it the impact? Or did he get it wrong and lie there in agony for hours, listening to the expectant rustlings of the Burrowers as they drifted around him, felt the first nibbles of the rats.

"You alright, Faith?"

Faith realised she'd closed her eyes and Helen was regarding her with concern.

"Yes, sorry. I was allowing myself to think a bit too much about…"

"About how they die down there? I often wonder that too. I would prefer to be dead before I fall but then I would need somebody's help…"

"Somebody's help. Josie!"

"Pardon?" Ruth looked confused.

"Josie could've helped him. She was the only person he was speaking to in the end, he was the only person, apart from Linda, she would ever leave the house for. Perhaps she was up here?"

"Perhaps, perhaps, perhaps," said Ruth. "You're making a lot of assumptions."

"I know," said Faith. "I'm just trying to figure it out, that's all."

"Well don't make too many guesses," said Helen. "That's not the way to come up with answers."

"I know," said Faith.

Ruth turned away and moved further down the walkway. Her father had done as Donald had only the previous year.

Faith never asked but from the hints Ruth dropped, she'd helped him at the end, given him what he needed before he jumped. Would Josie ever ask her to do the same for her? Could she ever do that for her daughter?

Helen and Faith caught Ruth up and the three walked along scanning the inner side of the Barricade, looking for breaches in the barrier, not finding anything.

Ruth looked around. "Shouldn't there be a patrol up here?" she asked.

"Probably over the other side," said Faith, scanning the barely discernible rim of the Barricade.

Ruth shook her head. "I don't see any movement."

"We'll bump into them," said Faith, but she felt disquieted. The feeling of something coming was growing stronger.

They continued to walk. Helen just ahead, as usual. She stopped suddenly, leaning over to scan below. Faith and Ruth joined her, peering down into the disintegrating mass. No one spoke. Linda's hair, white from the shock of the abandonment, was her most distinguishing feature. Now it shone out in the darkness. The strands drifted out like filaments, almost gave the impression she was floating in water. Faith could not see the wound to her throat but noticed a myriad of other injuries, suffered no doubt, as a result of her fall into the depths.

"I'll get the patrol," said Helen, looking around.

"Not yet," said Faith. "Please. Just one complete circuit to make sure…"

To make sure her daughter wasn't down there as well.

"She's gone. They come."

"Did you say something?" Faith was looking at Ruth.

"Me, no."

"She's gone. They come."

The whisper again. Floating up from below.

"Hello. Is there anyone there?" called Faith. "Did you see anything?"

"They're coming back," said the voice and then the rustlings stopped.

CHAPTER SIX

"Who's coming back?" called Ruth.

There was no answer. A sense of urgency crawled through Faith and she walked away from Linda and her friends, continued to frantically search the barrier for signs of another collapse, another fallen human. Helen and Ruth could see to Linda, report her to the Council. She needed to find her daughter.

By the time she completed the circuit, returned to where they discovered Linda, only Helen remained.

"Ruth went down to the guard hut," said Helen. "Couldn't raise anyone up here."

"I didn't see anyone either."

"Skipping patrol duty? Who's supposed to be up here. D'you know?"

Faith shook her head, wondered at how this was

becoming a habit, the reason why more people were taking the drop, nobody up here to talk them out of it.

"Do you ever think about those who went in?" asked Faith.

"Are you serious? How can you not think about them? When we walk this path nearly every day. Nor do I want to forget them and what they did."

"Not like that," said Faith. "I mean how they're living, how they fill their days, what it's like being stuck underground never feeling the sun or the wind on your face."

"Sometimes," said Helen, after reflecting for a moment. "When I'm taking a shower and the water cuts out again, I imagine someone below wallowing in a bath. When we have the same sludge to eat, I imagine their cordon bleu meals—I mean royalty is hiding down there as well. Then I get bloody angry and go for a run!"

"What would you do if you ever saw them again?"

"I don't know. My mum's in there. How could she turn her back on me and Dad? If she'd taken my kids, perhaps I could've forgiven her but she didn't even do that and they're dead. I'd like to be the one to give her the news, see her reaction. Then I'd probably kill her."

"Does it worry you that whenever we talk about those below, it's always if they survive and if we see them, we'll kill them."

"Well we can't just let them go unpunished. Somebody has to pay and we've certainly paid more than our share in terms of blood and loss. I doubt anyone down there has to get their precious hands dirty."

Faith found her eyes drifting over to the gate. The one point through which the Barricade could be breached. She would never allow anyone to walk through it. Those who went below gave up their claim on the external world when they turned their backs. They had no rights to it anymore.

"They speak." Another strange whisper from below. *"They talk. They return."*

"Do you hear that?"

Helen nodded, looked down to where Linda remained. Nothing touched her whilst it was light and most people generally walked above.

"Do you wonder about the Burrowers as well?" asked Helen. "I do. I try to imagine tunnels down there. What it must be like to live with the weight of all this above you. To inhabit a rusting world, away from the light. If they're human."

Faith had been considering the Burrowers more and more lately, even—unbeknown to anyone—searched the lower boundary, seeking out an entrance, only to fail.

"They've never spoken before," said Faith. "Why tonight, when Linda was found here and Josie vanished… and no patrol walking their path?"

"Perhaps we can ask the guards now. About the

patrol at least," said Helen, as the murmur of voices reached them and heads appeared.

"There she is," said Ruth, leading the two men over.

Faith remembered these two. They'd been at the Council meeting, occupying places that did not belong to them.

One peered over. "Yep, she's there alright." His tone was dismissive. His partner pulled out a reel of tape, fixed the marking in a bored manner. Then they nodded at the women before turning to go back the way they came.

"Hey," said Helen. "What about the Last Words?"

"What about 'em?"

"You need to say them."

The guard, his ID badge declared him to be Keith, shrugged. "No point."

Faith stared at him. "No point! No bloody point! This woman died because of them…"

"Unlikely. She was nuts back then, nuts now."

"No. She had a recognised condition," said Faith. "She was agoraphobic."

Keith marched up to Faith, his face barely a whisper's breath from her own. She could feel the heat coming from him, the look of hate in his eyes. The sudden animosity and rage puzzled her but it did not make her afraid, instead she allowed it to feed her own anger, exacerbated by the building heat which triggered the claustrophobic feeling of an internal pressure unable to find release.

"She was an idle bitch using up precious resources."

His words shocked her. How could he think of another human being in such terms and then she remembered the words used against her own daughter. How they viewed Josie in a similar light. It was that realisation which stoked the first flames of fear.

"Women like her," he continued, "and your daughter, and those men in Container Three. They need to pull their weight. They're weak and drag us all down. And I'm not the only one who thinks like this but I am one of the few brave enough to say it."

"Brave? You're pathetic!"

His eyes narrowed, his body pressed closer, his nearness pushing her back to the barrier and its gap. And then suddenly he was gone. Faith blinked and saw Helen had pulled him back in an arm lock, a furious expression on her face.

"You are a guard here to *serve* the community," she hissed. "Serve *all* the community. Remember your place."

Helen let him go and Keith staggered back to the steps, his companion, who'd remained silent, swiftly following him.

"Perhaps you should remember *your* place," snarled Keith back at them before he vanished from view.

"What the hell was all that about?" Helen asked,

gazing after them.

"I don't know, but I don't like it. Can we just say the Last Words and get the hell down from here," said Ruth. "I feel… exposed."

Faith felt it too, the sense of being watched, from above and below. The rustlings beneath them increased as they waited for the invitation to be given.

"I'll say them," said Faith. "I knew her best."

Helen and Ruth stood either side of her and the three women fixed their gaze on the doors beyond the gate which had been closed for twenty years.

"Let the world reclaim this body of a
   woman
Let her blood and bone seep into the
   earth below
Let her ghost haunt those who hide
Let her gift them Hell
Amen"

The rustlings grew louder as if the creatures were vying for their place. They'd been given permission but they would have to wait until night deepened further before they could act on it.

Once they were back on the ground, the three women took their leave of each other. The following morning, both Helen and Ruth had work to go to. Faith was due a rest day. All however agreed to meet up in the evening, to discuss their next move.

Josie. Faith's mind was still fixed firmly on her

missing daughter. She needed to sleep but she needed to know what had happened to her daughter even more. Malik had been acting strangely. He knew something. She had to get him to talk. If she could ever find him. He was not in his quarters or the aeroponics plant, a place where she allowed herself a brief pause. This plant was the one bright spot in her life. It was here, with her engineering skills developed from her days at FutureProof and the expertise of a few knowledgeable botanists, that they were able to bring the prospect of some fresh food into being.

There had not been much to celebrate at first but over time they progressed from lettuce to a variety of other vegetables, never as good as those grown in the soil, she had to admit, enough though to colour their dismal lives. It was also important community members could see something *grow*, remind them the end hadn't come and was still in fact, a long way off.

"Have you seen Malik at all, today?" she asked Samantha, the woman monitoring the humidity and temperature controls on the night shift. The plant was deemed so precious, a twenty-four hour staff worked there.

"Sorry," she said. "Tried the bar?"

No. She was reluctant to go to the one place where everybody was guaranteed to appear at some point during the day to exchange news and gossip.

She slowly made her way to the bar, two old

containers melded together, a hand-painted sign projecting from its side, as if a hostelry from yesteryear. It was a noticeable need of the British population to maintain such a community hub. Pubs and inns were an ingrained part of their psyche, a hub where they could meet and put the world to rights, feel part of society.

In a nod to tradition, it had been named the King's Head, although the image—a suitably gruesome illustration of a decapitated monarch— more closely reflected their feelings about the absent ruler.

She hesitated at its door. If Howard was in there, or any of his pet guards, she would not enter. Faith scanned the room. It was surprisingly empty. The days lacked structure for so many the bar was normally full day and night.

A handful of old men were playing dominos in one corner. Sylvie was at the bar as usual, wiping the surface down. She always declared she had little in life, but what she did have, she would look after. She kept the bar spotless.

"Faith! What a surprise!" Sylvie spotted her before she had made a decision. Now she had to go in.

"Sylvie. It's been a while."

"Too long," said Sylvie. "Last time was when my pump filter wasn't working."

"Everything okay?" Faith waved her hand generally in the direction of the lights and pumps.

"Oh, it's all fine. Your magic touch cured everything. Drink? You look as though you could do with one."

"Been up most of the night," said Faith. "Found Linda in the Barricade."

"Oh crap," said Sylvie. "You definitely need a drink then. I'm not surprised though. She was never really right in the head. Heard about Jenny and Harry as well. And Donald. Quite a spate."

Faith ignored the comments, the questioning stare, refused to be drawn in to the gossip Sylvie so evidently wanted to share. The cruelty of rumour was destructive and she wanted no part of it.

The woman pulled a bottle from beneath the counter and poured out a generous measure. "For valued customers only," she said. "And it's on the house."

"Thanks," said Faith, allowing herself to knock back the spirit, feel its warmth slide down her throat, into her belly.

"That's better," said Sylvie. "It's given you your colour back. Now, what really brings you here."

Sylvie was a shrewd woman, could read a customer a mile away. It made her a very good landlord but also dangerous. She could wheedle a secret from a person in seconds and then use that against them for the rest of their lives. She had, however, proved a very good friend and ally in times of need. They understood each other.

"I was looking for Malik," said Faith.

"He was here," said Sylvie. "But he wasn't drinking. Came in with Howard, Paul and that awful creep Keith. Couple of young women joined them as well. I've seen them together a lot lately. Looks like they're hatching a plan—and not a good one."

"Really? How come?"

"There've been a few others in that group. They seemed to have objections, disagreed with Howard, quite visibly at times. I don't know what about but you can tell a lot from body language. Anyway, those who spoke up like that disappeared. When family came looking for them, I went with them to the guard hut and we saw the pictures hanging up. They'd been found on the Barricade and the families hadn't even been told. An oversight, they said."

"Has Malik told you anything about all this?"

"No," said Sylvie. "I did try, I mean, having them in here was scaring all my regulars away. Must be losing my touch." Sylvie frowned and seemed to consider. "The atmosphere hasn't been that good lately."

"You've noticed a change too?"

"Yeah, everyone seems to have a secret, or at least more secrets than usual. And I don't like it."

Knowing secrets had been a source of power for Sylvie. Time and familiarity however, could weaken anyone's grip.

"And Andrew?" Faith scanned around for

Sylvie's husband.

"He's out, checking the distillery."

"You moved it further away, didn't you?"

Sylvie grinned. "Well, it does have a tendency to explode."

"But aren't you concerned about him?"

"Andy? Nah, the man's got rubber skin. And he's learned to run fast."

Faith smiled, the thought of this couple made her happy. To see a genuine and lasting relationship in the compound was unusual. When society fractured, trust died with it. But not these two. Andrew had actually been a leading research scientist at FutureProof but refused to go into the bunker when he'd been offered a place and Sylvie hadn't. He would take his chances above ground, he'd said, and so he stayed.

She remembered his last focus of study, soil conditions and beneficial organisms. Before the end, he'd shown her wriggling little nematodes under his microscope lens. He'd been looking at ways to engineer their DNA so they became even more useful in certain areas. Respiration and decomposition he'd said. If only he'd been able to see those particular studies through, they would be in a much better position to kickstart their natural environment, accelerate the enrichment of their wasted soil. She stopped herself. No. It was tinkering with such things which had brought them to the brink of disaster before. Human tinkering brought nothing but trouble.

Andrew had worked with Faith on the aeroponics, helped the doctors wherever he could, tried to apply his skills to the wreck of a population left behind but he'd also tried to rebuild community in the real sense of the word.

Before the crisis, Andrew and Sylvie had shared their dream of retiring to a country pub. The King's Head became their substitute and its customers, their family, where they had no other. Faith had vague memories of a young son and daughter somewhere but she assumed they'd died before the troubles. Sylvie never spoke of them and she never asked. Occasionally, they'd come round to Faith's for dinner, Josie hiding upstairs, unable to bear the sight of a couple whose delight in each other was so much at odds with her own parents' marriage. But that was years ago and no one was ever invited round any more. There was no point when you couldn't feed them.

"Did Malik say where he was going?"

"No," said Sylvie. "But he did leave on his own and when Andrew popped back earlier, he mentioned he'd passed Malik near the distillery, seemed to be heading towards the Barricade. He'd said hello but said Malik didn't notice him, he seemed preoccupied."

The far side of the compound, well away from everyone. Was he going over there to get away from everyone or was it something else?

"I'll head on over that way," said Faith. "See if I can track him down."

"Good luck," said Sylvie. "And we must get together soon, have dinner. It's been so long."

Faith nodded and waved as she left. Sylvie's invitation was genuine but she wasn't sure she would be taking her up on it.

CHAPTER SEVEN

SHE WALKED quickly past the sentry point, nodding at the guard who barely acknowledged her in return. The industrial estate was a huge concrete park, ugly like so many others built in those years of so-called progress. The further she moved away, the sparser the buildings and a wide-open expanse of parking for the containers routinely transported there. It was a central depot, a hub forming a lifeline of supply around the country—once upon a time.

It felt so empty, a bleakness of land matched only by the grim blocks of flats and multi-storey car parks framing it. To one side was the 'distillery', on the other rose the Barricade, its browns and greys, sepia and umber tones bleeding into the sky. She made her way towards it, walked slowly along its perimeter, occasionally glancing up to see if anyone was looking down. There was no one. Every now and then she would notice her hand had drifted out, was brushing the structure with her fingertips, as people do. She stopped when her thumb snagged a jagged edge, her blood dripping down to mingle on the rust below.

She continued to walk, sucking her thumb as she went until the bleeding stopped. The Barricade curved round and she passed the one set of stairs at this end. There weren't many ways up or down here as it was an area not many liked to come to.

Faith started to pay more attention to the structure, the jigsaw of scrap and plastic, brick and rubble forced together to make the construction. There were small gaps, tubular shapes, which drew in air allowing loose metal to sound like windchimes, their echo dancing around her as she passed. It was a mournful music and did nothing to lift her mood.

She continued on, a honeycomb of holes appearing but still not big enough for a person's arm to slip through, let alone the rest of them. She'd almost reached the most distant point of the Barricade, the curve going either way showing no one walking the same path as her. Had Malik not come out here, perhaps gone further back into the city itself? No, despite the secrets Malik had been keeping lately, she felt it was not a place he would go. The city held too many horrors for him. And that was when she saw it. A piece of corrugated iron, hanging like a hatchway door. She'd never noticed it before.

Cautiously, she approached, glancing around as she did so; previously sure no one came here, a paranoia started to grow, convincing her she was under surveillance. As quietly as she could, she picked up the hatch, lifted it so she could see inside. The smell immediately made her drop it again and she staggered back.

The noise echoed around the lot.

"Hey! Faith!"

It was Andrew. She waved. "It's okay, just poking about."

"You be careful over there. You might find it all comes crashing down around you!"

"I will." She gave him a wave and carried on her walk, glancing back occasionally, to see if Andrew had gone inside. Once out of view, she paused and slowly doubled back. Stopping when she noticed Andrew had gone over to the wall, lifted the hatch and seemed to be speaking to someone inside. Then a doorway to his left materialised from nowhere and he vanished into its belly.

Andrew? Quickly Faith made her way to the hatch, lifted it slightly and listened. She could hear a murmur of voices. Then she looked to her left to the area where the door had materialised. Straining her eyes, she tried to make it out but could see nothing. *You're trying too hard*, she muttered. *Relax*. She let herself drift, lazily scanning the material in front of

STEPHANIE ELLIS

her, swiftly realising it was a collage. Bits and pieces of scrap welded onto a single surface to look as though they were jumbled together like the rest of the Barricade. Carefully, she ran her fingers around its edge, found a nick allowing her to get a grip and pull it open.

She was prepared this time, pulled a mask over her face. Flicking on a pocket torch, she crossed the threshold. She was in a tunnel, low but still high enough she didn't have to bend. She took it all in. Allowed the light to travel across the floor, rough concrete, dry soil, occasional bits of debris.

The walls were compact. Seemed more solid than the exterior despite being built from the same materials. As she took it all in, she noticed struts and supports at regular intervals, reaching up and across the ceiling. It was like a miner's tunnel. The sight of it was reassuring. Then she heard voices, whispering and drifting, vague mutterings, a low chanting almost. Part of her wanted to leave, get out now. The other part wanted to see what the Burrowers were really like or if they truly existed, find out what Andrew's involvement in all this was.

A cold wind blew along the tunnel, as if a door elsewhere had been opened. It came from the left but she could see nothing in the wall, realising it was probably another concealed doorway. If anyone discovered her now, would they harm her? She didn't have her gun on her and tiredness would lead to mistakes. That decided her.

She would go home, rest a while, then armed, and hopefully with at least Helen on side, she would come back and they would explore properly. She was of no use to anyone at the moment. Not knowing Josie's whereabouts was a real worry, as was what happened to Linda but she couldn't afford to make stupid mistakes caused by lack of sleep.

Quickly she pushed the door open and slipped outside again. Walked back, this time deliberately sticking her head round the distillery's door.

"Andrew!"

He turned and smiled at her.

"Faith, lovely to see you. Enjoy your walk? Although a bit early to be out and about."

"Yeah," she said. "But it's quieter, no one asking stupid questions or hassling you for something," she replied, trying to work out how he'd got back over here whilst she was certain he was inside. "Not very scenic but you take what you can."

"You can say that again."

"Better get back," said Faith. "I've got a shift later and need to get some rest. Looks like you've a lot of work to do."

He nodded and smiled and Faith continued on her way, replaying how he looked, their conversation. Had he been inspecting her, trying to catch her out somehow? She didn't think so, the talk had been too banal, too mundane. She sniffed as she walked. That smell again, yet she was outside, away from the tunnel—but it clung to her. Had he been able to smell that? She needed to go home and shower first, just in case anybody else recognised the odour, realised where she'd been, started to ask questions.

As she walked, she understood she had already cast Andrew into the role of the enemy, even though she'd no idea what his part was in all this. He had only ever helped people, been friendly. Now she cast him as an arch villain. She was definitely in need of sleep.

Turning into her street, she glanced at Linda's house, noticed its door was open, yet she continued on. There was nothing she could do for Linda at the moment. Finding Josie and discovering what was going on was the most important thing for now and that could only be done with a fresh mind.

She slipped the key into the lock, entered her empty house, out of habit called out for Josie. Then she climbed the stairs to her cold room, climbed fully clothed under the sheets and fell asleep.

Around her, the house whispered with its creaks of wood and wind in the pipes. Others whispered too, visitors who'd seen her enter the Barricade and return home. They had followed her, wondering what she would do with the little knowledge she had gleaned.

They let her sleep though, she would be useful in the time to come. Andrew said so.

Despite her anxieties, her body cried out for rest. So many nights of broken sleep and horrific insomnia had built up a deficit and so her body closed down. By the time she woke again, it was night. She wondered nobody had come to check on her, make sure she was alright. Did they care?

She groaned at the time, her stomach echoing her voice as it reminded her she hadn't eaten all day. She sniffed. Ugh. The tunnel's corrupted scent still clung to her. Faith lifted her aching body from the bed and made her way to the bathroom. A jug of water remained for washing, it was ice cold but she didn't care, needed to feel clean. She quickly dried herself and pulled on clothes from a drawer scented by dry lavender. The smell of the tunnels thankfully vanished.

Food. There was nothing in her cupboards. It would have to wait. Her stomach growled yet again. She paused at the door and looked back at the stairs. "Josie," she called, her voice soft and pleading. Only silence answered. Nothing had changed.

She made her way, not to the guard room to find Malik who was on duty that night, but back to Sylvie's bar. Helen and Ruth were both there. Andrew was pouring their drinks and swiftly added a third for Faith.

"You look much better," said Helen, moving over to let her sit down.

Faith nodded. "I thought you would have come looking for me after what we agreed."

"We did," said Ruth. "You were dead to the

world…"

"Dead to the world. D'you mean you came in?"

"Yeah, sorry," said Ruth. "When you didn't show up we naturally came looking. I mean after Josie disappearing and what happened to Linda we had to check up on you, didn't we? And locks don't really stop Helen."

"You were sleeping like a baby," said Helen. "We've been checking back on you throughout the day."

"Thanks, I think." The idea they found it so easy to get in, and even worse, stood over her bed and she had been unaware was totally unnerving. At least these were her friends. It could so easily have been someone else. "Well, I'm ready to go now. Hungry though. Got any food tonight, Andrew?"

"Chilli."

"That'll do." She'd deal with the heartburn later.

"Well, you're definitely brighter," said Ruth. "No sign of Josie when you left?"

"No," said Faith, allowing herself a brief frown, "but I've found something I need to check out. It might give us some answers. What about you, heard anything?"

Both women shook their heads as Andrew returned with a bowl of something unidentifiable. Nobody ever asked any questions about the food. Provided they tasted the chilli powder, felt its fire, all was good.

"So then," said Helen. "What's with the

mystery?"

Andrew had gone down the far end of the bar and was serving another customer.

Faith shook her head. "Not here. Let me finish this and I'll show you. You both armed?"

"Always, at night," said Ruth.

Helen nodded. "Likewise."

"Not a word though to Andrew or Sylvie."

"Why not?"

"I don't want them getting involved in something which might bring them trouble."

It was a lie and one she would soon pull back but it would do to keep them quiet in the confines of the room.

"How was your patrol this evening?" she asked Helen.

"Quiet. Nothing to report at all. I tried to find out why no one was on duty earlier but they kept saying I was mistaken, perhaps the men were on a 'comfort' break! Can you believe that! If *we* used that excuse, we'd be mocked for being weak and feeble."

"Sewers were quiet as well, if you're asking."

Faith looked at Ruth, puzzled.

"I mean it. Dead silent. No rats, nothing. The little monsters appear to have abandoned the sinking ship. Think they know something we don't?"

"Perhaps they've died out at last."

"Would be nice to think so but rats always survive. Human or animal."

Faith wolfed down the remainder of her food and emptied her glass. She needed to get out of there, get moving. "Come on."

As the women scraped back their chairs, Faith felt as if all faces had turned towards them. It increased her feeling of exposure and surveillance. She shivered. People were just taking notice as they always did. It was a small place. You watched each other. She was nothing if not as guilty in that respect.

"Goodnight, ladies," called Andrew after them. Faith felt his eyes following them even after they'd left the container and were well away from the bar. Had she read suspicion there or was she imagining it?

"Where are we going?"

"You'll see," said Faith, guiding them away from the compound and back to the far side of the Barricade.

CHAPTER EIGHT

"SEEMS QUIET for a Friday night," said Helen, as they walked together across the wide-open lot. "No courting couples."

"Thank God," said Ruth. "I mean, how unromantic can you be, coming to this place?"

Security patrols would often find couples hiding in the corners, against walls, down alleyways beyond the lot. Some, the young, would blush and run away giggling. Others would bluster and demand their privacy, occasionally making a deal with whoever caught them not to tell their partner back home.

Lies and deceit continued in so many forms but this particular one was the most painful for Faith. She'd no time for such cheating. If they did not want to be with their current partner, they should say so, have the courage to split rather than continue in a lie which would one day be found out and cause so much more hurt.

"You can't tell him," said the last woman she'd come across, skirt hitched high, pale flesh supported by the wall.

"We have to log all unauthorised presence in these outer areas," said Faith. "Your names will go in the book."

"But not what we were doing?" asked the woman, rearranging her clothes, hiding her pasty skin with its mottling of cellulite.

"Sorry, we have to declare it."

"Couldn't you make something up?"

"What would you suggest? Birdwatching, trainspotting?"

"Don't be bloody ridiculous. Something simple, like taking a walk."

"And wouldn't your husband be suspicious of that?"

"What? A walk with my brother-in-law discussing my husband's birthday?"

Faith looked at the woman. There was a nervous energy about her, a sense of despair. She came across this in many of the men and women they logged on their rounds. All of them seeking something more from life, trying to fill that gaping black hole inside which was empty and cold and growing all the time.

"Sorry," said Malik. "We have to record what we find."

The couple had laughed then.

"Oh, don't give us that," said the man. "We've seen you lot, gathering in little groups, hiding in the alleys like us, seen things pass between hands. You scheme and plot like the rest of us. The difference is, we just seek a little comfort, a bit of human warmth where we don't get it from anyone else. What goes in the log for you lot?"

Faith had ignored his comment and filled in the book, ignoring the names and insults cast after them as they walked away. What the couple didn't know was their own respective partners had been discovered the previous day, their names written above tonight's entries. All were welcome to browse these records in the name of transparency and in hope the risk of naming and shaming would prevent greater breaches of community protocol.

Everybody came to read the books once in a while. Human curiosity never changed. They saw the names of their neighbours, found their own and then went away without comment. In the end the books served as a reassurance that everyone was alike, nobody could claim the moral high ground.

Faith too, often flipped through the pages and was reassured to find her own and that of her friends missing. But who was to say they hadn't made their own deals to keep their names off the page?

"It was getting busy back at Sylvie's, and it is cold out," said Ruth.

The temperature had dropped. For most of the

past twenty years, the weather had changed, refusing to allow the seasons their usual cycle. Either grim, grey rain clouds and constant rain or months of heat making them long for the bleakness preceding it.

Now it was December and she felt cold. "Feels like it used to," said Faith.

"And look at the sky," Ruth pointed.

The clouds were a murky, dirty orange colour hanging heavy and giving the night a strange illumination. Faith hadn't seen clouds like that for years.

"Snow," she said. "Do you think it could be?"

"Cold enough," said Helen, slapping her arms and stamping her feet.

They were all feeling the effects of the cold now they were talking about it. Hope rose in Faith.

"A snow day," she said. "I'd love that."

Ruth glared at her. "Alright for you, but think of all those burst pipes. I've been telling people to lag their pipes for years and they've all looked at me as though I'm mad. *What would they want to do that for? It's never cold enough*, they say. They're going to come looking for me now."

Faith looked up at the clouds again, could almost feel them preparing to open up. If pipes burst tonight and people started shouting for Ruth and couldn't find her, they'd come looking and she had to avoid that.

Ruth caught her look. "You think I should go

back," she said, "don't you."

"I can't risk anyone coming after us yet. Look, I'll show you what I found so if you need to come and find us later or if we seem to have disappeared, you know where to search."

"Makes sense to have someone on the outside," said Helen.

Ruth nodded in reluctant agreement.

They passed the distillery which lay in darkness. Nobody was working within its confines tonight.

"Here," said Faith, reaching the hatchway and lifting it. "I'm not sure where this goes but this is one way in and here," she turned to find the doorway, showed them how it was camouflaged, "is an easier way in. It's where I saw Andrew go inside earlier."

"Andrew! *Andrew*. Are you sure?" Helen looked confused, shocked.

"Yes, but I wasn't able to find out what he was doing inside. I mean no one ever goes in there, do they. The only ones inside apart from the rats are the so-called Burrowers."

"Then I'd say it definitely makes more sense for one of us to stay outside," said Ruth. "I can go and prop the bar up for the evening. Perhaps chat with Sylvie. Customers like to talk, I could get them to give me their opinions on the Burrowers, *without* giving you away," she added, catching Faith's look.

"You know, I've never known who or what the Burrowers are," said Helen. "Remember how we all used to ask, tried to find out when we heard the noises below, noticed the bodies being taken."

"I used to think it was people who didn't want to be part of our community. Those who preferred to have a bunker of their own, at least in their own mind, even if it was above ground. It meant they could hide. Although I wasn't quite sure how they survived, how they ate."

"Well, we all know what they eat now, don't we?"

"Are you sure?" asked Faith. "Bodies gradually went bit by bit, but we never actually saw them being eaten. Yes, I made that assumption as well but lately I feel as though a lot of things I thought once held true are no longer what they seem."

Josie. Linda. Malik. The Council. The guards. *The whisperings.*

"Then I suggest we go and do a bit of burrowing ourselves," said Helen, pulling out both torch and gun.

"I'll catch you later," said Ruth. "If I don't see you around tomorrow morning, I'm going to come looking and I'll be telling Malik where you've gone."

They said goodbye and soon it was just Helen and Faith standing beneath the looming monstrosity, preparing to pull the door open once more. Everything was quiet. Waiting. Faith felt a storm was coming both above and below.

"Put your face mask on, you won't want to get a lungful of this," said Faith, handing the woman one of the masks she'd brought in preparedness for the search.

Then she opened the door and the two women stepped into the darkness.

"Whoever built these tunnels, knew what they were doing," said Helen, sweeping her torch around. "I was worried we'd be pushing our way through piles of rubbish."

"They've had years to develop this," said Faith. "But it's an educated construction. And that makes me wonder about who's behind it."

Despite its height, the tunnel was only wide enough to allow them to walk in single file. Faith led the way, Helen checking behind them on a regular basis.

"We should've checked the hatchway," said Helen, after a little while.

"Thought about it but there didn't seem to be access to that opening from this tunnel, we could only go straight ahead remember. There was no forking of tunnels."

"Not back there," said Helen, "but there is now."

The women had come to a solid wall of debris but another, similar tunnel, to the one they'd walked, branched off both left and right.

"Toss a coin?"

"Left," said Faith. "Only because it's away from the compound. Go right and it'll take you to the part nearest the guards."

"Logical."

The women took a left, continuing to scan the

walls as they did so, this time noticing a loosening in the material lining the passage, small gaps through which they would see the occasional flash of a glittering eye, heard the chatter of the rodents both disliked so much. Ruth's disappearing rats. The smell was beginning to filter through their masks and it was becoming harder to ignore.

"Look," whispered Helen, shining her torch upwards. The ceiling stretched away from them, curving up into the darkness, moving back and opening up the structure. Solid lines appeared to run horizontally around its side. Walkways and ladders.

"That's not possible," said Faith. "I mean the weight above and on the sides."

"We need to get up there," said Helen, searching her beam along the passage, trying to find those first initial stairs which would allow them to climb up to this unexpected development.

They walked further, the ceiling still opening out above them until suddenly, the tunnel they were part of seemed to close in again and was like before, a solid mass above their heads.

"Did we miss something?" asked Helen.

"No," said Faith. "But we keep on going, I'm not going back to double check. Have you noticed the ground has begun to slope down?"

Helen's light scanned the track, it had taken on a downward gradient, a gradual incline.

They walked forward a little more, this time side-by-side as the tunnel widened out, would actually have allowed several people to walk abreast. It was a crazy construction and one which did not fit in with her understanding of the dimensions of the Barricade. She knew it was about a mile wide at its base but tapered up to a much narrower two metres at the top where the walkway ran around its summit.

And in the walls were recesses, big enough for a human to lie horizontally, to sleep perhaps. Faith turned away from Helen and moved nearer to the wall. Metal and brick had been beaten smooth. There were no jagged edges here, and the recess was lined with blankets, had a pillow. Somebody did indeed sleep here.

"Look," said Faith, as Helen appeared at her side. "People live here."

A shadow flitted across the far end of the tunnel, its cloaked form hiding everything but its eyes. Its smell reaching them even from that distance, however. The creature smelt rotten, decaying. It smelt of death. Surprisingly, it paid them no attention.

"Christ," said Helen. "Was that a Burrower?"

Shapes from imagination were beginning to take form and become a reality. Curiosity burned alongside a growing fear so much had been kept hidden for twenty years. What plots and schemes had been hatched within these walls as well as outside?

"We follow and find out."

But neither woman moved, both reluctant to approach the figure, discover the type of human living within the Barricade.

"How many of them are there, do you reckon?"

Numbers had never occurred to Faith. Although they were always termed the Burrowers, plural, she'd regarded them as solitary figures. Shapes who patrolled the darkness and formed their own style of protection to those above. She'd never had any sense they were huge in number, might pose a threat. Now she wasn't so sure.

Age old questions reared their heads. What did they live on? Were they carrion feeders?

She checked her gun and then moved ahead again, flashing her torch into the recesses which seemed to exist in only one side of the wall. Some contained blankets, others were empty and then she saw the first one.

A body reclined in the alcove, shrouded by its coverlet.

"Sleeping?" asked Faith.

Helen shrugged and reached out her hand to pull back the cloth.

"Don't," hissed Faith, "I mean…" She had entered the Barricade on a search for the truth and here was one about to be revealed and yet—and yet she wasn't too sure now. Scenes from old horror movies ran on fast forward through her brain. "Okay," she said at last, "just, you know."

She steadied herself, watched carefully as Helen grasped the blanket, slowly, gently, lifted it back. Two skeletons lay there, curled up together. They looked small, almost childlike. A glint of metal drew her attention and she looked closer. Each wore a locket around their neck.

"The twins," said Helen.

Faith stifled a sob. She remembered the twins. Sixteen-year-old Mair and Menna. Menna whose illness had led the two of them to jump from the Barricade. She had been on duty that day, tried to stop them. Somebody had brought the two here, laid them in each other's arms. Somebody cared.

Another alcove, mother and baby posed as Madonna and child. The decaying toy lying by the baby identified the pair. They too had been treated with respect.

It didn't matter how many years had passed. Each skeleton was marked by something which identified them, bringing their living form back to those who now examined their bones.

Then they came to a deep wide ledge, skulls laid out in rows across the terraced levels. At the back, the upper halves of four skeletons. A macabre ornamentation.

"You know what this scene reminds me of?" asked Helen.

"No," said Faith, taking in the odd scene again.

"Fun Fairs, the rifle range, or a coconut shy."

Faith looked at her for a moment and then back

at the skulls. At the end of one ledge sat a bowl containing a number of stones.

"Let he who is without sin," muttered Faith, picking up one of the stones and feeling its cold weight. "Wonder who they were?" She had an itch to throw it, a feeling which brought a sudden wave of self-disgust.

Her foot crunched on something. Glancing down, she saw she'd stepped on a skull and crushed it with her weight. It was small. Human. A child's. Other bones scattered the area, increasing the further down they went to where the shadow had been seen, the smell increasing all the time. Had these formed part of the skeleton range as she now thought of it. Did they throw stones down here at children's skulls in the name of entertainment? Were those earlier tableaus simply a way of exhibiting their trophies?

They'd come upon an area which didn't just hold bones. Human ribcages had been fixed into the sides of the wall and opened out to support decomposing bodies. Some ribcages were positioned horizontally on the floor or on small ledges. These formed baskets containing parts which had lost their original owner. The nearest one to Faith held two hands. Somebody had placed them together as if in prayer.

"Ugh," said Helen, taking in the scene. "Seems like some of those horror stories people used to tell are true."

"We don't know that," said Faith, despite the apparent evidence around her. She didn't want to believe it.

"Well, we've got the bones, must be hundreds here."

And there were the bodies, more than she'd realised. The number appeared to include the number who'd jumped recently as well as those who had simply disappeared. She wanted to turn and run, get out into the fresh air, try and scrub the sight from her mind. But she couldn't. She had to go on. Find out more.

Their torches were picking out flashes of white in the walls, a mosaic forming of metal and bone, skulls staring out. This was where some of their dead ended up. Always dropped into the Barricade to be 'disposed' of, so they didn't have to think about it. And what had they thought would happen to their nearest and dearest once they were left in this manner. That the bodies would be laid out somewhere and allowed to rot naturally, a respectful end. Had they really thought that? Faith doubted it. Most of them preferred not to think about the dead once they'd gone, or at least not their fleshly form. They discussed their lives, yes and remembered them, but preferred to forget their death and internment.

Another shadow moved beyond them. This time, Faith didn't hesitate. "Hey!" she called and sprinted towards it.

"Faith! What the fuck?" Helen ran after her. "You don't know what they are."

But Faith wasn't listening. She wanted to know, needed to know, who the Burrowers were. The tunnel narrowed again, she could hear Helen breathing heavily behind her. The shadow was still ahead but Faith was making ground, could reach out and touch, grab hold of the cloak. She pulled and the figure jerked to a stop as the hood was pulled back, making a choking sound as the ties at the figure's throat jarred it.

Faith just stared, unable to speak. Whatever she'd expected, it certainly wasn't this. Helen had gained her side, looking in the same direction, she too was silent, astounded.

"Josie," whispered Faith, as she shone her torch onto her daughter's blinking face. Familiar brown eyes gazed back at her, the cheeks, always gaunt, now seemed razor-sharp in the light. Her brown hair, formerly long and wavy had been hacked off, gave her skull only a light bristling. She looked almost as skeletal as the bones they'd passed on their way to her.

"Mum," whispered Josie.

And Faith recoiled at the smell of her daughter's breath, the same odour which she had sought to scrub from herself earlier that day, the same smell which reeked its way through the hatch.

"Josie, sweetheart. What are you doing in here? Like this? I've been going out of my mind with worry. Looking for you everywhere."

"Didn't you get my message?" Josie looked shocked. "I asked Malik and Andrew to let you know. When I saw Linda, I knew I had to hide. I couldn't find you so I went to Sylvie and Andrew. They brought me in here."

Faith couldn't believe it. "They knew and they didn't tell me!" Anger and distress reared up. Part of her wanted to get back outside and confront her so called friends. How could they have not said anything when they knew how upset she'd be?

"They said it was the safest place to be. Nobody comes in here, nobody knows *how* to get in here."

"That's debatable," said Helen. "We know, we also know about Andrew. I'm sure there are probably others."

"You could've come out again. I'd have kept you safe."

Josie shook her head. "No. You'd have been in too much danger. Andrew said Howard was gunning for you anyway. There was a chance you'd end up like Linda…"

"Howard? Was he behind Linda's death?"

"Yes," said Josie. "He was there with a small group of men. I couldn't see their faces. But I'd recognise Howard anywhere. They were cutting her…"

Josie's voice trailed off and her eyes grew distant. There was pain and trauma in that look. One many had worn twenty years ago.

"Josie."

Her daughter looked startled, as if surprised to see her mum there. Faith cast her mind back to Malik, barely vocal at the Council meeting, keeping secrets—as was Andrew. Secrets and lies every way you turned.

"You saw them kill Linda?" interrupted Helen.

Josie nodded, the traumatised expression remaining on her face.

"I don't think we should ask her anything more," said Faith, pulling her daughter closer to her.

"No, I'm sorry," said Helen. "We have to know what's going on. We came in here for answers after all."

Helen spoke the truth. They had to know even if it meant Josie reliving the horrors of Linda's death.

"I'd spent the morning with Linda. She was like always, nervous, twitchy, pacing. This time though she kept on about those bloody worms, more so than usual. Kept itching and flicking at her skin, saying she needed to get them off her, *out* of her. There was nothing on her of course, I checked and reassured her and eventually got her back to bed. As soon as she was fast asleep, I came home, had something to eat and then went back. When I opened the back door, I heard voices, Linda's, she was crying."

Josie paused, appeared to struggle as she pulled herself under control. "I crept around outside to her bedroom window and looked in. That's when I saw them. They were holding her down and she was shrieking and howling. Howard was leaning over her, saying something but I couldn't make it out. Then he... then he... he stabbed her. Then two other men started to cut open her stomach and they... they... they pulled something out. I thought, I thought it was her stomach or something but it was something else and it moved, wriggled in their hands. They shoved it in a bag and left. When they'd gone, I just stared in at the window. I couldn't move, couldn't go to her. There was no point. And then I got scared. So I went looking for you and found Malik. I told him everything and he took me to Andrew, then they both brought me here.

"And they didn't tell us," said Helen.

Faith still couldn't believe it. Whatever was happening sounded like the stuff of nightmares. She continued to hold her daughter tightly as Josie sobbed against her.

"That man you found in the carpark this morning," said Helen. "You said his stomach had been ripped open. Do you think there's a possibility..."

She didn't need to finish her question. Faith knew exactly what she was getting at.

The sound of voices drifted up to the small group. Faith turned in their direction to see more shadows gathering in the distance. They moved as one, spoke as one. The angle of the heads indicated they were looking up as they sent their whisperings up into the Barricade.

"No, Mum." Josie was whispering now, pushing them back the way they had come. "Malik's spoken to them and they let me stay on condition I don't go near them. They leave me alone."

Faith could hear someone walking up above them, imagined them looking down and considering Linda or Donald.

"Josie, no matter what Malik said or implied, you are safe with me and I'll always look after you and if anything does happen, well…" Faith nodded at Helen.

Faith looked again at the group. She knew she should take Josie and get out but something inside her was pushing her on, forcing to confront many of the black holes of her knowledge of her limited existence. "Stay here," she said and pulling out her gun, marched up to the cloaked group.

"Mum, don't." Faith shrugged off her daughter and continued towards the figures.

"They will return," whispered the voices. "They're coming back and you have to let them out."

"Let who out," demanded Faith, pointing her gun directly at them.

Her voice must've carried because from above came someone calling her name. "Faith? Faith is that you? What are you doing down there? How… Hey, let go of me, what are you…"

There was a thud and a jolt from above, as flakes

of rust drifted down on them, merging with a scattering of white.

"Who was that?" asked Helen, running up behind Faith. "I don't like the sound of it."

"That was Gary," said Faith, finally recognising the voice. "He lives next door to Malik. One of the good guys, I've always thought."

"Sounds like he's in a bit of bother," said Helen. "As are we, I think." She jerked her head towards the group who had turned to face the intruders. Cowls covered their faces preventing identification.

"You shouldn't have come," hissed one.

"You've no place here," said another.

"You've no place *anywhere*," said a third.

"Now if that's not a threat, I don't know what is," said Helen.

"Yes, but it's who's making the threat that's not so threatening. Isn't that right, Andrew?"

The figure nearest to her, cast back his hood, as did those next to him. There were five in all and she knew every one of them, although she hadn't seen four of them since they'd vanished a year before.

"You really shouldn't have come down here," said Andrew. "You've messed everything up."

"Everything? You hide my daughter and don't tell me, even though you know I'm worried sick. You're sending messages up to the walkers to frighten them…"

"That bit was just pretend," he said. "Keeping up appearances. We have to play a part to frighten people away, demand an offering, you know, scare people with tales of cannibalism and things that go bump in the night."

"And Josie?"

He had the grace to look embarrassed at that. "She's safer here than she is anywhere else, and it was only temporary until…"

"Mum." Josie had not remained as instructed, had instead followed Faith and Helen as they approached the group.

"And Malik's been helping you?" Malik, her *friend*, was fast becoming a stranger to her.

"Yes. Look, we know Howard's up to something, you think so too but we needed more information so I asked Malik to get more chummy with the man. It meant deceiving you, but it was the only way to give the impression he really had come round to Howard's way of thinking. And it gave us more time to block off all the exits."

"I don't understand," said Faith, as she processed Malik, and Andrew's, apparent innocence against her earlier condemnatory thoughts. Then she processed his final words. "Block off exits?"

Andrew sighed, dismissed the men with a look. "May as well tell you everything now you've found your way here. We've known for a long time that those below want to return and we, like you, have no intention of allowing that to happen. We found there were additional entrances and exits to the bunker complex built within this Barricade. We don't know who built them or who helped them, it was all done so long ago, but when the last of the Burrowers came to us, risked coming out into the light to let us know what was going on, we discovered they could leave the ground below at any time. The only reason they chose not to was because of the presence of the Burrowers in the wall. They carried infection and those hidden couldn't risk that. The Burrowers were as much a barricade as the iron and steel around them."

"So you've been pretending to be Burrowers," said Helen. "What sort of people were they? I mean were the stories true?"

"You mean did they eat the bodies dropped down to them? Yes, yes, they did. There were never that many of them. Usually poor souls who had lost their way somehow. We don't know where they came from but they viewed coming into the Barricade as a sort of penance and they regarded eating the flesh as a way of honouring those who died. They were very peaceful folks. They never talked much, sometimes they'd try to explain what happened to them but it was always confused. Stuff about being put to sleep and waking up in a room with orange lights. Never made sense."

Orange lights. It was an image from her own nightmares. Had she heard something, a whisper perhaps?

"It was us above, who made them out to be monsters. Making up stories and beliefs about them because they were hidden from us. What you can't see does have a habit of becoming monstrous…"

"Unless you know what went in there in the first place," said Faith, thinking of her husband.

"We've at least blocked the last possible way for those below to return. Apart from the one above, that is."

"So all those whispered messages were just a form of subliminal communication? An attempt to start warning people?"

"Yes, trouble is, some of those above have a more direct communication with the bunker."

"Howard."

"Yeah, Howard. He's been staging a bit of a takeover lately and nobody seems to be standing up to him. He's been buying people off with promises for when the return happens."

"When the return happens, not if," said Helen. "And Malik told you this?"

"Yes. We know the world is righting itself. You've felt the seasons re-establish; no one really expected it. I mean it's snowing up there for Christ's sake. The farmers have even been trading us some hops as a gesture of goodwill and I've been trying to establish a proper agreement with them, despite Howard's best attempts to undermine me. It means those below think they can return and take charge again, carry on as if nothing ever happened in the interim."

"They expect to rule?"

"Rule. Set taxes. Dictate our lives. Control us. As they did before."

"Over my dead body," said Faith.

"And mine," said Helen.

Then Faith had a thought. "That smell down here. What is it?

"Another little bit of role play. We pull the dead down here as has always happened but lay them out in a chamber." He nodded his head in its direction. "To make people think we still − eat - the bodies, we make sure we spend some time in there, let our clothes and skin absorb the smell, touch their hands, their arms."

Faith shuddered. "So you don't…"

"Good God no."

"What can we do?" asked Faith.

"I think you need to go back above. I'll join you shortly and we'll talk more. Josie should stay down here. I really don't think it's safe for her up there. We'll look after her. And if you want, we'll hide her away from Howard and his cronies. Trust me."

"You promise to look after her?"

"Promise."

"You believe all this?" asked Helen.

"Yes, although I'm finding it difficult," said Faith. "You?"

"Strangely enough, I do too."

"I'll be fine, Mum. I'm not as weak as you think I am," said Josie as they took their leave.

Faith nodded and hugged her daughter. She no

longer felt frail, she felt like steel. Faith left her daughter behind, more reassured than in a long time she would survive. Her feelings about Andrew and Malik however, were in turmoil.

"You know we're taking an awful lot on trust," said Helen as they made their way back past the skeletons.

"Yes," said Faith. "But my gut says they're telling the truth."

"At least you're looking a lot happier," said Helen.

"Yes, and it's not just finding Josie. It's knowing Malik and Andrew are still the good guys in this. At least I'm hoping they are."

They continued through the tunnels, beneath the opened-out ceiling where they'd spied walkways and ladders. That exploration would have to be for another time.

And then they were outside, to be confronted by a figure running towards them, feet crunching in the layer of snow which had fallen in the few hours they had been inside the Barricade. Torches were not needed in the strange light to see who it was.

"Faith! Helen! Thank God," called Ruth. "You've got to come with me. You've got to come and see this."

Ruth took hold of both their arms and started pushing them towards the steps which would take them to the Barricade's summit.

"Up," she said. "You've got to get up there now!"

The three women made their way to the top, slipping slightly at the dusty coating and then gripping the barrier at the peak.

A chill wind whipped round them. Faith could feel it biting at her cheeks pinching her nose. It was like old times and that was when she knew, understood why Ruth had demanded they come up here. In the strip of land below, the gap between the bunker entrance and the gate in the wall, a figure could be seen. The door behind it had opened and Faith understood she was looking at someone from below. Andrew was right, they were coming back and coming back now.

"They will not be allowed out," she snarled and headed off to the gate. From what Andrew had said, there would be people in place to help them get out and she could not allow that.

"Come on," she said to the other two. "We have to make sure the gate stays locked. Keep Howard and his cronies away."

The three women made their way towards the central part of the walkway, found it harder and harder to push through as more and more headed up to join them and look down on those beyond. Faith briefly wondered how the structure could bear the weight of the population and then dismissed the thought. She had to focus.

Eventually, they got to the steps which would take them down to the gate. It was even harder now to fight against the tide of people making their way up. But they managed it, although it was a bruising experience.

Howard and Keith were already stood at the gate. Malik and another man with them. Faith and Helen approached.

"We let them out," said Howard. "It's the human thing to do."

"No," said Malik. "It's the law. You don't get to do this."

"You forget it's I who makes the law," snapped Howard.

He really believed that, thought Faith. The man was delusional.

"You like to act as if you are," she said, "but you're wrong. Helen, do you think you could round up some of your more reliable soldiers?"

"Already on it," said Helen running off.

"I'll go back up there," said Ruth. "A little reminder of our Law could come in useful. *They chose to go in. They can never come out.*"

Ruth too was soon gone but it wasn't long before they could hear a rumble of voices, quiet at first but growing with rage and indignation. The chorus of '*They chose to go in. They can never come out*' echoed round the walkway. Howard would find it harder now to attempt to open the gate. She knew he could buy people but she doubted he had enough to buy the entire population of the community.

She manoeuvred herself behind Howard so she was between him and the gate. Then she turned and peered through the small windows of reinforced glass. It was grimy, made the vision blurry, but it was enough to see more of those who'd abandoned them come blinking out into the wintry world. After half-a-dozen adults, smaller figures ran out. Children. Their cries echoed around the arena as they whooped and played in what they had only read about, never seen until now. Faith noticed how the chant got a little less at this sight, seeing small children pulled at emotions many had buried. Then she heard Ruth cry out.

"What about our children?" she called. "What about my two children? They're both dead. They never got to run and play in the snow, build snowmen or have snowball fights. They didn't get your sympathy or smiles. Don't you dare dishonour our own with this false feeling. *They chose to go in. They can never come out.*"

"Thank God for Ruth," said Helen. "They'd be breaking down the door from this side if she hadn't said that."

As the voices rose, the children stopped playing and looked up, then back at the adults with them. Faith saw them gestured back inside. The ploy had not worked. Then the adults also vanished. All except one male. He strode over to the huge gate, peered through the blurry glass directly at Faith. He looked familiar.

"You will let us out," he said. "We are your government and you will obey."

She remembered now. The Prime Minister. But no such title existed anymore. There had been no election. No vote which would have continued his term. They might have had something below but without a large part of the population taking part, that was invalid. No. He was not her Prime Minister. He was nothing.

"No," she said. "You are not and we won't. You chose to go in. You can never come out.

He stared at her for a moment longer, sought to look past her as if searching for someone and then he turned on his heel and marched back into the bunker. A cheer from above rose up at his retreating form.

"You think this gate is the only way," sneered Howard.

"I know about the doors inside the Barricade," said Faith. "They've been destroyed."

Howard laughed. "People climb you know."

At that moment, Helen returned, not only with the whole of her watch but the remainder of the community who were not up on the walkway.

"Easily sorted," said Helen. "I'll post a guard around the top and we'll also have guards around the base. They won't get out."

"You think everyone's on your side?" asked Howard.

"No," said Helen. "I know you've made promises, bought people. But not everyone's like you. There are people with morals. Actually, come to think about it. If people are desperate to get out, perhaps we should allow you and your friends to go in."

"No," said Howard backing away slightly, before he recovered himself. "I think however the situation is not as clear cut as you may think."

Faith turned her back on him and looked through the glass. Would any more appear that night? It was late so it was highly unlikely, unless they'd wanted an element of surprise. Now people knew what was happening. The complex was going to be alive tonight with people ripping open old wounds, many like herself, keen to see her husband suffer in some small way for what he had done. Although how did she feel about her son? She wasn't sure about that. And would Josie want her brother back? There would be arguments in cubicles, at the bar, in alleyways and warehouses. Festering wounds, long-buried, all bubbling to the surface ready to erupt. Twenty years of pain was not so easily dealt with.

But if they wanted to come out, did that mean they'd used up their resources below? If that was the case, how were they supposed to be supported? She did not relish working to keep those who had abandoned her alive. Could *she* leave *them* to die?

She stood back and watched in admiration as Helen swiftly and efficiently organised the guard, noticed her authorising the use of live ammunition. Most guards carried blanks. Beyond her, voices carried.

"I'd like to see her just one more time."

"Well you can," came the unsympathetic reply. "From up there."

"But I want to speak to her, say I forgive her."

"Forgive her? Are you bloody nuts? She went in there without so much as a look back. Your mother left you behind."

The voices faded as the couple moved away. Faith could empathise completely with their feelings. Everyone had been hurt in a similar manner but she knew whilst there were many who wanted them to remain below ground, there were plenty of others who wanted to forgive. They were the ones Howard would be seeking out now. She knew that's what she would do if she were in his position. Even Josie had shown a similar tendency, not for her father, but for her brother. *I was a brat to him*, she said. *And I paid for it.*

"You can't deny you're curious though," said Ruth, when Faith joined her again on the walkway. Many had since descended and gone home for the night, unwilling to remain in the cold and thinking, probably correctly, no more would appear.

"True," said Faith. "I'd like to see what they look like now. I want to see them pale, gaunt, wizened. I don't want to see them come out fresh-faced and in perfect health. That would be rubbing salt in the wound."

"Did you know about your husband and his

secretary before they went in?" asked Ruth.

Faith cast her mind back. Remembered the increasing number of late nights, for a campaign he'd said, but she had smelt the perfume. Constituents, he'd said. Graham had become more evasive than usual, his politician's persona, seeping into their family home. And Callum had seen how his dad could manipulate people and get what he wanted with very little effort and had wanted that for himself. Faith loved her son but she had felt an increasing dislike for the person he was becoming.

"Yes, and perhaps we'd have split eventually, but I wanted it on my terms. I wanted to be the one to walk away."

"Do you think they're still together?"

Faith laughed. Graham and Shirley. "No, they'd have got on each other's nerves in no time. I hope they have a law in there that the person you chose to take in with you, is the person you must remain attached to—as long as you both shall live."

Ruth chuckled. "I don't really want to see my mother. I used to think I'd have all sorts of things I'd want to say to her but now, the kids are dead and gone, nothing's gonna bring them back. She's not worth expending the effort for."

"Sad though, that families have had to come to this. What sort of people have we become?"

"Realistic. Desperate. Suspicious."

"You'll be back up here tomorrow?"

"Yes, don't think I can keep away now. It's like an

itch."

"And a whole lot of other people will be scratching the same sore," said Ruth as they said goodbye.

Faith made her way back down. She needed to speak to Malik, to Sylvie, to Andrew. To thank them and apologise for her mistrust.

CHAPTER NINE

SHE WASN'T surprised to find the bar packed, the customers spilling outside despite the chill. Children were running around a little distance away, shrieking and laughing as they made their first snowballs, pelting each other, and the occasional adult. They did not go too far however, preferring to stay in the safety of the limited beams of light illuminating this section of the lot.

All adults monitored the children, making sure they didn't go too far. Their numbers, as Howard had said, were low. Faith did not disagree with that, but she preferred the population to grow naturally and carefully. Dying in childbirth was a very real issue and needed to be taken seriously. Especially as it was the women taking the risks. They needed to redevelop the appropriate care for all members of the community and that would only come with more nurses and doctors, both in short supply and few wished to give the time to be trained.

Since when had the human race become so selfish, she wondered. Since they went below ground, came the reply as she remembered seeing those first few appearances on the other side of the Barricade. That had been the ultimate act of selfishness.

She pushed her way through the door, leaving behind the sharp, clear air for a room muggy with the breath and odour of its occupants. Sylvie noticed her immediately, quickly finished serving her current customer before coming over and pouring her a drink without Faith even opening her mouth.

"That was quite something," she said. "For them to appear like that. I wonder why now? What prompted it? If I'm honest, I never expected to see any of them again."

"Perhaps things are becoming difficult below, power, food. I mean, we don't know how any of that was planned or engineered…"

"Or perhaps they've learned things are improving above ground, want to come back and stake their claim before we re-establish ourselves properly."

Sylvie had just given voice to the thought now uppermost in her own mind. It seemed to fit with the behaviour of those who ostensibly claimed to have the best interests of the community at heart.

"Is Andrew around?" asked Faith. She wasn't sure if Sylvie was aware her husband had been spending time beneath the Barricade, amongst the dead. Perhaps Andrew hadn't told her in order to protect her.

"He's just coming in now," she said. "Sent him home to wash and change. If he came in smelling like he did earlier, the bar would've emptied in no time."

"What's he been brewing then? Must be powerful stuff."

"A new beer, with the first of the hops the farmers gave us recently. Has to be brewed in the dark, away from everyone if it is to ferment. He's said it'll be strong enough to strip the flesh from your bones. Even his clothes had to go in for a boil wash, especially that old cloak of his."

"Why don't you just bin the cloak if it's that bad?"

"Oh, can't do that. Become a bit of an heirloom. Wears it when he's working to keep the cold out. I've told him he looks just like those old monks when he's got the hood pulled up."

Sylvie was telling her she knew.

"Is Malik here?"

"He went with Andrew to help him bring the bottles on his way back. They should be here soon."

As Faith sipped her drink, feeling, despite the change in circumstances, a lot more relaxed with the knowledge Josie was safe, she allowed herself to scan the bar, eavesdrop a little. She wanted to know what the general feeling was. It surely couldn't be good, old feelings of anger and abandonment being raked up again. Dead bodies and stomachs ripped open were no longer the subject of discussion.

"The kids would get to see their grandpa," said one man.

"I don't want them near him," said his wife. "He left us behind, didn't want to take them."

"They were given a hard choice," said the man. "It must've been hard..."

"Hard! Hard to go below to comfort, warmth and safety! Hard to sleep well at night knowing no one's going to come crawling out of the shadows to try and cut your throat or you're not going to choke on the poison in the atmosphere after all those fires! Why the change, Brian? When he turned his back on you, his only son, you swore you'd kill him if you ever saw him again."

Faith noticed how the husband avoided his wife's eye, seemed to suddenly appear shifty, sly. She remembered his face now. He was one of the members of Howard's attempted Council coup.

"I've had time to think," he said. "Perhaps it's time to heal on both sides, move forward together. We can only do that if we let them out, hear them speak."

"Brian? This is not you unless... what exactly have you been up to lately?" His wife had moved closer to him, was peering at him in an attempt to get him to look at her directly. She suspected something.

"Up to? What do you mean?" His tone was injured, his face a mask of innocence, but still he couldn't hide that look in his eyes.

"You've had a lot of meetings lately with Howard…"

"Yeah, well that's Council stuff."

"Council? You're not Council. You weren't voted for."

"Votes aren't everything. I'm Council alright. Ask Howard." He got up then and left the bar. Faith could see other men following him, some of their faces she also remembered from the meeting.

The woman looked surprised and annoyed at his sudden departure. She caught sight of Faith looking and came over.

"You're Council, aren't you?" she asked.

Faith nodded.

"What's going on then? What's Howard and my husband up to? You bringing them back?"

"Never," said Faith. "I'd never bring them back. My feelings haven't changed. I'm not sure what Howard's up to although I'm trying to find out. And your husband is most definitely *not* Council."

"You'd better start telling people that," said another woman joining in the conversation. "He and my Pete have gone round telling people so often they're new members everyone believes them. They don't seem to remember there were no elections."

"Wrongfooting you," said Sylvie. "We need to start putting people right."

Faith was surprised at how quickly this had all happened, how much everybody else seemed to know what was going on whilst she, who should be at the centre of things, was most definitely on the outside. Josie, she thought. So much time had been taken up with her she'd missed all this.

The door was wide open to allow air to circulate and over the heads of the throng, she could see the meeting portacabin across the way. The lights were on.

"Looks like a meeting's in session," said Faith. "Perhaps now is the time to start doing a bit of digging."

"Do you want any backup?" asked Sylvie. "Andrew and Malik shouldn't be long."

"No," said Faith. "I'll keep any flak directed at me for the moment. Keep them out of the spotlight a little longer."

"Okay," said Sylvie, but her voice belied her worry and as Faith left, she saw one of Sylvie's bouncers move at her friend's direction, follow her across the lot albeit at a discreet distance. Did she need that sort of physical protection? It was worrying they thought so.

Nearing the door, she noticed some of the younger guards outside, leaning against its walls. They straightened as she approached, shifted position so they were blocking her way.

"Fraid you can't go in," said one. "Howard said members only."

"Well as I seem to recall," said Faith. "I am a Council member, at least until the next election."

"You're not on the list," insisted the guard, "you can't go in."

"And you can't stop me." Faith moved to push her way through but they formed a solid wall, stopping her progress. "You will get out of my way," she said.

"Or else?" they sneered.

"Or else I'll make sure you get some of the worst jobs going for the rest of your lives."

"Yeah? You've got no say. Things are changing. Have changed, Howard says. We've got a new order now."

Faith tried again and this time one of them pushed her back with a determined shove. She would've ended up sprawled on the floor if Sylvie's protection hadn't come up behind her and caught her in time. He gave the men a look and moved in on them. For the first time they looked scared but then they realised their numbers and edged closer together, felt braver.

"Thanks," she said, freeing herself from his grip, heading towards the cabin again.

"Faith! Hey, Faith!" A voice carried across the night, above the hubbub of the crowd who seemed unaware of the altercation at the portacabin.

It was Andrew and Malik.

"Come and join us for a drink!" they shouted. "Got the special brew in. Want to be the first?"

Faith looked back at the guards who just smiled at her. "Sounds like your friends would rather you were with them. You'd be better off over there you know. Go and enjoy a drink. It's been a long day."

Ugh. They were coming up with the same old comments, using the ploy so beloved of the old ruling elites. Repeat a lie often enough, people accept it as the truth.

She made her way reluctantly back to the bar. Andrew and Malik steered her inside to a corner hidden by a mass of regulars. It was as if a deliberate protective ring had been thrown around them.

"You need to keep away from them," said Andrew as she sat down beside them, giving them both an angry and annoyed look.

"I've every right to be in there."

"Perhaps, but he's got his bully boys onside now. Is telling people what to do, not asking. He's had a plan for some time now. Still not quite sure what but I think it's about to come to fruition."

"You think he's been in contact with those below?"

"I know he's been in contact with them," said Malik.

"How?"

"Because I helped set up their communication lines."

Faith choked on her drink. Malik helped set this up! He really had been playing the inside game.

"Don't look at me like that," said Malik. "Andrew's told me you know everything. This way we fight back from a position of knowledge."

"Knowledge which you did not presume to share with me?"

"I wanted to do a proper survey of the community first," said Malik. "I needed to know who I could call on, who would still stand against a return. When there seemed to be a number in favour, albeit still in a minority, it got me worried. Why would people change their mind when they'd been treated so badly?"

"And?"

"And the usual. Promises made of power, of wealth, or the possibility of wealth. Appeal to a person's selfish self-interest when they've had years of austerity, of trying not just to live but to survive, when everything was bleak and grim. Who wouldn't want to change things for the better and even more, become top dog?"

"I don't think Howard wants anyone to be top dog except himself."

"You're not wrong there."

"So?"

"So."

The two men fell quiet and contemplated their drinks. Both seemed reluctant to speak any further.

She knew what they were going to say, however.

There was a sizeable group in the community who were preparing to help those below return to society above and not just to return but reclaim their old positions and force people like her to work for them. Faith had no intention of slaving for them, they did not deserve it. The people they left behind deserved better.

"When?" she asked.

"Not sure," said Andrew. "But soon."

CHAPTER TEN

For the remainder of the night, it seemed as if Andrew was trying to convince Faith he was on her side. Sylvie and her husband kept refilling her glass but still, despite the amount, a part of her mind remained cold and clear, stubbornly keeping a mistrustful eye on those she considered friends but who had been living a double life without her knowledge. That much of what they'd been doing was to protect her and Josie made it harder in a way to accept. She viewed it as a sign of weakness and although she understood her unspoken anger which directed at them should really be pointed at herself, she found it easier to blame others.

She pushed back her chair and rose to her feet. "I need time to think," she said.

"Why don't you stay in the compound tonight?" asked Sylvie. "There's room."

Sylvie's words made her pause. The compound had always been cramped, very little space for others. "How come?"

"They've moved out," said Andrew. "Howard, his cronies."

Thinking of her own home, she doubted they would be neighbours. Someone with ambition like Howard would be going much more upmarket.

"'I've been to their new homes," said Malik. "They've settled themselves in to some pretty fancy buildings. They've been working on them for a while to make them suitable to live in again."

"Claiming the best, just like their buddies below," said Faith. This grabbing of pole position in everything was beginning to rankle. All the little inequalities were creeping back in, and also the not so little instances. It was going to become a society of haves and have nots once more if they were not careful.

"And isn't that what they've always been doing, even after all this time?" queried Sylvie. "The rest of us have been so busy just trying to survive, we never even noticed. When this place was set up we all agreed it was going to be a community with everybody being supported equally—but it's never been like that has it? There's always been those who shaved off the cream of whatever resource we have whilst proclaiming they were just the same as us. Remember the old saying, 'we are all equal, but some are more equal than others'? Those days of communism and then the socialists trying to take the moral high ground with the evil money-grubbing capitalists? They were all at it. All selfish, greedy. All trampling on those of us further down the pecking chain. You, of all people, should remember, Faith."

Faith did, and she didn't like it. She had allowed the lifestyle her husband's contacts and position had bought to cushion her guilt, felt they were merely getting what they deserved, what they'd worked for. But her husband hadn't worked like the miners and firefighters, the sewer workers, the nurses. He'd never got his hands dirty, merely rode on the backs of others. He, and she, had been hypocrites but she hoped she'd wiped the slate clean; her efforts on the community's behalf exonerating her for failings before.

"I thought we'd put all that behind us," said Faith. "Hoped we had."

"Seems some can't change their spots," said Sylvie as Faith headed out.

The crowds outside had dispersed, only a few still stood and chatted, eyes fixed on the Barricade, their thoughts remaining with the happenings on the other side.

Faith didn't want to think about it anymore, at least not here. Josie was safe for the moment. Inside the Barricade had been a revelation. The absence of the dreaded Burrowers even more so. It made her reconsider the legend. She doubted, however, she would ever know the whole truth. And those other doors. Did they mean people had been going in and out of the bunker complex all these years? *Get a grip*, she told herself. You're seeing conspiracy theories everywhere. She made her way to the gate, noticing there was no guard on duty. The door to their hut was open and the lights inside off.

All gone to the Barricade, she remembered. To stop those inside getting out. The absence of guards made them vulnerable to those who'd chosen to live beyond their bounds—not those like her who inhabited nearby homes but the gangs who scavenged in the forbidden zones. Far fewer in numbers these days, you still could not take any chances. Ragged men and women, brutalised by their struggles, refusing to conform to any idea of community. They remained dangerous. She'd regarded them as little more than beasts, a cruel, although accurate, assessment.

Now though, who was the beast? At least those beyond were honest in their brutality. Faith realised she hadn't been in those parts of the city for a long time. Focussing merely on their little bubble, they were wide open to strangers and now the idea of an unguarded gate began to worry her. But Howard wouldn't let them be overrun would he, unless...

Had he organised something? Faith shook herself. She was dreaming up problems left, right and centre. Sleep woman, you need sleep. Exhaustion was spreading its ache once more through her body. Waves attacking her at the worst possible moment. It didn't matter the time of day, such assaults were merciless. Unless she was due a break, the only way to cope was to simply power through the haze and that was getting harder and harder to do. Her body sought to betray her at ever more inopportune moments.

With an effort, she sped up, forced herself to walk briskly along familiar streets, make the short journey to her home, passing Linda's bungalow with its door wide open. Howard. He needed to pay for what he'd done—after the more immediate problem of the return. She felt slightly guilty but nothing was going to bring Linda back. She wished the same could be said for those below.

Faith walked past the bungalow, kept her eyes fixed firmly on her front door, reassuringly closed. The windows however, were all dark; without Josie home, there was no welcoming glow to greet her. She turned the key in the lock and entered cautiously, jumpy with thoughts of Howard's scheming, envisioning her husband being above ground already. Why couldn't he have stayed dead and buried?

Instead of turning on the few lamps dotted about, she flicked on her torch, scanned each room as she passed it. All were empty, the backdoor double-bolted and most definitely locked. She looked up the stairs and decided against her bed. Tonight, she would crash on the sofa. It was as comfortable and warm as anywhere else. *And it'll be easier to escape if you hear anything,* whispered a little voice. It was the little voice that kept her company on her patrols. *Look behind you, do you see the shadow move? What's out here really?*

Faith slumped onto the sofa, made sure her gun was loaded, safe under her pillow. Then she closed her eyes and let her mind drift. Orange light and strange burrowing creatures moved through her dreams. Noise and confusion. Temperatures rising. Strange ideas worming their way into her subconscious, wriggling.

She woke with a start. The unbearable heat blazing through her and forcing her to fight with the window catch in an effort to open it as quickly as possible. It panicked her, the intensity of these attacks, the way they swept aside all conscious consideration of anything else. It made her vulnerable and she didn't like it. Eventually, the cold air touched her skin and she cooled down, was able to take in the outside world once more.

With the curtains open, the strange light filtered into the room making her think for a moment she'd forgotten to turn off a lamp. She gazed at the window, saw dots of white appear, freeze slightly in position and then slide down the pane, melting as it went. It was snowing again and she wondered how deep it would be tomorrow. Other flakes danced just beyond the glass, not wanting to come any closer. They created a swirling, hypnotic pattern which held her gaze until her eyelids grew heavy and she finally slept.

The following morning, she woke to a deeply blanketed world. She had not seen snow like this for a long time. It made her feel like a child again, and she suddenly wanted to call Josie down, come outside and build a snowman. Then she remembered, Josie wasn't here but others might soon be. Faith made her way upstairs and dug out the last of her fresh clothing, the few remaining thick jumpers and socks. She paused at her bedroom window, gazed down at the snow below, expecting to see a pristine blanket, untrod by anyone.

The footsteps leading up to her door and around her front garden made her start. Someone had been out there and she'd not heard them. A prickle of unease ran up her spine. She pulled on her coat and boots and cautiously returned downstairs, gun in hand. She peered through the window at the side of the door, nudging aside the net curtain to try and get a view without being seen.

The footsteps were beginning to disappear beneath a fresh flurry of snow but it was enough to see the steps which approached the house also led away. Why had they come? She had nothing, except a voice in the community and if they wanted that then they would have broken in and either killed her or dragged her off somewhere. But she had been left alone.

She opened the door and allowed the cold to wash over her, wake her up. It didn't take long. A quick look left and right revealed no one hiding to leap out and grab her. She headed off across the road towards the entrance to the cul-de-sac, a swift look at Linda's house showing the door now closed.

Faith shrugged. She was not going to think about it anymore. Most likely, it was Ruth or Helen checking up on her as they had before. The proposed return was all consuming. Again, there was no one at the gate but it didn't matter. For once everyone was up and about, milling in crowds at the base of the Barricade.

Faith walked over to the stairway and found it closed off. "Not safe," said Gary, with a worried look at the numbers behind her. "All that snow and ice, the people here. It's asking for trouble."

"Who says?" she asked.

"I just thought it would be safer."

"*You? Not Howard?*"

"That git, no." Gary's hurt tone convinced her.

"Look," she said. "People want to know what's going on. If you don't start letting them up soon, you're going to have a crush and people will most definitely get hurt. Get the guards clearing the steps. Show people what you're doing, they'll wait then."

His look was doubtful but he waved a couple of guards over and soon brooms and shovels were being handed out to those who were above them. Faith also took a shovel, made her way to the top, started to throw spadeful after spadeful over the other side of the barrier as if she would bury them again. As she worked, however, she noticed movement on that side, saw the door open and this time more than one came out. Body after body stepped out into the open, hesitantly at first but then seeing no danger with more confidence.

"Gary," yelled Faith." I think you should let them up now. We need to show those bastards we don't care about them. Whatever hell they've created for themselves below ground, they can just go back there, like the worms they are."

The structure started to vibrate, groaning beneath the arrival of its visitors but it held firm. An angry murmur accompanied those who swarmed up its sides and around its walkway.

Soon she was surrounded on all sides as the community joined her, standing shoulder to shoulder, staring down on the returned. Those who'd emerged looked up and started to smile and wave. Faith felt an anger like never before and soon realised how much others felt like her as howls of rage and pain descended on those below whose expressions turned to one of shock.

One of those who'd appeared held a megaphone. "Aren't you pleased to see us? To know we survived? Isn't that what you wanted?"

What they wanted? Faith could not believe it. The sheer narrow-minded, egotistical selfishness of it. How dare they.

"Go back to where you came from," she yelled down.

"Crawl back into your hole," screamed another.

"Liars!"

"Murderers!"

"Bastards!"

"Go back. You are not welcome here. This is not your world."

The man with the megaphone appeared to collect himself and then spoke again. "Don't you recognise me, friends? Your Prime Minister."

Faith stared hard. The man was about sixty, old, pale but his skin was remarkably unlined, showed no sign of the lines which ravaged those above ground. That alone indicated a life of relative ease and comfort. He wore no badges of suffering. She remembered him. Lionel Grey. Her husband's, her ex-husband she corrected herself, boss.

He was looking her way. She didn't want him to pick her out from the crowd, claim a relationship which didn't exist. It felt dangerous. As if she was being set up for something. She wanted no part of it and turned her back.

"Faith!" Another voice and one she thought never to hear again. She continued to walk away.

"Mum." Another man's voice. She paused but did not look round.

"Mum!"

Oh, how she wanted to turn round. Look at her son once again. Tell him how much she still loved him, how much she had missed him. The crowd had fallen silent and was looking at her curiously. What she did now would show whose side she was truly on. She had no choice. Faith blinked back tears and continued to walk away. Descended the steps ignoring everyone.

Despite the open sky, it felt almost claustrophobic amongst the press of bodies, so it was with a sigh of relief when she left the Barricade behind her. The bar was open as always. Andrew and Sylvie sat inside quietly drinking and chatting. Their customers were all at the Barricade but they had no one to look for, to throw accusations at.

"Faith! You look like you've seen a ghost!"

"Heard one," she said. "Graham called after me as I left. I heard Callum shout Mum."

"Your son?"

"I kept walking," said Faith. "I didn't look back. I cannot speak to them. I couldn't betray the rest of us." Mum. The name ripped at her heart.

Sylvie and Graham reached across and each took a hand, squeezing hers tight. They were her family. They hadn't betrayed her.

CHAPTER ELEVEN

"Name?"

"Olivia and Rupert Fellowes."

"Relation?"

"My sister and her husband."

"No children?"

"No. They left them behind with me. Both died in the first few years of the crisis."

Faith watched as Malik filled in the names, recorded those of the ones who reported them. The information would help build a picture of who was still below ground. Their numbers. What to expect.

"Name?"

"Charles and Lauren Morton."

"Relation?"

"My parents."

"Anyone else?"

"No. They left me and my siblings behind.

Turned their back on their grandchildren."

Gradually the names of all those seen were recorded in the book. Some names, however, were missing. These were of the children, the youths, anyone who appeared to be under the age of twenty. These had no names, were not recognised by those above.

"Faith!"

She looked up and could see Ruth at the top of the barricade gesticulating wildly. Her friend had barely left her spot since those below had reappeared. She had not yet seen her mother and was determined to remain there so the first thing she would hear, should she reappear, would be her condemnation.

"*He's* coming back. Wants to speak."

"Who?"

Ruth didn't answer, instead she turned to watch those on the other side of the Barricade. Faith made her way up the steps to her friend's side. Looking down into the clearing before the entrance to the bunker, she saw him. Lionel.

"Crawl back under your stone," cried a voice.

"Go back to where you belong!" shouted another.

"You chose to go in. You can never come out." The echo rang around the barricade.

The man stood there, gazing up at them with an expression not of the fear she expected, but one of contempt. She added her voice to the chorus.

Nobody who went below should be allowed to look up at the rest of them like that.

Then a voice broke away from the co-ordinated chant.

"Hey, where's His Majesty then?"

"Yeah, where's the bloody king?"

Faith noted they called for the King. Elizabeth, when she went below, was in her nineties. What could she offer the future? That had annoyed her. She had expected her to stay above ground to share the suffering of her subjects. As she had done so famously during the war.

Would it be Charles though or William who was king? She found she didn't care. Whoever wore the crown forfeited their right to rule when they abandoned their people.

"Who's going to say sorry?" called someone.

"Yeah. Who's gonna crawl on their knees to us? *Beg?*"

Faith felt the ugly mood solidify around her. There would be no forgiveness from these people, and whilst it had always been what she wanted, she felt depressed at what they'd been reduced to. No forgiveness. It brought no joy.

She heard a scuffle further to her left.

"Get your hands off me!"

The cry focussed her attention.

A small group of guards were pulling spectators back, urging them to return to the ground level, their words backed up by a hand on a shoulder, a grip on an arm. The movements became more forceful as she saw someone spun round and pushed down the stairs. Ewan. One of the older members of the community. He slipped and fell, crying out as his head cracked against an old panel.

"Ewan! Hey, what do you think you're doing to him?" A woman, Ruby, his wife, pushed past the guards to get to her husband.

Friends around them started to push back at the guards, men and women she recognised as being part of Howard's clique. Those on the Barricade turned away from Lionel towards the disturbance.

"People, people. Friends. Please." It was Howard's voice coming through a loudspeaker. "Fighting amongst ourselves will do no good. Please come down from the Barricade in an orderly fashion. We don't want people to be hurt."

"Why should we come down?" A question echoed by many.

"Because it's in your best interests." Howard's voice had changed tone and it didn't go unnoticed.

"Think you're getting a bit too big for your boots."

"I am the Council Leader…"

Murmurs and unflattering comments greeted this statement, their resentment transferred from Lionel to Howard. Faith watched as more men and women of the community gathered behind Howard. He'd built a small army right under their noses but something told her he hadn't wanted to reveal his hand just yet. He looked uncomfortable, slightly worried.

"Come on, people," cried Ben, another of Malik's container friends. "He wants us down there. Let's go. Been pushing his weight around too much if you ask me. Needs to be reminded what democracy means."

"Yeah," shouted the woman at his side. "Let's give him some democracy in action."

They swarmed down from the Barricade then, made for Howard and his group who built a hasty retreat as they saw how clearly they were outnumbered, how much they'd misjudged the situation. Others remained on the Barricade, returned to watching those from below, but they too had vanished.

An angry buzz rose as the crowd sought out Howard. He had disappeared. Faith scanned the complex from her vantage point. Something caught her eye near Andrew's distillery. Weaving in and out of those who remained on the Barricade she rushed over to the nearest steps which would take her down to that spot. She could hear Ruth and Helen calling after her, knew they would follow. It didn't take long before she was scrabbling down the stairs, half-running, half-falling, trying not to get snagged on the rusted outcrop.

Eventually she hit ground level and raced around to where she'd discovered the entrance to the structure. Howard was nowhere to be seen. Faith bent over, gasping for air as the sprint took its toll on her. She took a few deep breaths to steady her breathing and tried to compose herself.

"Shit." Ruth had caught up with her. Helen was just behind, as was Malik. "Do you think he's in there?"

"Where else," said Faith looking at Malik. "Malik?"

He nodded.

"We need to go in again."

A crowd had found them by that point, Ben leading the way. He looked furious.

"He's gone in there?"

"Possibly," said Faith, "but I think we need to keep an eye out for him up here. Do you think you can organise people to search the zone and make sure everyone's alright?"

Ben nodded. "I didn't think he'd be in league with those below. All these years he's been playing some sort of game, biding his time. Why now?"

"Because they want to come back up," said Ruth. "He saw an opportunity and took it. To hell with the rest of us."

"Well, it's backfired on him," said Ben, with grim satisfaction.

"Perhaps," said Faith. "We need to find out exactly what he was up to though."

"In there," said Malik, "and out here."

"Well, we've got those two men of his," said Ben. "I'm sure they'll answer some questions."

"You do that," said Faith. "We, in the meantime, will go in here." She pulled back the entrance to the Barricade drawing gasps from the onlookers. It wasn't a time for secrets, there'd been too many in recent times and it threatened to bring down the Community. "I found it the other day," she said, by way of explanation. "I didn't say anything because Josie is in there and I wanted to keep her safe. I hope you understand."

"She's gone below?"

"No," said Faith. "She just wanted somewhere to hide, to feel safe."

"But the Burrowers," said one.

Shocked faces looked at her and she knew what they were envisaging.

She shook her head. "I haven't found out much at the moment but I don't think the Burrowers exist, at least anymore."

A few approached the entrance and were looking past her shoulder into its darkness. Despite the risk to her daughter, she was not going to prevent them coming if they wanted to.

"What you do," she said, "is up to you. I think we are all entitled to discover the truth. I want to do a proper sweep inside of this rust heap, see exactly what it's been hiding. It's about time we knew what we were dealing with."

If Howard had made his way into the bunker below via the Barricade, she was determined to make sure he wouldn't get out again. Faith could feel the crowds pressing in behind her to get a better look, not that you could see anything in the darkness beyond. As they pushed, she shifted her balance to remain upright, fearing the jagged metal to the sides of the entrance. Should she fall, she would become impaled on spikes and blades, like so many had done. It didn't matter whether you fell from above or were already at ground level—the Barricade was lethal.

"Oh my god, what's that smell?"

"Fuck. It's like someone's died in there."

Those around her fell back a little, choking and gagging as they were assaulted by the stench.

"Course someone's died. All those jumpers. Went somewhere didn't they?"

Faith winced as a woman next to her shrieked. Little orange eyes had appeared at the door. Rats. A brave scout had come to the threshold and was sniffing the air cautiously, seemingly oblivious to the crowd of anxious humans before them.

A foot was raised to stamp down on its head but the rat seemed to sense the danger and dashed away. Not back into the Barricade, but out amongst those gathered. Nor was it on its own as a mass of furry brown bodies followed their leader.

Gasps of horror and revulsion echoed around her and Faith soon found herself part of only a small group remaining at the door.

"Wonder why they've come out," she said.

"Rats leaving the sinking ship," said Helen.

"Either no food or they sense danger."

All eyes returned to the tunnelling gloom within the Barricade.

"We need to go in," continued Helen. "Something is wrong. Out here. In there. Below."

Once more, Faith entered the curved corridor, fitting the mask over her face to lessen the effect of the noxious air. A placebo probably, albeit a reassuring one. Others followed her actions, pulled out torches, poised weapons. A few had guns, bullets being strictly rationed. Most had blades, short daggers, serrated shanks, brutal machetes.

Helen took the lead with Ruth and Faith flanking her. The tunnel, initially cramped before, felt claustrophobic now, the presence of bodies behind her creating the feeling of a wall being pushed towards her.

Voices muttered as they noticed the construction, theories bandied about as the tunnel widened, silence as they came to the chamber of bones allowing them to spread out.

This time, Faith allowed herself time to take in the area properly. Before, she had been guided by Malik and Andrew, her movements directed. Skull and bone embedded the walls, bordered recesses where someone had slept. She placed a hand on an old blanket, felt its rough chill on her skin. Pulling it back revealed thin padded sacks making a poor mattress. Ignoring everyone around her, she wriggled into the space and lay down.

"Faith?"

"Just trying to get a new perspective on this."

"Looks like a bloody uncomfortable one," said Ruth peering down at her.

"Yeah, I doubt anyone slept well in this."

She swung her torch up. The roof of the recess was of the same construction as the barrier it was carved from: rusted metal, sheets pierced with broken pipes, coils of wire. The more she looked, the closer it seemed until it was as if she would be pressed beneath it. She struggled out, pushing Ruth in her haste.

"You okay?" Helen had joined them.

"Yeah, got a bit claustrophobic." By now, her breathing had steadied, her heart stopped thrumming. She felt stupid as she looked back at the alcove. It hadn't changed.

They passed three more adult-sized recesses and Faith pulled back the blankets, revealed the same sad bedding. A low hubbub followed her progress as their companions spread out and inspected the chamber. No doubt they were offering up their own Burrower theories, recounting old stories.

They'd reached that part of the chamber, shrouded in the same dense pitch, where Andrew had met them, kept them, before directing his visitors out again. Faith had assumed one path led away to the right but as additional light gathered around her, she noticed two more paths—one to the left and the other straight ahead.

"Split up and report back?" asked Ruth.

"No," said Faith. "I need to see it all for myself. All this time I thought I knew everything about the zone but it seems there's been a lot hidden from us and I don't like it."

There was no argument from her friends. She paid no attention to what anyone else might be doing, but asked they look out for Josie as they went. Her group turned left, leaving the low murmur of anxious, but excited, voices behind.

The passageway felt as if it was following the curve of the Barricade once more, albeit further in, nearer to its inner perimeter and then they hit a solid wall, broken only by another door hidden away on their right. There were no handles, nothing to indicate how it could be opened.

By this time, a handful of people who'd entered the Barricade with them had caught up. Two carried axes.

"Here," said Faith. "See if you can break down this door."

The two, large burly men who served as members of their small fire crew, came forward. The sound of axe heads striking the mix of wood and metal was painful in the enclosed space. The vibrations clanged and echoed, setting her teeth on edge. Eventually, they broke through, discovering their way had been prevented by a simple beam across the other side.

Faith pushed her way through and saw a flight of

concrete steps heading down. A string of lights lit their route. Helen ran her torch along the walls and ceiling, picking out a small surveillance camera as she did so.

"We go on," said Faith in response to her friend's raised eyebrows. "If they've seen us, they've seen us. Makes no difference."

She was determined to go as far as they could. Down they went, feeling the temperature drop as they did so. Gradually, they saw more light appear ahead as they reached the bottom step and came to another corridor. Barricades of solid concrete were wide enough apart for them to walk six abreast. They made their way silently to the doors which, from their construction, would need more than an axe to gain entry.

"Malik?"

"I haven't been this way, but I assume it's fingerprint activated like the others. And I'm not cleared. Howard never allowed me full access rights."

Faith stared at him. "You've been playing up to him all this time, to be 'in the loop', and yet you remained on the outside?"

Malik looked embarrassed.

"I thought he'd let me in eventually."

"You seriously thought he'd let you know what he was up to? I wouldn't be surprised if he knew what you were doing all along, was actually playing *you*."

Faith directed her attention to the door. There was nothing there to indicate what lay beyond. Curious as she was, she needed to know about the other passageways above, get a clear picture. They couldn't afford to leave themselves vulnerable due to lack of knowledge. It was bad enough as it was.

"We'll leave it for now," she said, even though she wanted nothing more than to batter her way in, blow it up if necessary.

They made their way back up the stairs, sharing angry theories about Howard and those below. The idea they had never been as isolated as they thought, although still abandoned, still betrayed, roused tempers.

She heard the group's angry mutterings at each of the other doors.

"We need to scan the rest of the Barricade," said Helen. "A proper close search, see if there are other places like this. We can't risk being open to whatever they've got planned."

"You reckon they'll risk forcing their way up?" asked Faith.

"When they realise they can't win us over," said Helen. "I'll go and organise it now, get people to report back at Sylvie's."

"Not at the Council room?"

"No," said Helen. "Anything we do would be tainted by association. Secrets and lies. There's no room for that anymore.

Faith nodded her agreement. There was a

nervousness surrounding everyone. From a future which had begun to look bright, one they could rebuild slowly, in their own way, it had become one filled with threat and an order they had not agreed to.

CHAPTER TWELVE

Everything had changed even as nothing had changed. The following day it was as if they were back at day one when nobody knew what they were doing, could quite believe they'd been left to cope on their own. A strange sense of displacement and unreality had settled over them then, as it now did once again.

The whole community was focussed on one thing and one thing only, the Barricade. Large numbers occupied its upper reaches, watching for activity from the doors to the underground complex. Others stood guard at any entrance found either internally or externally at the Barricade. The outer doors were kept open to allow air to circulate within its walls, get rid of the years of stale air which sat, almost solidly, inside.

"Come on," said Helen. "You look exhausted."

"Can't seem to summon the energy at the minute," said Faith. "I know I should keep going, that I need to keep going—and I will—but part of me just wants to sit down and cry." It was an admission she would not make to just anyone.

"I know how you feel," she said. "I went through all that crap a couple of years back. Remember? I think I was lucky we weren't facing the issues going on now."

"I remember," said Faith. "Your face was like a flashing beacon, switching between red and white. We used to tease you. You laughed though. I don't seem to be able to."

"Different circumstances," said Helen. "I wasn't facing the pressure you're under or all this shit with Howard. I still felt like crying at times but I had the space to go off and do it, get it out of my system. You'll get through it. It means you're on the home run to freedom."

"I suppose I have to look on the upside," said Faith. "I'm officially becoming an old crone."

Helen punched her arm. "Don't you dare call yourself that. We don't call the men names which define them by their age. We shouldn't either. We are mature ladies."

"Now you make us sound like ripe cheese." Faith laughed.

"At least I made you smile," said Helen. "Come on, let's go over to Sylvie's and compare notes with everyone, get something to eat and then crash for a bit."

The bar was full. A constantly changing mass of people who came in to report on the areas they'd searched, give any additional names of those they saw on the other side of the barricade, denounce anyone who'd gone over to Howard's side.

"Where's he holed up?" asked Faith. "Anyone find out?"

It was a question asked of everyone who came in and all shook their heads. Sylvie and Andrew did their best to raise spirits, offered drinks and bad jokes, moral support. So many had been forced to confront their ghosts, face torments they'd buried long ago. Some, on the other hand, had to come to terms with the possibility their relatives hadn't survived. Many would mutter 'serve them right', but you only had to look at their faces to realise they didn't mean it, the conflict within their hearts unbearable. Those folk went away into quiet corners to mourn anew.

Faith rested her head on her hand and allowed her mind to drift, the air had turned muggy, the voice level, a gentle hubbub. She could feel her eyelids drooping.

"Come on," said Helen. "You can get a few hours at our place. Tomorrow is another day and all that."

Ruth and Helen pulled her up and supported her back to their digs. She barely paid attention to her surroundings, allowed herself to be dropped onto a bed where her eyes closed immediately. It said something not just about her exhaustion, but also her trust, that she allowed herself to sleep so easily.

When she woke, it was to a lighter dawn. Although winter, the quality of the light was improving as clouds lifted slightly. The air was fresher.

"Come on," said Helen, sticking her head round the door in response to the creaks from Faith's bed as she moved. "No rest for the wicked."

With a groan, Faith pulled herself up and followed Helen and Ruth to the communal kitchens. It was the place everyone migrated to. She didn't care she hadn't washed, was wearing the same clothes as yesterday. They were all in the same boat and had got used to the smell. She could have done with a few more hours but even so, she'd experienced the best night's rest for a long time and the fog in her mind had at last cleared.

"Any news?" she asked her friends as they walked.

"No," said Helen. "We took it in turns to go out last night, made sure one of us stayed with you. In case Howard decided to pull some sort of stupid stunt."

She hadn't thought of that. "I suppose he doesn't like being made an idiot of at the meetings," said Faith.

"No," said Helen. "We think he might try and use you because of Graham, your links below."

"In what way?"

Helen shrugged. "Haven't figured that bit out yet, but I don't trust him."

They'd reached the kitchens and found the facilities maintaining a mere skeleton staff offering only the most basic of food. This was to allow the cooks to rotate their shifts in order to go to the top of the Barricade and look at the scene as it unfolded. After she'd eaten, she kept herself deliberately away from those who would talk to her, so they did not ask the question she knew sat on their lips, 'Why didn't you want to speak to your son?'.

And now she found herself back along the walkway. She did not see her friends, had left Ruth and Helen behind, as she sought to face up to events. She knew they understood, were facing, and attempting to resolve, their own inner conflict. Having compartmentalised so much of her life, locked memories away, she needed to finally face things, including her rage and misery which had been so heavily tamped down until now.

She stared down into the area beneath the Barricade. The snow which had stopped falling in the early hours turned to slush beneath the feet of those who'd come out with the sun, weak and wintry as it was. They'd gone now, back inside as more crowds gathered. Faith assumed the numbers glaring down at them, the sensing of animosity and incredulity pouring towards them caused them not a little concern, triggered a greater caution in their reappearance. Time to regroup and rethink. Faith could imagine Graham involved in that. He had always been good at PR, knew exactly what angle to take. It was probably his idea to send those children out the previous night to tug at the heartstrings. Would he do the same again, risk their safety?

As she looked alongside her, she noticed many of her companions held objects, stones, bottles, whatever they could lay their hands on. They were ready. And although she understood their feelings, in fact itched to have something in her own hand to hurl over the barrier towards those below, she hoped they would refrain. To throw such things at children would be beyond the pale.

But then again, they left the children behind, didn't they? Wasn't that beyond the pale in an even bigger way. They had assumed the children would die. That they would all die. And they nearly did.

Faith frowned as she stared down. There was something puzzling her and then she realised. The area which had been so soundly booby-trapped and mined had not exploded or harmed anyone. It was as if a switch had been flipped to make it safe. But there were bodies down there, some whole, some scattered across the surface, rotted down to bone and scraps of cloth. No one had ever gone to reclaim the corpses on that side; if you missed being pinned against the Barricade, and fell onto open ground, it was regarded as bad luck. No one would claim the body for burial, although relatives, if there were any, might come up and say a few words to acknowledge the passing. Then they would drown their sorrows in Andrew's moonshine. For those who died in the community at large, things were barely more civilised.

Funeral rites were spartan. Nothing more than a big pit formed from a crater a few miles away. Someone died, they would be dragged on a cart there and tossed into the hole, a spadeful of lime thrown in as well. Nobody stayed to monitor what happened to the bodies. Once you'd been trundled down that road, you ceased to exist.

Any last words were said over the body as it lay on the wagon. Most would see their loved one from a distance, notice its destination and simply shrug and turn away. Feelings were cut short with a blade as sharp as any knife.

Since she'd been left with only Josie, Faith had never allowed herself to have any other form of family. She didn't want to suffer the same pain and humiliation as before. That was something everyone wanted, she realised. To humiliate the inhuman community below. Make them feel as they themselves had done. Turning the other cheek was not an option.

It was still cold and Faith stamped her feet to get the blood circulating. She wondered how the movement echoed within the structure. Did Josie hear her? Feel the vibrations of the feet of all those above. How did it feel to have so much weight hanging over you? She wished Josie could be up here with her, allow her to see she too had a say in what happened to those who were demanding to return. That it was her turn to turn her back on her brother if she wished.

Would it make them feel any better though? No sign of Josie had been found on their additional inspections of the Barricade. Faith hoped she'd simply slipped out and disappeared into the outer reaches of their zone. She tried to ignore the possibility Howard and his crew had swept her up and taken her inside along with them. If that was where he had gone. Without any proof, she could only guess. It seemed the most logical course of action considering his recent behaviour.

Across the strip of encircled land, the grey, squat building at its epicentre stared at them with its ugly eyes, harsh and dark. Those windows were tinted. Had never allowed anyone to see inside but they knew the people within could look out as much as they wished. What had they thought as the Barricade went up in response to their abandonment of family and friends. Did they just laugh at something which did not affect them in the slightest? Well, look who's laughing now.

There was a crackling in the air, a sudden blast of static. The public announcement system remembered from that time was sparking back to life. It shook Faith out of her reverie.

"People gathered on the Barricade. You have not seen or heard from us for many years. We know you harbour a deep and bitter resentment at how you perceive yourselves to have been treated…"

Perceived? They were twisting things already, turning the tables on the abandoned people. Soon would come their reasonable excuses.

"Feelings I can understand. All of us suffered from the separation. The bunkers also housed families torn apart."

"Turn that shit off!" came a voice a little way down.

"They suffered? They don't know what suffering is."

"No! No! No!"

Shouts echoed all around the barricade as the muttered remarks and quiet anger erupted into a wall of noise washing down in front of them to pound on the doors of the building. As if in response to their knocking, the door opened.

They were taking a risk. If people started throwing things… but as the figures emerged, she realised they were repeating the same tactics as previously. First came the children, then women and the elderly. The men, the stern-faced politicians, stood behind them, way at the back. Hiding behind a shield of the vulnerable was a long-recognised defence tactic in war.

It beggared belief.

Faith looked at their faces. The children

appeared frightened, occasionally looking back to seek reassurance from a parent who would nod at them and gesture to them to turn their heads round, face those who studied them.

"Go back!" cried a watcher.

"Go back in your hole! Run away. This isn't your world any more. It's ours.!"

"Ours, ours, ours."

"They chose to go in. They can never come out." The chant reverberated around the complex, this time as if it would never end.

Faith looked down and met the eyes of a little girl. She had put her hands over her ears to shut out the sound, blinked briefly but was unable to stop the tears, in the end screwing her eyes tight shut and trying to close out everything around her. A woman just behind her, moved forward and pulled her into her arms, soothing her.

"How can you do this?" she called. "How can you make a child cry like this?"

"As easily as you made our children cry when you did more to them than raise your voices, when you condemned so many of them to death."

"My daughter was five when she died," cried one. "Starved in that first year."

"My son was only ten," shouted another. "Shot by scavengers."

"My baby died at birth because we had no medicines." Another.

"Why should your child's tears be worth any

more than the blood of ours?"

The woman's anger turned to fear then as if she honestly hadn't expected so much hatred to still burn in the hearts of those they left behind. That or she expected them to be pathetically grateful for their return.

"We did this for you," she cried. "We had to survive. We were told the whole human race would die. Somebody had to sacrifice themselves!"

Told, thought Faith. They had all done as they were told, believing the politicians, the armies, the bloody computers. But people weren't computers, would behave in ways which ensured their survival. Fight back in ways never considered by any model. The human spirit was a rare and dangerous thing.

"You don't know what it cost us," she cried as she took her child back towards the bunker, shouting up at those listening. "You don't know what we went through below."

"But you saw us, didn't you," yelled the man next to Faith. "You could watch from those windows or those fucking surveillance cameras. You had ringside seats to our hell and you could've helped and you never did. Sacrifice! You don't know the meaning of the word."

Other children were starting to cry, were moved back to the mothers, back to the bunker. Most of the men doing likewise until just a small group remained, wisely out of throwing distance of the crowd. Lionel, Graham and a few she recognised but couldn't quite name. They stood there as if they owned everything around them already.

Their stance drew howls of derision. Despite the distance, someone threw a stone at them. It was the signal for all to join in and soon a tidal wave of stone and glass, metal and plastic was hurled at the group. None of it hit and the men just stood there with smug expressions on their faces.

"You people need to think things through," called Lionel. "We've already made a formal agreement with Howard, your leader. He's promised to make sure we can all work together. You need to listen to him."

"What promises did he make?" called Gary. "That man doesn't speak for us. He is not our leader as you put it. In fact, you could say he's been deposed. You want to make deals, you deal with the people you see up here. *We* are the people, the community. It is for us to decide whether you join us or not and at the moment, I can most definitely say, it is a not."

Faith scanned the Barricade, she could not see Howard. He had holed up somewhere like the rat they all knew him to be.

"We know where the gates are to get out of this place," said Lionel. "We do not need your permission."

"You will find," said Malik, "those exits have been closed off and are guarded. There is no other way out."

Faith was suddenly anxious, were Howard and his men already at some undisclosed doorway, getting ready to lead Lionel and his people out and stake their claim anew? They would have weapons. The people here had just wood and rocks. She hoped they'd found all the exits at the Barricade. She tried not to think about tunnels which may possibly lead out into other parts of the zone, beyond the barrier. The extent of the underground complex had never been made clear and they'd never been able to work it out.

Graham moved away from Lionel, stepped closer to the crowd. She looked down at him now, knew he'd seen her and was studying her. No doubt measuring her against that bloody girlfriend of his. How many pounds had she gained from her cushy life below ground?

"Faith," said Graham. "I am so pleased to see you alive."

Pleased? He didn't seem pleased although he had shaped his mouth in a smile.

She returned his smile. "You'll forgive me if I do not reciprocate the feeling. In fact, I had rather hoped the opposite for you."

Had she? As she searched within herself, she realised the truth. The understanding lifted a weight from her shoulders as she let her feelings towards him go at last. There was general laughter at her words and she was pleased to see a flicker of annoyance cross his face. He quickly recovered however. He never did let anything faze him.

"Faith, I think a private talk between us would solve many of the issues facing our communities."

"Issues? We aren't the one facing issues. That's your problem and me? Why me?"

"You're my wife."

"Ex-wife," said Faith.

"Our vows still stand," said Graham.

He had a nerve. "You must be kidding. We had lawyers left amongst us when you went, one of them divorced us on grounds of desertion. You'll find it's all legal and above board. According to those laws you still seem to think we all have to abide by."

"Faith, I understand you're still a bit upset…"

His tone was irritating. He was patronising her. Like he used to do. Oh, how she had hated that about him, put up with it for the sake of the children.

"A bit upset! You make this sound as if you'd forgotten to put the bloody bins out or something stupid like that…"

CHAPTER THIRTEEN

THE BANALITY of his words, the implication their suffering had been no big deal roused the watching crowd. They let rip with the missiles and with their anger, the group below retreating beneath their onslaught. Faith noted with satisfaction how Graham, so confident and arrogant a moment ago, immediately turned tail and ran back to the shelter. He'd run away before and now he was running away again. Some things didn't change.

Yet despite their withdrawal, Faith and many others remained along the top of the iron structure, literally on top of the scrapheap, staring down into the space, still fathoming the extent of what was transpiring in front of them.

"Faith."

Helen and Ruth appeared at her side.

"We heard your husband crawled out from

under his stone again. What'd he have to say?"

"Nothing much," she said. "No one let him speak."

"Yeah, gave it to 'em good and proper," said a voice from behind them.

"Howard's calling a meeting," said Ruth. "He wants you, and us, to attend. He's got a nerve. As if he's got any authority."

"Howard's back? Where did he slither out from?"

Ruth frowned and shrugged. "I don't know and that worries me. He's got a small army protecting him. He's outnumbered but can still cause a lot of damage if it comes to a fight. I don't want to see people get hurt unnecessarily."

Shit. He'd wrong-footed them again but he still needed something from them. An uneasy feeling began to claw its way through her. Everything was building up again. Change was coming.

"We know he'll be scheming as usual," said Helen, "but we need to go and find out what he's up to. We might even be able to turn it to our advantage."

Faith felt that was highly unlikely but she had to agree with Helen.

"They might come out again," she said, looking at the closed doors. Much as she hated seeing the people appear it was hard to drag herself away.

"And? They're not going to be able to go anywhere are they? We've got everything covered.

Literally."

Helen had a point. Faith allowed herself to be guided down to ground level and back to Helen and Ruth's quarters. They shared a container with two other women, the two who'd considered the idea of having children by some sort of community decree, a good idea. Their housemates weren't there. They hadn't been there the previous night when she'd fallen asleep either.

"Haven't seen them for a few days," said Ruth. "And to be honest, I haven't missed them. Reckon they were two of the little grasses who went running back to Howard whenever they had some juicy tidbit of news for him."

Faith sighed. The camp was polarising but it had been an invisible splitting and it was as if, apart from a central few, most were unaware of this happening. Insidious tweaks in routine, subtle whisperings, nothing overt. It was the Council Leader's hallmark methodology. Like refusing to rotate the Chair as they'd always done.

"So. Why do you reckon we've actually been summoned?" asked Faith.

"Hostages?" The idea was laughable.

"Hostages to be handed over to Lionel."

"I didn't think we had any value, except to cause trouble. He might just want us in one place so he can get rid of us all in one fell swoop."

She could picture that. Turning up innocently expecting a meeting, only to be faced with a gun, bound and then shot. Dropped into the sides of the Barricade to be left to the Burrowers. Only there weren't any Burrowers any more, not that she was aware of. Only those who pretended, those who sought safety, like her daughter and they had all vanished. She wondered if Josie had heard her father's voice, had she been able to see him, had he seen her? She shook herself. Dwelling on it was leading to conspiracy theory after conspiracy theory.

A knock on the door frame to Ruth's room roused her from her thoughts. Malik appeared bearing bags appearing to contain food. It was food she hadn't smelt for a long time.

Helen, being the nearest, lunged at one of the bags and was tearing it open. "Oh my days, teriyaki chicken!"

The words were a nonsense. They were able to make a fake teriyaki sauce but there were no chickens above ground.

"Don't eat it until you know where it comes from," said Ruth. "That's the rule. So, Malik. Where did it come from?"

He shifted uncomfortably beneath their gaze for a moment. "From below," he said eventually. "They sent it up to us as an offering. Howard told me to bring some over to you before the meeting. A gesture of friendship, he said."

Friendship? Faith reached for a piece and sniffed cautiously. It smelt and felt exactly like it was supposed to but they shouldn't have been accepting such gifts. It was a sign of weakness. And was it really what it appeared?

"It could be poisoned," she said doubtfully, dropping the piece back into the bag.

Malik shook his head. "This came from a large box and I watched the others eat theirs before I left with this bag. They were all still breathing when I left. Eat this and then we all go back."

Faith's stomach was growling at the presence of a food so long denied. With a final shame-faced look at her friends, she dived in. Pushed the question as to how they still had chicken below. *If it was chicken.* The small group ate quickly and quietly, trying to savour the long-forgotten flavours for as long as possible. Hating Howard all the time they did so.

"They can't be short of food then," said Ruth as she licked the sauce from her fingers.

"Or they might simply want us to think that," said Faith. "Give the impression of plenty, that they're doing us a favour by returning."

"Then I suppose we'd better get going and see if they're offering anything else. Dessert for example. Or perhaps a fine wine?"

Despite their reluctance, their curiosity drove them on and sent them back to Howard, just as he'd asked. Faith was annoyed at what would be their perceived obedience but they had no choice if they wanted answers.

The four walked to the meeting room, noticing the small huddles of groups standing about, their gazes continually turning towards the gate in the Barricade, others peeling away for a moment to climb the steps and look down before rejoining their group. The atmosphere reflected the unease they themselves were experiencing. It was as if the carpet had been pulled from under them yet again.

It made her angry. The world had been an uncertain place but they'd survived, created their own certainties and expectations. Understood the way things now worked. They no longer felt there was much to fear from the planet itself. The cause of most people's fears however was to be found closer to home, amongst friends and family. Apart from Sylvie and Andrew, nearly every other couple or friendship Faith knew of showed each retaining a small part of themselves as private. An aspect of their personality and emotion nobody was allowed to be privy to. With that came distrust.

They entered the Council room. Howard had taken the seat he claimed as his at the head of the table. His cronies flanked him as usual.

"Ah, Faith. I'm glad you agreed to our meeting today." As if she had any choice.

"I'm glad you remembered to include us," said Faith. She looked him directly in the eye, refused to show any sign of subservience.

Howard said nothing to her reply, just stared at her, trying to assert his authority, then turned his smile on her friends. She was pleased to see they too, didn't respond. The four of them took their seats at the table and waited expectantly.

"Firstly, I should say we won't be here too long, in fact most of our meeting will be held elsewhere but I just needed to go over a few things with you beforehand."

Howard's faithful lapdog, Paul sat to his right. A smug expression on his face. Ruth and Helen's housemates sat in their seats. Four seats remained empty.

"Where are they?" asked Faith gesturing to the seats. It was not a full meeting of the Council unless they attended.

"Setting things up," said Paul.

"Setting what up? asked Helen.

"Now I don't want you to get all het up," he said.

Patronising bastard, thought Faith.

"We have been receiving some communications lately from those below and they have been anxious to establish a dialogue between us…"

Faith looked at Howard. No doubt he expected stunned disbelief, and she decided to play along, let him have his moment as if she hadn't already worked out what his little game was. Well, she hadn't quite worked it all out but she knew part of it, thanks to Malik who appeared to be studying the table.

"You broke the law," she said. "It's always been agreed that we would never have anything to do with those below unless the whole community agreed. Every single man jack of them."

"We thought it more prudent to keep the contacts discreet," said Howard. "You'll understand why when we meet them."

"Meet them? Are you mad? You're not letting them up here!"

"No," he said. "We're going into their bunker."

Faith's mouth dropped open. Did he seriously think they would agree to such a thing?

"You must be fucking kidding me," said Helen. "How are you going to be discreet with us all walking in through the gate? And if we don't want to go, will you be forcing us at gun point. I can see how well that'll go down."

Howard merely smiled. "Do you think that's the only entrance?"

"No," said Ruth. "But the others we know of are all blocked."

Paul grinned. "Not all of them. Not the important one."

"I know you don't want to be anywhere near me," said Howard. "But you must admit you're curious. You want to know what's going on. What it's like below. And most of all you want to know why now?"

Faith didn't like to admit it but he was right. She wanted to know. You could never make a decision unless you understood all angles. Too much had been built on doubt. It was time to remove the foundations of sand. Society needed something much more solid to stand on.

CHAPTER FOURTEEN

FAITH FOLLOWED Howard silently back to the Barricade, they kept to the background, tried to avoid catching anyone's eye. It didn't work. How Howard thought he could just walk through the crowds now was beyond her. He'd played his hand too early, shown his true colours.

A man saw them, pushed forward and spat in their direction.

"Changing sides, Faith?"

"Why you with them?"

Angry faces were directed at them.

"No!" shouted Faith. "It's not like that. Please, believe us. Let us go below, find out what they want. I promise, when I come back you'll hear everything. I promise. You know me. All of you. I've never lied to you. Done everything I can to make life easier for you."

Heads nodded, voices murmured agreement. The sense of distrust around her lessened. Another disturbance attracted her attention and her heart plummeted.

"Better had come back!" shouted another man, stepping up beside the one who'd spat at them. He was dragging someone behind him. Josie. "You don't come back and tell us everything, she's done for."

"Josie! Let her go." Faith rushed forward but Helen restrained her.

"We can't do anything now," she said. "We've got to go down there, even if we don't really want to."

"But…"

Faith looked directly into her daughter's eyes, saw her fear but also that strange strength which had been slowly re-emerging.

"I'll be alright, Mum."

Two more people stepped out from the throng. Andrew and Sylvie.

"Don't worry, Faith," said Andrew. "We'll look after her. I'm sure this gentleman won't mind coming along to our place." Andrew had a gun and was pointing it at Josie's captor and then someone pulled out another gun and aimed at Andrew. Things were spiralling out of control.

"Stop it!" shouted Helen. "All of you. Put the guns away. That's what they want. For us to turn on each other, leave the way open for them to return and take over. We won't let them do that, we promise. But we need to find out what's going on. Enough of us have died over the years, do we really want to wipe each other out now, when the planet seems to be righting itself. When we have a chance! And do you think, Faith of all people, one of those betrayed as much as any of you, would go against us?"

The man looked ashamed at that and lowered his gun, but he still kept a grip on Josie's arm. "We'll go to Andrew's," he said. "But she will answer if you double-cross us."

Faith nodded, although she could not imagine how they thought she would do that. She was in exactly the same position as the rest of the community.

They continued on their way. The looks of the crowd returned by glares from Paul and Keith, causing those who watched them to turn swiftly away. Rumours had been circulating recently about 'punishments' taking place in dark corners, beatings at the hands of unseen assailants, bruises to be displayed as unexplained. Despite the mismatch in numbers, the crowds didn't seem to realise they held the upper hand, preferred to stay out of reach. When it came down to it, so many of them remained cowards, preferring people like Faith and her friends take the flak, fight whatever battles came their way.

Laws had been established and most were respected, occasional lapses often caused by the effects of drink or a sudden build-up of despair, the latter something all sympathised with being only a hair's width away from their own current condition. When you took the time, or the risk, to consider your situation, the danger of slipping into that void was magnified. She had allowed herself to look over the edge, almost fallen but had pulled herself back when she saw Josie, realised how much her daughter needed her presence in order to just survive. If Faith sank then she would be taking Josie down with her. It always pulled her back.

Howard was leading them towards the far side of the Barricade, much further she considered, and they would soon be near the first entrance she'd found. He stopped before then however, on the one side, the towering rusting mass of the barrier, on the other, an old hut, once used for storage but long empty.

"In there?" queried Faith.

"No," said Howard. "Here."

He turned towards the structure and ran his hands over the surface, just as she'd seen Andrew do, as she had done when she followed him. This Barricade, supposedly built with the intention of stopping a return, was the site of all secrets. Had it ever been a barrier or was that just an illusion they'd created for themselves?

Howard pulled the panel back and looked at them expectantly. "Through here, unless you've any objections?" He wanted her to challenge him, again she refused to bite.

"Paul."

The name was an order. Paul stepped ahead of them, switched on his torch to cast its beam down the corridor ahead.

There was a difference this time however to the other entrance. There was no smell. A small, albeit welcome, difference—one which immediately rang alarm bells. This was something not built on a whim, this was a proper structure. Although why Howard would send someone else first was a puzzle. It was as if he expected danger to come towards them from somewhere. Yet she'd seen no danger in her previous visit. Yes, there'd been bodies and bones, but those who'd caused this were no longer present.

Again, the question of the Burrowers came to mind. They had disappeared according to Malik. That to her, still remained doubtful. The corridor, unlike the others, led straight on. There were no forks into dark corners, no widening or narrowing. It was just a regular, straight on passageway, almost clinical, an impression that grew as the materials lining the wall became gradually more uniform and structured. Like the newly-discovered passageways, this was not random. This pathway was deliberate. It made her wonder when and how this had all been planned.

The Barricade. It had appeared to be borne from the rage and hurt of those left behind. Now, for the first time, Faith began to consider other reasons behind its construction, other minds plotting a use for its being. Suspicions began to form and as they did, the world was taken from under her feet.

"How long ago were these tunnels constructed?" asked Ruth.

Faith was happy to leave her friends to ask the questions. She knew Howard would be curious as to her next move, her relationship with the still living Graham, her link to Lionel, had, she supposed, given her an unexpected boost in the pecking order.

"Nineteen years."

Howard stated the fact without explanation, without apology.

"And where does it go?"

"You'll see."

She already knew the answer. He also knew that she knew. She could challenge him now, or wait until they'd got to their destination. She would wait. She had been waiting twenty years, so it seemed for this moment, a few more minutes wouldn't hurt.

"Who built it?"

"Us and…"

"And?" prompted Helen.

"Them."

"Them? The people who abandoned us? You cannot be serious."

"No. Not the people in the bunker. The others, those who came out of it first, before…" He paused, appeared to reconsider his words. "The ones you called the Burrowers."

So they had come from the bunker complex, had spent time in the world below. What on earth possessed them to come back up in those early years and live within the metal monster? Sacrifice or punishment? It had taken skill to build what she had seen of the Barricade's internal structure.

"Some of the people fell victim to a virus, an unpleasant disease which threatened the community. It was a strain we'd never seen before and we could not contain. They were given a choice. Voluntary euthanasia or to work above in the Barricade. They could not join your community however because of the risk they posed to you."

"Risk?"

"The... um... virus, plays tricks on the mind. Creates severe psychological delusions. We made sure they stayed within the Barricade, nobody ever saw them. Occasionally heard them. And of course, it became easy to feed them."

"You mean we fed them," said Helen.

They looked at each other. The rumours of cannibalism had been true. The thought made her sick.

"Where are they now then? The Burrowers?" asked Ruth.

They'd all seen the bones in the other corridors, smelt the stench of decay. It was missing here but in its own way, that made it all the more horrific.

"Those earlier residents of this structure are long

gone. Others however have taken their place. They are… elsewhere."

"This virus?"

"Later," said Howard.

Faith wanted to push the question but kept quiet. Attempted instead to make sense of what he'd been telling her. She wondered what this meant for the nature of the survivors in the subterranean world. It was the first time she'd even thought of the word survivors in the same breath as those who had left. She'd never bestowed the word on them before and berated herself now for considering them in that manner. Yet there was a virus which had endangered them sufficiently to cause the expulsion of infected members whilst apparently protecting those above from the diseased.

"Will we run into them?" asked Ruth.

"No," said Howard. "They are otherwise occupied."

"Have you met these people, these Burrowers?"

"Of course," said Howard. "They gave me permission to travel this path and provided access to those below. This—and the lowest level of the complex—is their world, not mine. It was our—concession."

They continued to walk straight ahead, all the while Faith keeping herself on alert, eyes flicking side to side in rapid succession. There were no recesses in these walls, no spaces for the creatures to sleep, no piles of bones to line their way. So, where were they?

"One thing I would ask however, should you ever meet them. They were, are, people, just like you and me," said Howard, finally pausing as Paul stopped ahead of them. They were at an apparent dead end.

Then the wall slid aside.

Ahead lay another corridor—but this was wide, curved into smooth walls, low lights at intermittent intervals. This was a civilised world and it finally hit home how they'd never been truly alone. They had been watched and monitored, perhaps examined as they went about their daily lives. For twenty years.

"This passage gives access to us!" Ruth sounded angry and Faith could understand why. "Did they come amongst us when we slept? Those stores of ours which mysteriously disappeared, did they steal those to add to their own stockpile?"

Howard's silence was the only answer they needed.

"And you knew," said Helen. "All this time and you knew. Yet back then you never attempted to run for Council, said you preferred to stay well away from politics. Now we know what you were doing. Digging down here to be with your friends. That would make you one of the original Burrowers..."

She suddenly paused and Faith noticed the horrified expression on her face. "Were you a Burrower?"

"Not quite in the sense I've described," said Howard, smoothly, "but I suppose you could say I am a spokesman for their community. An honorary member."

They had come to a stop by another door and were waiting as Paul tapped a number in on the keypad. The door slid open.

There were four of them. Ranged in a row in front to prevent further access. They wore a uniform of boiler suits and face masks. But despite the clothing, she could still detect a faint scent, the smell which had enveloped her in the other tunnel. Here it was bearable but it was still there and that was disturbing enough. Were these the Burrowers?

Howard's next words answered her. "Here, Paul," he said, "are your comrades. These are our supporters. They have been active for months, years. Above and below ground. They have paved our way to the top and for that we will take them with us. We have agreed that their confinement will come to an end. We still owe them and our bill is becoming due. I know the terms of payment and soon we'll have to pay. There is plenty of room above for all."

"You said they were diseased," said Helen, voicing Faith's new concerns. "How can you promise them a life above ground if they are a danger to the uninfected?"

"The land they take will be well away from us. I see no issue." With that, Howard closed down any argument.

"We could just hand this bunch over," said Paul,

laughing. "An extra payment so to speak. Reckon they'll find them pretty tasty."

Faith was getting ready to jump in but Howard beat her to it.

"These representatives? What do you take me for, Paul? I am a man of my word. And these people are from our Council, here to discuss the future with the Prime Minister."

Paul's expression soured and he stared at Howard with something almost akin to hatred. Not everything in the garden was rosy, then.

"Ex-prime minister," added Faith.

Howard gave her a look but said nothing.

"Regardless. They are here for a meeting and we will all be attending as a measure of good faith. We will discuss settlement with the Burrower community at that meeting."

One smiled, apparently appreciating Howard's acknowledgement. That chilled Faith more than anything. It implied a balance of power she'd never considered before. Especially, as it appeared they were all, including Howard, in the power of this group—at least in this area of the complex.

The boiler-suited guards moved closer, ran scanners in their hands over their bodies.

"Why?" asked Ruth. "There's no radioactivity around us."

"We know," said a distorted voice. "This does not detect radiation. It is a pathogen counter. It can detect the presence of many strains of virus."

"Virus? We are all well and healthy as you can see," said Faith, no longer worried how she appeared to Howard.

"You could easily be exactly that," said a boiler suit. "You could also be carriers. That is the problem we have experienced below ground. It took us a long time to sort that out. We have adapted, some are immune. You, however, have suffered recent exposure above ground. Regrettable but now it has to be dealt with."

Sort it out. Those words sounded ominous. One part of Faith wanted to turn and run, back to the safety, if it could be called that, of her world. At least she knew what that was although his words about recent exposure were disquieting. Could that be a reference to Linda? But how had she been exposed, if it was her? More and more questions were being raised the deeper they went. She could not return without solving the puzzle once and for all, learn exactly what had happened to those who had abandoned them, learn the truth of the Burrowers.

She thought of her family. Graham was no longer worthy of that consideration. Which side of the underground community was her son on? Burrower or… or whatever else Lionel and Graham claimed to represent.

"Which pathogens?" asked Helen, curious now.

They'd fought many diseases above ground. Vaccines had vanished along with the drugs which made modern life bearable. Diseases, once beaten, had made a virulent and triumphant return—until immunity rebuilt itself on a more natural basis.

The men in suits did not answer. Cold eyes merely looked at them as if they were nothing.

"You know if we do not return, there will be trouble,"

"And who says you will not return?"

The reassurance was not reassuring.

CHAPTER FIFTEEN

"BEFORE WE GO to the meeting," said Howard to the boiler suit who appeared to be in charge, "it was agreed we would give our new arrivals a tour of the complex."

There was something in the man's tone implying another message being passed on, a query made.

The masked face nodded. "Of course," he said. "I was aware. Preparations have been... made."

There was a lilt to his voice which nudged at her memory. So much was crawling out of the corners of her mind, demanding her attention, attention she couldn't afford to give right now. She pushed it back.

"I don't like this," whispered Ruth, at her side.

"Neither do I," said Faith, "but I doubt we'll ever get a chance to see for ourselves what they've had and what we've been missing."

"I'm not sure I want to be reminded of that," said Helen, catching their conversation.

To witness every safety net, every security they'd been denied would be to have their suffering compounded. Faith could already feel the familiar bubbles of anger and resentment start to rise—and they hadn't even got beyond this first entrance yet.

"Lead on," said Howard, to the guards.

Faith wondered if they would like to punch him for his arrogance as much as she had always longed to do.

They continued down the arched hallway with its cold concrete floor and smooth steel walls gradually narrowing to what could almost be described as a pinch point. She looked back down the passageway. Imagined hundreds of people breaking through, a flood washing up at these doors, only to find themselves jostled and herded into a smaller and smaller space so that those at the front would suffocate or be trampled on by those behind. Piles of dead building up and no escape.

It brought back memories of nightmares mingled with vague recollections of the final day when the doors closed on them, on her. She had watched, shaken and disoriented, as hundreds hurled themselves into that strip of No Man's Land. Smoke had filled the area as booby traps were triggered; the smell of flesh, wood, metal and gunpowder mingled as they burned.

This initial setback hadn't stopped the assault

and a further wave clambered over the carpet of corpses to get to their pinch point—the doors. This in turn triggered automatic firing from above by unseen hands and so more and more died, piling up until those tinted windows always so visible as cold brooding eyes were hidden from view.

Eventually the firing had paused and a disjointed voice announced they would disconnect any remaining booby traps so the dead could be reclaimed. No one stepped forward. They decided to leave the bodies as a grim landscape for those who'd gone below to view should they ever peer through the cameras or return to those tinted windows. A slowly decomposing reminder of what they'd wrought. Far from saving humanity, it felt as if they wanted to wipe it out.

The bodies did however, gradually disappear over the following days and despite all the watches put on the complex, it was never discovered how or by whom they'd been taken. It was then, the stories of the Burrowers evolved, becoming more and more outlandish over time as tales of murder and cannibalism were thrown into the mix.

At the doors, the boiler suit took off his goggles and pressed his face to a black scanning pad on the wall. He had his back to her the whole time so she was unable to see what he looked like, his mask replaced swiftly as the doors opened. What disease had they succumbed to which necessitated the hiding of their faces? Or maybe they were people she knew.

If they wanted to infiltrate the complex, it looked as though they would have to gouge out somebody's eyes. If Howard was found to be cleared for access at any entrance, Faith knew she would take great delight in that particular aspect.

The doors slid smoothly back, no sound, no juddering, just a whisper of movement. A crossroads presented itself but lacking any signage to indicate what lay down the other three passages. If they chose one way, what would they miss from the others?

"You will get to see each level in turn," said Howard, as if reading her mind. "Nothing will be hidden from you."

"How do we know?" asked Faith. Howard had never been famed for his transparency and to suddenly appear so willing to share information after his aborted coup above did nothing to allay her suspicions.

"You don't," said Howard. "Perhaps you should finally trust me."

"I would say your timing is a little off in making that request," said Helen. "You've done nothing but manoeuvre people for your own benefit and I doubt you would have brought us down here if your plans hadn't gone awry."

Faith held her tongue. Continued to remain alert, file away their location, seeking out any markings she could use as reminders in the absence of signs. She did not want Howard's preaching to distract her from their surroundings.

Howard directed them down the first corridor on their left. It ended at another set of steel doors, this time the doors to a lift. Paul pressed the button and the doors slid open to reveal a huge steel box. The sides were mirrored with hand rails running alongside. A numbered panel lit up, showing the floor levels. It seemed normal until she studied the floor numbers. Three floors. She'd expected more than that, for those who lived below to have been moved much further from the earth's surface.

Even so, humanity had become a dwarf burrowing into the soil to create this warren. The thought of burrowing again brought her back to considering the men in the boiler suits. She shuddered. She watched the numbers change: 3, 2, 1. They were at the bottom. From here the only way was up.

"Look out for any other means of getting back out," murmured Helen as they exited. "Other lifts, stairs. I hate the idea of feeling trapped. And there's got to be a backup plan. There's always a backup plan."

Unless it was deliberate. A policy of containment should something go wrong and they had to seal areas off to protect the rest of the community.

They stood in a tiny lobby, just big enough to hold their group. It was a concrete version of the steel box which had brought them there. Doors stood closed and silent opposite. There were no tinted windows, nothing to suggest what lay beyond. Only two small circles either side near the top of the lintel. Tiny dots which moved. Cameras taking in the visitors and assessing them.

A sudden whoosh caused Faith to look up and that was when she noticed little holes in the ceiling. Gas was seeping through, small tendrils of vapour becoming denser. She started to cough.

Howard did not look at all worried. "Please don't be alarmed," he said. "It's merely a disinfectant. We need to sterilise all who have been above or had contact with them."

We. This put Howard firmly on the side of those who dwelt below the ground. Still, the vapour tickled her throat, her nose and soon they were all coughing and spluttering, sending the germs they were apparently anxious to avoid, out into the small space.

"Good," said Howard, noting their reaction. "Better out than in, I always say."

"Why doesn't it affect you?" asked Ruth.

Neither Howard or Paul, Malik or Keith, showed any reaction. Only Ruth, Helen and Faith choked on the gas.

"Because they've all been here before," said Faith, staring at Malik, who turned away from her gaze. "Some of you might not have been allowed free access but you've all been here, got used to it, or become immune or whatever."

Her comments were rewarded with silence.

After what seemed like an eternity but was probably in fact only a few minutes, the blind doors slid back as noiselessly as those above, and the group entered Floor -3. The sign was posted clearly on the other side, above another panel which appeared to show the layout of this level.

Faith edged forward to study it more closely. It was a giant warehouse.

"This is where stockpiles of food and supplies were built up before we finally came down here," said Howard. "Most of that food is now gone for obvious reasons but we also brought down seedlings and chemicals to allow us to grow what food we could in this environment. Much like the aeroponics plant above."

As Faith gazed along the empty bays, occasionally interspersed with an odd sack or sad-looking solitary drum, she realised how low supplies had become—if this was the truth of their situation. It made her wonder at the food sent up before. Synthetic after all? Must've been, what other source could it have come from?

"Looks as though the cupboard is bare," she said.

Howard nodded. "That's part of the reason the residents want to return to the surface. The farmers have told us the crop cycle is re-establishing. The planet can sustain us once more. Something we never thought possible. It'll be hard at first, all those extra mouths to feed but eventually there'll be enough for all."

"You're assuming you will be allowed back," said Faith. "Why should we, or the farmers, now sustain those who did the exact opposite to us, in fact took all the best supplies and left us to starve. Do you really think we should be so forgiving? The idea of turning the other cheek has long since passed. Nobody is going to forgive easily."

"Perhaps," said Howard.

His tone remained steady, confident, as though her rebuttal did not interest him in the slightest. Oh, how she wished she knew what was going on. All that she saw raised more questions than answers.

"Well, the attempt to gain our sympathy isn't working," said Ruth as they walked along yet another empty bay.

Howard ignored her comment and paused at a panel at the end of another set of shelving. It was a touch-screen display of the whole warehouse. "You've seen this bit for yourselves but this area is huge, miles long. I doubt you want to walk it. But you can see the rest of our storage area and what it holds here."

He slid his finger across the screen, giving them a panoramic view of the warehouse. It was all exactly as they had seen for themselves.

"You could have edited that," said Helen, sceptically. "Fed in your own images."

"True," said Howard. "But we didn't. Today is about total honesty."

Faith's mouth dropped open at that.

"Yes, Faith. Today is the day Hell finally freezes over," said Howard with a smile.

And still she didn't trust him.

"Is the bottom floor down those other passages the same?" asked Ruth. "Do they all lead to warehouses?"

"They all lead to this warehouse," said Howard. "Each sector has access to this place. I could take you along to those lifts now but I thought it best to do one sector at a time and do each floor within that sector thoroughly. I don't want to be accused of hiding anything, now do I? Obviously, if you wish to walk around more and examine further, you are quite free to do so. Time is of no concern down here."

For the moment. Time on the bigger scale of things seemed to be dwelling on the inhumans as she still regarded them. The clock had not stopped ticking despite Howard's words.

The companions looked at each other, raised their eyebrows, shook their heads. All had seen enough for the present. They could always request to come back later, perhaps make their own way down here. And if the lifts from the other sectors brought them to this particular warehouse then they would see the parts they had missed at that point.

"No, we're good for the moment," said Helen. "Next stop?"

Howard took them back to the lift. He pressed -2

as they piled in. The men in the boiler suits remained behind.

"They're not coming with us?" asked Ruth.

"No, they have other tasks more important than babysitting us," said Howard. "They don't regard you as a threat."

Faith didn't know whether to feel insulted by that remark or not. She didn't want to be perceived as weak but that was apparently how they had been viewed.

"We haven't seen any other people yet," said Faith, dismissing the thought with some annoyance.

"Access to the warehouses has always been restricted and only certain personnel have clearance for obvious reasons. Now there is little point in going down there considering how empty it is and so restrictions have been lifted. Our population is free to wander those bays as much as they wish. We believed transparency was vital to prevent discontent and accusations from our community. *You* can understand that."

Faith understood alright. When a community had limited resources and had to guard them, there were always others, suspicious and bitter, assuming those who guarded it were syphoning off some for themselves, that there was more there than they were letting on and so they were being deliberately starved. Yes, they had had those situations, occasionally becoming a threat of all out riot until they had given in and opened up the warehouses with the proviso that anyone stealing what they saw would be shot on sight. A threat which unfortunately had had to be carried out on more than one occasion.

The lift doors on the next floor opened onto a lounge area. The floor of the large lobby was marble, sofas dotted about, a few paintings and photos hung on the walls. In one corner was a large desk with a computer terminal. Over it hung a small sign which said *Reception*. There was no one there. It was a throwback to a more civilised time.

"This floor is living accommodation. Bedrooms, small studios, family suites. All kitchen facilities are upstairs."

They were guided down more passageways, carpeted and silent. Faith felt as if she'd been transported back in time to the old chain hotels, Travel Lodges and Premier Inns.

Howard took out a card and swiped it at one door.

Inside, it did indeed resemble a hotel room. Comfortable bed, built in storage, small shower room. It was the sort of accommodation many of those above would give their eye teeth for.

"Nobody living here?" she asked, taking in the slightly stale smell, the dry atmosphere. There were no traces of human scent.

"Sadly, not anymore," said Howard. "Come on, I'll show you the others."

They were led down the corridor, admitted to

empty room after empty room. Some were single occupancy, others double or family. Some were suites with a small sitting room.

A thought struck her. "These weren't empty when you first came down here, were they?" If it turned out they would have been able to house a greater number, Faith knew she would not be able to contain her anger.

"No. We had people down here, families, individuals. All sorts. Those who remain are now all living in A wing. This wing is D."

"You're saying there are four accommodation wings, all were full once but now only A houses the population? What happened?"

She had expected population change of some sort, maybe one similar to theirs with the death rate outstripping the birth rate, but she had not expected this level of decimation.

"Natural wastage was part of it," explained Howard. "The old got older and died. Not many children were born so the population stagnated but there were other things. We had cycles of suicides, huge numbers. Never could, and still can't, figure out why those happened. Psychiatrists have simply put it down to mass hysteria sweeping them all up but we reckon there's more to it than that."

Suicides. A feature of life above and below. Those committed above ground had been carried out with a purpose. They had become a ritual, a rite of passage. Did those who lived below carry out a corresponding rite, one of contrition and remorse? If this was the case then how wrong had both societies been? They needn't have waited for the planet to wipe them out, in the end they were too busy not just turning on each other but also themselves. Or perhaps they weren't suicides, simply made to look that way to cover up something else, another need.

It sounded as though he was being open, he was telling them so much. Still she had the feeling there was more he was keeping hidden.

"Kept the Burrowers happy though," laughed Paul. "Natural wastage meant we didn't have to make decisions. They got fed by both sides."

Another need. The old tales of cannibalism returned to her. She couldn't suppress a shudder.

"We. Again," said Helen, noticing what Faith had already taken on board and giving voice to it. "How long have you been 'we'? Since the beginning?"

Of course, it had been since then. Those below needed a contact above, someone prepared to take a chance with survival beneath the sky rather than the earth. They would hedge their bets. What had been the promised rewards, the pay off? Stay above ground and we will boost your rations. Stay above ground and we will give you weapons. Medicine. A safe passage down here whenever you needed it. Keep your head down though so people don't get suspicious. It all fit now.

Howard had gone pretty much unnoticed during those first ten years, even though they had formerly worked together, they barely acknowledged each other. She had seen him around, apparently suffering like the rest of them—except he'd never worn that familiar haunted expression she'd seen on so many others, including her own, whenever she had gazed in a mirror. He'd blended into the background, as had his cronies. Until more recent times when he'd gradually spoken up, put himself forward for Council. Their man in power. That's what she would have done. What they had done. Played the long game.

"You never had to fight for anything did you?" she accused. "Whilst we monitored every scrap, you took yours uncomplainingly so everyone would figure what a good guy you were, yet all the time you were getting everything you needed literally handed to you on a plate."

It explained his plump figure, the fat coating him whilst others were skin and bone. Howard didn't answer but his expression was enough to admit the truth of her statement. Nor did he look ashamed. All he had done was what so many had done since time immemorial, continued to plot and scheme not just to survive, but become master of all he surveyed. Those old webs of political intrigue which brought the world to its knees had continued to be woven in the darkness. The spiders were still here.

"Next floor," said Faith, suddenly wanting to get

their visit over with as soon as possible. Discover what Lionel wanted—apart from access to the sky above, and get out. For twenty years, they'd been played and it hurt. So far, Howard had barely mentioned Lionel and she began to think the power base might not be what she'd imagined.

Ruth and Helen looked furious but kept quiet, mouths set in thin straight lines.

Another ride back up in the steel coffin. This time another lobby but more workmanlike. A reception which gave on to school rooms, gyms, a cinema. Places to learn and keep body and mind healthy. Again, all were empty.

Howard took them back to the lift and they returned to Floor -3, took another passage to the warehouse at the bottom of Wing C. It replicated Wing D, as did B. Then it was time for Wing A and Faith could feel herself holding her breath.

The warehouse provided no new information, this sector of it was as empty as those lying beyond.

Floor -2. Living quarters. Finally, there was signs of life. As they stepped out into the lounge reception, she could hear the occasional murmur of voices as doors opened and closed, shouts and cries from children, a feeling of movement in the air. The reception desk was manned.

"Good morning, Sonia," said Howard, approaching her. The group followed behind. All swinging their heads round at the slightest sound, eager to catch sight of those whose voices they heard but those below must've been shy because nobody appeared. It began to spook Faith.

"Good morning, Howard," said Sonia. "Lovely to see you here again. Will you be staying long this time?"

Faith noticed how Sonia smiled at him, her expression one of someone eager to please, slightly nervous, but not surprised to see him.

"Not sure yet," said Howard. "I'll let you know, although could you make up a room for our guests here. Only for the one night," he added as he caught Faith's look. "They are expected back above ground and we wouldn't want anyone to think they'd been kidnapped or come to harm."

Sonia had turned towards the group and was staring at them with undisguised curiosity. "I hope you don't mind me asking," she said. "But what's it like up there. I was only little when I came down here. Four years old…"

Faith had been preparing to snap back a sarcastic answer until the knowledge of the woman's age stopped her. She was someone who'd had no choice. Her knowledge would've been informed by whatever lies Lionel told her.

"It's tough," admitted Faith. "Harsh, unforgiving."

"But things are improving," butted in Howard. "Life is returning." He sounded as if he didn't want Sonia to be put off. What *had* she been told?

Sonia nodded but her smile seemed a little sad.

"I wish my parents were still alive to even just hear those words," she said.

"I'm sorry," said Ruth, her sympathy evident. "At least yours will not have experienced the violent deaths we had above or the loss to a disease we could've once treated with access to the right medicines. Natural death, though hard, is easier to come to terms with."

A surprising spark of anger flashed in Sonia's eyes. "Natural death! What do you mean…"

Then she looked at Howard and quickly shut down. "Yes, yes of course. I'm sorry. It's just still painful. You know?"

All those unexplained deaths, ostensibly to suicide. Not so natural then.

Howard guided them down the familiar corridor. This time knocking on doors and waiting for the occupants to admit them. Individuals, families, couples, they met them all, were welcomed each time and invited in to look around. Around them were the sights and smells of occupancies. The place felt alive. It all seemed so normal, and yet…

When they shook hands, their contact was brief as if they wished to drop the proffered hands almost as soon as flesh was touched. Faith had images of them running to hand sanitiser as soon as they'd gone, to rub themselves clean. Eye contact was also minimal, a quick look and then away, trying to distract from this apparent rudeness by indicating things around the room, how the families fared, talking whilst doing seemingly unimportant tasks which would take their attention away.

And then Howard would whisk them out of the door and onto the next.

"How many families did we see?" asked Helen as they moved towards what Paul denoted, the singles corridor.

"Several," said Faith.

"Not many."

"No, but we're not going into every room and meeting them all. There are miles of corridor with these quarters along them. We're over the warehouse remember."

"Yes, but still. I get the feeling there really aren't that many at all. Less than even Howard hinted at."

"But what about the numbers which appeared above ground last night?" asked Ruth. "When they all came out. Seemed like hundreds."

"Yes, but that space isn't big any more. The base of the Barricade's encroached on the gap over the years as people chucked rubbish over. It wouldn't take many to fill it and if they sent everybody up there, then it would look like huge numbers. We were all too worked up to count properly, weren't we? Just accepted what we saw."

They wandered the singles corridors, met people in their twenties, thirties, forties. No older though.

"The elderly have their own section," said Howard as if reading her mind.

"Since when has fifty been regarded as elderly?"

asked Faith indignantly.

He didn't answer.

"I'm afraid, however, you won't be able to visit them today. They are our more vulnerable group, more prone to panic attacks and outbursts. We had discussed your visit with them but they said they did not want to meet you. You'll agree we really shouldn't force your presence on anybody."

"*You* were the ones who asked us down here. *You* are the ones who need *our* help and support if you wish to return above ground. Now you make it sound as though it's our fault for them feeling the way they do, although perhaps they're ashamed. After all, wouldn't they have been amongst those who fought for places to come down here? Turned their back on their families above? No wonder they wouldn't want to see us." Faith was furious at the way he was turning things round to imply they were the ones causing the upset when it was really their own appearance above ground which had opened old wounds and caused deep distress.

"Please, please," said Howard. "I didn't mean any offence. We're hoping they will see you tomorrow before you leave. Perhaps such a meeting might even be cathartic for both sides."

Faith doubted that. Then she had a thought. "Wait, my ex-husband's fifty-five. Like me. I assume he's in those areas you mention?"

For the first time, Howard looked ill at ease. "He has... separate quarters... because of his station."

"His station? So he's still part of the great and the good?"

"What about the royal family?" asked Ruth, butting in suddenly. "They're here aren't they. Shouldn't we be allowed to meet them? Get *their* apology."

Faith didn't think anybody was going to apologise any time soon. A familiar wave of tiredness washed over her. It felt as though they had walked for miles. Uncomfortable heat prickled her skin, as it always did at inopportune times, forced her to really have to concentrate on those around her. She didn't want this, someone else should be taking over, leaving her be. After all this time, she still found it hard to understand why so many would naturally look to her for answers and help. At best because they genuinely needed her, at worst, she often felt it was simply down to idleness. Her thoughts had not been very charitable of late and she realised she had become more bitter and judgemental.

"I think," said Howard, "it might be a good time for you to take a break. You've had a lot to take in and I'm sure you want to discuss it amongst yourselves. I'll take you back to your room and get some food sent to you. Then we can head off again in an hour. I'll take you to the research floor."

That sounded more promising. Part of Faith wanted to continue their tour, not allow any let up but she so desperately needed a rest, the sweat had become a river down her back and another wave of heat was building up to take over as soon as the other one faded. It built up unwelcome feelings of claustrophobia, a desire to lash out at anything and anyone.

"You're right," said Helen, after a quick look at Faith. "I think we could all do with a break, digest what we've seen and heard."

"Thought you'd want to see everything at once," said Malik, puzzled at this sudden desire to break off the tour.

"We need to rest," said Ruth. "And I've been on my feet for days. They're killing me."

"Faith?"

Malik was looking at her now. She didn't want to reply.

"We all need a rest," said Ruth, jumping in as Faith started to open her mouth.

Her tone was sharp though and stopped Malik asking another question. Faith was relieved. She didn't want to have to explain how she was feeling to him, in front of Howard. Something so normal would be used to belittle her. But even though it was normal and not an illness, it *was* a major upheaval for the female body, a complete readjustment in hormonal levels, something that was too often regarded by those who had not experienced it as being no more incapacitating than a sneeze or a hiccup. It was the sort of thing which caused untold misery to the sufferer but was used as a joke by everyone else.

They were taken back to the suite Sonia had assigned to them. It had a large sitting room and four bedrooms. Sonia, Faith, Helen and Malik remained, the others took their leave and said they had their own rooms to rest in, confirming Faith's suspicions about them being part of the link to above ground.

They sank gratefully onto the sofas and chairs. Sonia appeared with a tray of tea and biscuits. Food apparently would be along in a minute, empty warehouses but still able to produce meals on demand. It didn't make sense. Faith leaned back and allowed her eyes to close, not even listening to the conversation of others. She just wanted to disappear inside herself for a moment.

The sound of a long-forgotten theme tune roused her. Helen was waving a remote at the huge flat screen on the wall opposite. Old programmes appeared on a guide listing. Hundreds of films and tv series.

Helen was almost beside herself with excitement. Coronation Street! Eastenders!

"Never took you for a soap fan," said Faith.

"Guilty pleasure," said Helen, looking slightly sheepish. "Come on, you've got to admit, it's pure escapism. But if you don't like it, let's see what else is listed."

Helen scrolled through a whole host of channels when Faith suddenly told her to stop.

999. Public Service Channel.

"That one," she said.

Helen obediently pressed select.

A host of tiles scattered across the screen, each relating to some public announcement or other. The most recent were only a week old and so related to life underground as did the majority as Helen scanned back through time. Eventually, she came to the point where, twenty years ago, those final announcements which would split their society for ever, had been made. Faith recognised the headlines from then and previously. She watched them the first time, she did not need to see them again. Many were burned into her mind, forever to haunt her dreams. The most recent though… that roused her curiosity.

"Go back to those last announcements," she said. "Let's see what they've been telling everyone down here."

"Do you reckon it'll be the truth or will there be some whitewashing going on?"

"Let's press play and see," said Faith.

Malik sat quietly with them. He'd said very little since they'd come below and had now lapsed into total silence. Whose side was he really on? Could it be possible he was like Howard, playing both sides to ensure the most favourable outcome for himself? It was not something she had ever thought him capable of, but if Howard had been able to play the long game, who was to say Malik hadn't as well.

"Have you seen these?" she asked.

He shook his head. No.

The tiles vanished and a face appeared. A woman Faith recalled as being some presenter or other on tv back in the days when there was a television service. She looked older, the lines were more visible, but it was still her. Familiarity bred trust, another little propaganda ploy. The woman was a digital security blanket with her bland reassurances.

"Today is the 30th of November, 2040. Twenty years exactly to the day we came below. This anniversary coincides with an exciting new development which may ease some of the problems we have been facing in recent times. You will soon hear of contact being made with those above ground who survived the war."

War? What war? Unless this woman was counting the almost civil war which had marked the announcement of the selection of those who were to go below. Her script was nothing if not disingenuous. What had they been told?

The announcement ended without giving any further detail.

"Short and sweet," said Helen. "I wonder what the 'problems' were?" She selected the previous broadcast.

"Today is the 29th of November, 2040. We would like to remind you that for your own safety, you must remain in A Wing and access only your residential and work floors. Whilst we do not bar you from travelling to other parts of the complex, please remember that in view of recent... disappearances... we cannot guarantee your safety. Our security personnel are continuing their investigations."

Disappearances?

The previous day:

"...Ricky O'Mahoney is twenty-five years old, brown hair, brown eyes, five foot eight and last seen in the Warehouse accessed via A Wing. If you see him, do not approach but report to Security. Please remember, the Reappeared are not what they seem."

Reappeared?

"Malik. What do they mean by Reappeared?"

She could see an anxious look already settling over his face.

"I'm not sure. That's one thing Andrew and Sylvie and me have been trying to find out. A lot of people have just 'disappeared' from this place. I know, I know, all the usual rumours of cannibalism and the like have been bandied about but we don't think it's that so don't worry about any meat you might get offered. *That* isn't real meat by the way, just a protein substitute, easily grown, easily digested although you'd soon get sick of it.

"No, the Reappeared are people who've disappeared and then come back. They carry on as if nothing has happened, claim to have been going about their normal business for however long they've been absent from the complex. They look normal but there's something not quite the same about them. I *did* discover the disappearance was really a period of hibernation. Something Howard had put into place to lift the pressure on supplies. I think the amount of time they've been in suspension does something to their minds…"

"Suspension?" Faith saw her own shocked expression mirrored in her companion's face. "Malik?"

"When things got bad down here. Food and medicine shortages, worries about the planet, the community voted to put some of its members into suspension, a guarantee against the rest of us not making it. When the crisis passes, the people who hibernated were revived and everything went back to normal."

"Normal? I assume they had a full medical," said Helen.

"Yep, body scans, the lot," said Malik. "Nothing's come up."

"And are people still put into hibernation?" asked Faith.

"Yes," said Malik. "At first they used to worry but once they saw people come back the same as before, it became an accepted routine. They even created a rota so everyone spent some time in the suspension chamber, eased pressure on resources."

"Where are these chambers?" asked Helen.

"Another level not marked on the lift. Howard is being quite receptive at the minute, which I must admit is a surprise, and I daresay he will let you see the Hibernation Room if we ask."

"He didn't forbid you to talk about it?"

"No. Said I could answer your questions with whatever I knew. So you see, he is being pretty transparent."

They left the topic for the moment, putting humans into a form of hibernation was something from a sci-fi film. If it worked as well as it appeared then it would be an amazing advance. Except that feeling something wasn't quite right with the Reappeared.

Ruth continued to select the announcements, stepping back in time. Faith began to feel her energy levels rise again, more able to deal with the revelations and discoveries. Watched with more concentration as reports of disappearances and reappearances cropped up with great regularity, intermingled by warnings of rationing and shortages. Obituaries and funerals.

"They have cremations," said Malik, in response to Ruth's query about disposing of the dead.

Faith was about to ask where when there was a knock at the door and Howard reappeared, not even waiting for them to allow him in.

"You're to come with me," he said, his expression was serious, slightly more cagey.

"What about that food we were promised?"

asked Ruth, as her stomach rumbled in mutual complaint.

"You'll get it but we have to move you out for now. This corridor's being evacuated so we can do a sweep."

"Sweep? For what?"

"We don't know yet but our sensors have picked up an alien presence. And by alien, I mean stranger, not some little green man."

The attempted humour fell flat. As Howard guided them out of their corridor and across the reception space, Faith could see people in protective gear walking the corridors. An invisible door slid out of the wall and sealed the passageway. Through its small window, Faith could see more of the smoke which they'd experienced in the lift lobby. Sterilising perhaps, or poison? Why else would those who searched be wearing gas masks.

CHAPTER SIXTEEN

HOWARD SEEMED surprisingly calm despite the activity going on behind him, as if this kind of thing was mere routine. Then the sealed door suddenly swept open again and two of the workers in protective suits appeared, holding the body of a young man between them. The gas behind the doors had already vanished, leaving only a faint trace of something indistinguishable.

"Ricky O'Mahoney," said Helen, in surprise.

"Ah, I see you've been watching our Public Announcements," said Howard, unperturbed by her comment.

"That doesn't bother you? I mean we've already heard the lies about the supposed 'war'."

"There's a reason for everything," he said, smoothly. "Young Ricky here was quite the lad. He thought he could go above but he couldn't, now he's reappeared and look at him."

Faith had thought Ricky dead but as the workers laid him on the floor, his body began to twitch and jerk and a strange rash travelled across his face. Howard's calm expression suddenly changed and he grabbed them all, pushing and shoving them into the lift, closing the door on the workers who'd handled him, ignored their banging on the doors as he punched at the buttons to get the lift moving. It was the first time she'd seen him agitated.

"What's wrong?"

"Nothing, I hope. We'll all need a body scan but I think we're okay."

"Scan for what?"

"Looks like Ricky went into the Burrowers quarters, picked up a bug."

"The virus you mentioned earlier?" asked Helen.

"Yes."

"And those who helped him?"

Norman shook his head. "The level of their protective clothing isn't any good against that particular virus, they should have taken more care," he said. "I'm afraid it's too late for them."

"And you're leaving them down there?"

"The Burrowers will look after them. Help them adjust. It's for the greater good."

"Now where have I heard that phrase before?" asked Faith.

Whatever she had thought of about life below ground, it had never included any of this. How many real survivors were there and could she even imagine allowing them back above? She shook herself. That had been a red line. Nobody was coming back. But now there was a faint chance, she might, just might, allow herself to be talked into it. It would, however, be on her own terms. She wondered how her friends felt.

The lift stopped at Level -1 and Howard guided them along yet another corridor, this time one with the faces of past prime ministers and kings and queens and into what looked like a drawing room from some distant gothic age. It was as if they'd stepped out of time.

Low leather armchairs dotted the room with small coffee tables alongside. It was like a gentleman's club.

"Are women allowed?" asked Ruth.

"For today," said Howard.

"I meant that as a joke," said Ruth.

"I didn't," said Howard.

They would most definitely not be coming above ground without some changes, thought Faith. This sort of room and thinking was a relic of a past she did not want. She remembered the comments from Paul about having babies and supporting elderly parents and now this. There would be no place for misogyny if they were to establish a new world order.

There were two oak doors to the left and right of the far wall. One of these opened and Faith smelt food. Her stomach rumbled its own acknowledgement. Sonia stuck her head round the door and announced dinner was served. The meal Howard had promised them.

"She seems to be everywhere," said Ruth.

"Probably cooked it as well," said Helen.

They made their way into a similarly gothic dining room. Small polished wooden tables covered with pristine white linen tablecloths dotted the room. Low lamps glowed and silver cutlery shone.

Sonia led them to a table for four.

"Won't you be joining us?" Faith asked Howard.

"I had intended to but I have a little business to attend to first. I'll be back soon though and after dinner you'll have those scans I mentioned, then you'll meet up with Lionel and discuss the way forward. All will be explained by that point."

"Why aren't we having our scans now? You made it sound urgent."

"The facilities aren't quite ready but here you are isolated and Sonia is at no risk. Don't worry, you'll soon know everything."

He kept saying that but everything he had told them so far had only thrown up question after question. Howard left them, ignoring the comments they made as he walked out the door. Faith considered the scans but there was nothing she could do and so turned her attention to the plates in front of them. Strips of fake beef alongside peas and carrots, roast potatoes, filled the plate. A gravy boat sat in the middle of the table. Fake friends. Fake appearances. Fake foods.

"Who's going first?" asked Ruth, looking suspiciously, although longingly, at the meal in front of them.

"I will," said Malik. "I've eaten this stuff before. It's quite good actually and as you can see, I'm still here."

They watched him cut the beef, pop it in his mouth and chew. Then he swallowed. They watched and waited and he just smiled at them. That was the signal for their own attack. Faith decided she had not eaten anything as good for a long time. Yes, you could tell the beef wasn't real, but it was close enough. She hoped to meet the technicians who grew this protein to discover their secret, perhaps replicate it above when she returned.

"It's good," she agreed, wolfing down both meat and veg. It was bringing back childhood memories of a Sunday roast, memories she wanted to forget.

They all ate in silence, allowing themselves to enjoy their food as their brains processed everything they'd seen, their worries and their concerns, none of which affected their appetites in the slightest. When you had fought so hard to survive as they had, you learned to enjoy every single meal, regardless of when and where you were.

"Dessert," said Sonia, appearing as if by magic and placing small plates of gateau in front of them, complete with a scoop of 'ice cream'. "Enjoy. It's not real ice cream but our synthetic version is pretty good. We all cheered the day the scientists managed to do away with the weird aftertaste you always got with things like that."

Their dinner plates were cleared and again silence fell as they indulged in their dessert. Eventually all dishes were empty and the four made their way back to the drawing room.

"I'm stuffed," said Faith with a yawn. "That meal's made me sleepy." Her little burst of energy had evaporated. She put her head on the arm of the chair and found herself drifting off.

The others continued to chat around her, the words occasionally filtering through but she paid them no heed. Despite their strange circumstances, she felt content. Howard was winning her over, she thought crossly. She would have words with him when she woke…

"Faith, Faith."

The sound of her name snapped her out of her sleep. She sat up quickly, felt her head spin slightly. Looking round vaguely, she wondered where she was. Then she saw her friends looking at her. They too looked drowsy.

"We all fell asleep," said Ruth, "do you think we were drugged?"

"No," said Helen. "A warm room, a heavy meal, comfortable surroundings, safe. Our bodies merely responded to circumstances. Although considering we've been on our guard since we came down here, that is a touch embarrassing."

"What's the time?" asked Ruth, yawning.

"The clock… says exactly the same time as when we entered," said Faith. "It must be more than an hour though. Where's Howard? He was supposed to come back. Malik?"

Malik had stood up, was circling his shoulders, rubbing his neck to get some sense of movement back in them.

"He should've come back by now," he agreed. "Those times I was left guarding the door in the Barricade, he always came back when he said he would."

"Proves you can't trust him," said Faith, grumpily. She had a pounding headache and the consequences of that unexpectedly good meal had triggered a bad case of heartburn, the acid rising up her throat, forcing her to breathe slowly for a moment until the pain went away. A jug of water stood on the sideboard and she quickly made her way to it, gulping down a glassful and topping up the container she always carried tied to her belt.

"You okay?" asked Helen.

"Yeah, just the usual," said Faith.

"Usual?" Malik looked at her with some concern. "Something I need to know about?"

"Not really," said Faith, marching over to the door. Whilst her symptoms at times proved alternately embarrassing, occasionally dangerous and often downright painful, she had no wish to discuss them. She did not want to discuss the perceived 'weakness' of women. Yet in a strange manner, the fact women were prepared to put up with such agonies in silence whilst continuing to fulfil their role in society meant they were actually not weak, but extraordinarily strong. To be able to cope in extreme conditions when you felt as if your own body was at war with you demanded a threshold of tolerance she had yet to see in most men.

"We don't have to wait for him," she said. "Let's go and find him instead. Malik, you seem to know more than we do. Where do you think we should go first?"

"To the labs," said Malik. "When he said Ricky had been to the Burrower's quarters, they would have started running checks on the complex to see if the infection barrier had been breached."

Faith saw signs pointing to the corridor containing the laboratories and she walked past him.

"Medical Research, Environmental Research, Integrity Monitoring... I would assume the latter, if you're talking about a possible breach?" She raised her eyebrows at Malik who nodded back. She turned the corner and they found themselves entering a small white room with a door the other side. As they walked across, the floor lit up beneath each step so their paths were tracked across the room. After two or three impressions were taken the lights beneath their feet stopped and instead strobes appeared, sending beams of light over their heads, into their eyes.

Ruth gasped. "What the…"

"Don't worry," said Malik. "This happens at all lab entrances or sensitive environments. I should've warned you. The pads beneath your feet gauge your weight, the beams your height and proportions. The measurements are used to ensure the optimum dose of sterilising gas is directed at you. Paul told me," he added in response to her look. "Took great delight in telling me everything he knew about this place, the fact *he* was allowed in before me."

On cue, white vapours began to trail from the ceiling, these, unlike the lift lobby, did not drift around but homed in directly on each person, whirling around them so that for a moment they were each cocooned in a flimsy veil, shrouded from each other's view. When Faith tried to move forward she couldn't. The vapour had the strength of iron chains. Then it vanished and Faith, still straining to get out of its grasp, almost fell over.

"We've been passed," said Malik. "We can go on."

"And if we hadn't passed? What would've happened?"

"You would have been… contained. It's not a pleasant sight, Paul showed me a clip on his tablet. The last time, it was Kamal. I don't know what he'd picked up or how, but something was found on him and..."

Malik didn't say any more. Faith remembered
Kamal, one of the few guards who did his job
properly. Had been up on the wall when those from
the complex first appeared above ground. Only now
did she realise she hadn't seen him for a couple of
days, an absence she hadn't remarked on assuming
he was either on the far side of the Barricade or
gone on a scavenging run. The latter more an
excuse to escape the claustrophobic confines of the
community these days than in the hope of finding
anything. Now it appeared he too had been in
Howard's clique.

The door the other side was simply an entrance,
currently plunged into darkness. It lit up as they
walked along the corridor. Motion sensors. Lights
were evident at the end of the corridor which
stopped directly at the threshold of the lab. Inside,
white-coated technicians were peering down
microscopes, looking up at screens. Howard could
be seen studying a readout on a monitor alongside a
human-sized capsule lying horizontally next to him.
The only assumption she could make was that the
body of Ricky lay within, although how they would
have brought it up here when the level had been
sealed off, she didn't know. Especially if the
protective gear he'd referred to as being useless
meant nobody could go and recover the body.
There were so many questions spinning around in
her head.

The four made their way over to him. So much seemed to be happening that Faith was beginning to forget the main reason for their visit, the discussion about a future merger, above and below combined once more beneath the sky.

"Howard."

The man looked up from the screen, took in the group's arrival. He did not seem annoyed. In fact it appeared as if their presence wasn't even worth commenting on as he turned back to the screen again.

Faith looked into the capsule, its curved glass surface clear, allowing the person within to be observed without obstruction. Wires and probes were attached at various points. She was shocked however to see it wasn't Ricky, it was Paul. And he wasn't unconscious, but was staring back at her although not with that usual smug, superior expression of his but one of outright terror. And he didn't have just wires attached to him, his hands and ankles were bound by restraints.

"Howard. What's wrong with him?"

"Hm? Wrong? Oh, nothing's wrong. We just needed to test something and Paul kindly volunteered."

Faith looked again at the man imprisoned in the capsule. It was evident he could hear every word and he strongly disagreed with it. His mouth kept opening and closing but nothing came out.

"Can't he speak?" she asked.

"Sadly, no," said Howard, but he was smiling as he said it. "I'd have thought you would appreciate that little benefit. I know there's no love lost between you."

Faith shut him out for a moment and scanned the room. Ever since they had come below ground she had thought it was with the intention of meeting those in charge, including Lionel and Graham. She had yet to see these two, or anyone else from the underground government. If anything, it seemed as if Howard himself was in charge down here. As above, so below. How could that possibly be? The world had turned upside down.

"So, what is it you need to test and which he seems so unhappy about."

"It's a vaccine. It doesn't seem to work on those who've lived below ground for long periods of time so we decided we needed to test those who live above ground. If this doesn't work, we'll have to start again from scratch."

"That's not why you brought us down here?" Helen, now as suspicious as Faith.

"Good God, no. We still have that meeting scheduled, had to delay it slightly however due to that little incident down below and the need to move this research along a bit more. I thought you'd appreciate the time to rest as well."

Howard had never been obviously considerate before.

"What's it a vaccine against?" asked Faith.

"Oh, just a bug," said Howard. "Nothing major in itself but it has a nasty habit of taking over, weakens the respiratory tract of the infected person and we can't have that. Everyone has to be a hundred percent fully functioning when we go back up."

A bug. Hadn't one of those triggered all their original problems. And back up. Again that certainty. Before she could ask any more questions however, an intercom buzzed.

"Ah, they're ready for us now," said Howard. "Time to get these talks started. Let me know of any developments," he said to an assistant as he turned towards them. "Immediately."

Faith felt as if she'd been wrong-footed time and again. It was hard to focus on what lay ahead. Graham and Callum. So many conflicting emotions tore their way through her, long-suppressed, this was not going to be easy.

"You okay," asked Helen.

"Yeah, but if you think I'm about to lose it, get me out of there as soon as possible," said Faith. "I do *not* want to give Graham the satisfaction of breaking down in front of him. And I don't want to upset Callum."

"Done," said Helen.

Howard led them back down the carpeted corridors, past the room where they'd had dinner and on. Two huge doors appeared in front of them. A guard stood either side. On the walls were emblems of the Union Jack, the different flags of the island nation, an engraved crown. Images denoting this was the seat of power. One of the guards murmured into a wire and the doors were slowly opened from the other side.

Howard went first, walking into the room as if he owned it. Before him was a huge rectangular table. Highly-polished oak with high-backed chairs running down each side. At its head was an empty chair.

Faith noticed Lionel, but he didn't occupy the position at the head of the table, instead, as she'd begun to suspect he would, Howard made his way to it and sat down, gesturing with his hand that her group take their places in the free seats on his left. His actions confirmed her vague suspicions about his status.

Across from her, sat her ex-husband. It was unnerving to find herself gazing directly into his eyes. She shifted uncomfortably, distracting herself by taking in his companions. Lionel was on his left and then two others from those long-forgotten days of government. Her son was seated behind Graham, paper on his lap as if to take notes. He was staring at her.

The last time she'd seen him was when he had been a fourteen-year-old boy. Now he was thirty-four. A grown man, careworn but with the same hazel eyes and brown hair—although the unruly mop was now a buzzcut. The puppy fat she remembered was also long gone, replaced by gaunt, almost haunted features. What had happened to him, all those years below ground? Oh, how she wished she could speak to him on his own, hold him again. Be his mother. Reluctantly she looked away.

On his left sat a woman. The woman. The bitch who'd split her family. Although to be fair, if it hadn't been her, it would've been someone else. She certainly hadn't been the first. The blonde hair had vanished, replaced by a mousey nondescript colour. The face was no longer perfectly made up. What you saw now, was the real Shirley. As nondescript as the rest of them. Nor were there any curves, only angles. Sharp and pinched like her face.

Faith felt herself start to rise, but Helen's restraining hand on her arm, pulled her back to herself. Her friend had noticed them as well. A ploy to disturb her, confuse her thoughts? She would not give them the satisfaction.

She looked at Graham, surprised to notice he too appeared uncomfortable, almost scared. Glancing down at Lionel and the other representatives, their expressions were similar. She risked another look behind at Callum. He looked as if he was going to say something and then stopped. She allowed herself to give him a small smile. It wasn't much but it was a start.

Shirley too, was a surprise. There was no gloating there, that smug smile on departure had vanished for good. Instead, anxiety etched itself across her face.

"Right, let's get this meeting to order," said Howard.

"Firstly, I'd like to thank our guests, Faith, Helen, Ruth and Malik for agreeing to come below and speak to us. Secondly, I'd like to thank Lionel, Graham, Colin and Jeremy for having the good sense to agree to this meeting and especially to Lionel for stepping aside and allowing me to chair it."

"Lionel is still Prime Minister then?" asked Ruth.

"An empty title these days," commented Faith. "It demands a country, a population. You have neither, have not been elected as such by those above for many years. When you abandoned us, you gave up your right to such a title."

It didn't hurt to remind them of their real place in the order of things. Get rid of any presumptions.

Lionel said nothing. His eyes flicking left towards Howard, Howard giving a slight shake of his head, an apparent instruction forbidding him to respond to her words. Howard was very definitely the puppet master here.

"Lionel is still our First Minister, as we like to call the position," said Howard. "We thought it best for continuity in a time of great upheaval, social and emotional. It gave stability."

"For those below," said Malik.

"Yes, for those below," said Lionel. "It was a very difficult time."

"Difficult? Difficult?" snapped Ruth. "You had food, shelter, medicine, security. What was so bloody difficult about that? We had disease, bombs, guns, natural disaster. You expect us to feel sorry for you?"

"Ahem," said Howard. "Whilst I appreciate there is still a lot of unresolved conflict which will have to be dealt with at some point, now is not the time."

"On the contrary," said Helen. "If you want to discuss a return above, we will have to resolve this 'conflict' otherwise it will lead to violence. You've seen them up there."

Helen made it sound as if going above ground *could* feasibly happen.

"You won't even get into that patch of No Man's Land again," she said. "You saw what happened when you went above. The sky isn't yours, it's ours."

"You say condemning people to die, abandoning them to their fate is inhuman. I know that's what you call us," said Lionel. "Yet by doing the same to us, would surely make you our equal in terms of human monstrosity."

Ruth stood up. Faith could feel the waves of fury emanating from her. "How dare you. How dare you compare us to yourselves, use such an argument to force us to take you back."

Again, Helen intervened. She was the calmer one of the three women, her military training allowing her to assess situations, steady as needed. She touched Ruth's arm lightly, continued as Ruth sat down.

"I sense some desperation or urgency beneath your requests to come back up. We know you've heard of the recovery of the crop cycle, the soil, the seasons—something we never thought to see again. But it's early days and not established. I would've thought in your position you'd wait until things were more certain—*if* you held the upper hand. I suspect, however, you don't. Something else is driving you.

"We've seen the warehouses, yes pretty empty, yet you haven't shown us your aeroponics plant, your freezers, the labs where the microprotein is grown. So it's still possible food is not an issue. Particularly as the population level is a lot lower than we anticipated. How many are there here and what happened to the remainder—or did you never fill those wings originally, turned your back on us because we couldn't pay the same price as those who made it here. And finally, you're testing a vaccine for a disease unknown to us, also with a degree of urgency. My senses detect a threat has built against your community and your only chance is to evacuate the complex. Am I correct?"

Faith stared at her friend open-mouthed. She'd run through an assessment only just beginning to form in Faith's own mind.

"Impressive assessment," said Howard, "and absolutely correct. Think about my motives how you will, but we have a situation we need to discuss. Firstly, our population is a mere five hundred people. Men, women and children, although like above, not many of the latter."

Faith thought back to the Public Announcements. The declarations of who would be selected and how many. A sprawling underground ark which would house thousands. Five thousand had been the apparently impossible figure.

"Too many to maintain? asked Helen. "Did you have to cull numbers?"

She said it bluntly. A brutal consideration which hadn't even occurred to Faith.

"No. We had a storage facility, or Sleep Chamber, if you prefer a more palatable name. Malik must've mentioned the Hibernation Room. We'd made huge advances in cryogenics and were able to put a large number into suspension. At least we did back then."

"Did they agree to it?" asked Faith.

"Yes, you know that. All were volunteers."

"What happened to them?"

Lionel looked serious, sad even. "It was a tragedy. Something happened in their wing, the access tunnels collapsed and we couldn't get to them. We still can't get through. We've never really been able to get to the bottom of it."

"So, they're still there?" asked Helen, incredulous now.

"Possibly, although I would say the system was probably compromised. We've assumed they died."

"But you didn't actually check?" demanded

Faith.

"No. Our resources are precious and you have to weigh up the benefits of any action which will involve effort and manpower."

He was lying. She knew just by looking at him. There was something more and he still didn't want to tell the truth. Whatever it was must've been bad. Were these the ones who originally left the complex, the Burrowers who lived in the Barricades?

"Okay, so let's say we accept your tale of low numbers, no food. What else? What's the vaccine for? If you are suffering some virus or other, surely we'd need you to stay down here as a form of quarantine. We can't risk spreading something to our own people."

Faith wondered if they'd indeed walked into a trap, one whose chains were forged in morality.

"Which is why we need the vaccine, to immunise those above."

"No," said Helen. "The onus is on *you*. You need to wipe out whatever it is here. You do not put *your* diseases on *our* shoulders."

"Look, we're almost there," said Howard. "There'll be no risk to anyone and we can come above ground and be a proper community again."

There was no such thing. Never would be again. Faith had understood that for so long, she was surprised they didn't seem to understand it down here.

"What would the advantage be to us above?"

asked Malik.

"A rebuilt society. No more secrets, no more assumptions. True equality."

Still it didn't ring true.

"We are being entirely open with you," said Graham. But he didn't look her in the eye.

Faith didn't want to sit there any longer. She needed to move, to see, to discover what lurked in the darker corners of the complex. He'd glossed over the collapsed tunnels, regarded the subject of the Burrowers as done and dusted. Something remained hidden.

"The Burrowers quarters," she said, standing up. "I think you should take us to them now. I want to know who and what the Burrowers are and *where* they are. Then I want to see where this so-called collapsed tunnel occurred. I also want us to be given some of those tablets you are all carrying around with you with full access to the plans and security codes for the different levels."

She'd glimpsed the tablet on Sonia's desk, watched as she swiped the screen and the Wing in which they'd been allocated a room, had appeared. Small dots flickered along these passageways and rooms and she noted, as they were guided around the area, how those dots seemed to reflect the presence of people.

Howard looked across at Shirley and nodded. The woman got up and left the room, returning with four of the digital pads.

Faith did not acknowledge the woman as she was handed hers. She tapped the screen. Saw a line diagram appear immediately. An icon on the top right indicating the level. Each tap of the icon toggled between the different levels, the different wings. Another icon toggled between the diagram and real-time view.

"See," said Howard. "No secrets."

"Oh, I'm sure there are still a few," said Helen. "We just haven't discovered them yet."

CHAPTER SEVENTEEN

FAITH CONTINUED to scan through the floors, the levels, searching for an indication of the Burrower's quarters.

"Level -4," said Howard. "When you get to Level -3, keep your finger pressed on the number for four seconds. It'll switch view. You've already been cleared for access. Most of our residents are not allowed these permissions."

"We're privileged, then," said Ruth.

Level -4 was dark, low tunnels ran along earthen walls occasionally reinforced by steel girders, the ground too appeared to be no more than soil. Strings of lights hung along their length. It reminded Faith of the passages through the Barricade, had the same sort of claustrophobic atmosphere. It was a maze of tunnels with an incline taking you down, down. She saw no chambers, nothing to indicate living quarters.

"They hide," said Howard. "When you go down there and try and track them down, you can hear them, smell them, almost feel them, but rarely see them. Except for those on duty. The ones you saw in the boiler suits."

"You've been down there? Even though when you saw that lad, Ricky, earlier, you abandoned him for having been down in the tunnels?"

"It was a long time ago, and I was lucky," said Howard. "Once we realised what we were up against, we decided to leave well alone. Cut them off. But we had to make sure we could still monitor them, see how the tunnels were progressing. I mean, we'd built them initially, carved them out in case we needed extra storage or... something. They took them over though, moved them out further, under the Barricade, under——"

"Us," said Faith. "They're under our homes."

"Why don't you reintegrate them then?" asked Ruth. "If you want to make us all one happy family?"

"Should've killed them," said Callum. "It would've stopped the spread of the virus in its tracks. He had the chance and blew it. Now they're taking over. They've taken control of access to the Barricade, to——"

"Silence," snapped Howard. "I told you, you could attend the meeting provided you kept that mouth of yours shut. You forget yourself. Now get out."

Callum rose to leave.

"No," said Faith. "Let him stay. It seems he's being a bit more honest than the rest of you."

She looked directly at him, saw in his eyes traces of the little boy he'd been mixed with a man she didn't know at all. The old antagonisms, the teenage pride and machismo were all gone. Instead, mixed in with hope and shame was love. He was still her son. She was still his mother.

A light flashed on an intercom to Howard's right. He pressed the button and listened carefully via an earpiece.

"It seems our vaccine didn't work," he said.

"Paul?"

Howard shook his head. "He's being disposed of as we speak."

The words were cold, dispassionate. Strange when Paul had been Howard's right-hand man for so long. This had been his reward for his loyalty. It made her skin crawl.

"And the tunnel collapse?"

"Floor -3, Wing D. Scan further right. There's nothing hidden there. Everyone can see it."

She followed his instructions and saw more doors on the far side of the Warehouse, their cameras showing a collapsed wall, completely blocked with brick, soil and metal. Like the Burrowers' tunnels, she calculated these too ran under their own compound and beyond. All this time things were happening right beneath their feet.

But what if some of those Burrower's tunnels led up and out? That was why they appeared to go nowhere. They were misleading the eye, confusing the watcher. Letting their occupants crawl to the surface unseen. The disappearances in the city, those strange deaths. Linda. Her friend's death had never been far from her thoughts, another mystery to be solved. She knew who, but not the why. How deep had the manipulation of their society truly gone?

"I want to go down there," she repeated, heading to the door. "The collapsed wing first and then to the tunnels."

Her friends followed her lead.

"Have you been to either?" she asked Malik as they set out, not even waiting to see if Howard was giving permission or not. She didn't care.

"No, I only gradually found out about those and they were never discussed even to the limited extent just now. But I know he won't let you go into the tunnels."

Well he hadn't stopped them yet. Might even be serious about being open and honest. Faith shook herself. Who was she kidding?

"Why, what's he really frightened of?"

"The disease. From what I can gather they reckon it's from the tunnels."

That again. A vaguely-hinted at disease, not explained in full. A smokescreen?

"But if the tunnels lead up and out, then it could be from above which means it's something probably affecting us all already," said Faith.

And below wanted to create a vaccine to make them safe to the subterranean community, put their own interests first—again. Yet if not a disease and the talk of vaccine merely a cover, why were they so keen to examine them? The scientist in her understood the need for observation. Were they looking for signs of genetic mutation as a result of exposure to those toxins so virulent in the atmosphere twenty years ago? Checking to see there were no hidden killers in the surviving surface population?

"I know," said Malik. "It's been going round and round in my head. I don't know what to think any more. And there are other tunnels, ones we know nothing about."

He stabbed the panel to summon the lift. The remainder of the group had caught up with them by now. Howard and his group also. He looked resigned.

"You know you really won't find anything except a lot of debris," he said.

"Perhaps," said Faith. "But these days we need to see the evidence with our own eyes."

"Always so suspicious," said Graham. "Some things don't change."

"Do you blame me?" she asked. Her husband had the decency to look away.

Shirley was there too. Faith found herself stood next to her in the lift. She'd imagined the moment they'd meet for years. Seeing her in person however, showed her there was nothing to challenge or gloat over. Whatever had happened, this was a defeated woman. Still, she couldn't resist.

"So," she said brightly. "How's family life?"

Shirley and Graham looked at each other and then away.

"Still together?" she persisted.

"No," said Callum. "They rowed non-stop for the first six months and that was it."

"'Ain't that the way," said Faith. "If it hadn't been Shirley, it would've been someone else, like the time before and the time before that. By the way, neither of you have asked after Josie."

"I didn't know how, Mum," said Callum. "I've felt guilty every day I've been down here. I was childish, getting my own back because she'd pinched something of mine. I can't even remember what it was now, something really petty. And then I turned my back on her. Can you imagine how I've felt all this time?" He could barely hold her gaze, kept dropping his eyes, shame evident in the flush of his skin, the slump of his shoulders.

"Good," said Faith. "I'd imagined you not giving her a second thought but if you've been feeling like that, I'm…" she almost said glad, but changed it, "relieved."

"You thought I was a monster, didn't you? Well, I

was, I won't deny it, but most of all I was a brat. I don't blame you for what you must have thought of me and Dad. You know they promised us Paradise but it's been nothing but Hell."

"Now, Callum," said Graham. "It's not been all…"

"Crap, Dad. Don't keep spinning the lies. Isn't it time for the truth to come out, for all truths to come out?"

"Turn over a stone and all sorts of things crawl out," said Helen. "Nothing ever changes does it?"

They were coming to a converging point in their history, like the pinch points in some of the corridors, facts were piling up and they were falling over them. Skeletons were falling out of the cupboards and as she thought of those supposedly in suspension, she wondered exactly how literal this statement would prove to be.

The lift stopped and the group disembarked, found themselves retracing their earlier steps. Faith no longer felt as tired. Those spells came and went but the nagging headache remained. She felt irritable, a mood she couldn't shift despite everything else going on around her. The internal conflicting with the external.

"Here," said Graham, eventually.

They stood in front of yet another set of double doors where heavy wooden beams inserted into iron handles prevented access. A mediaeval measure in a high-tech world. Out of place.

"Keep people out or something in?" whispered Ruth.

Graham and Callum slid the beams out of their supports. The panel to the left looked damaged. Graham prised the cover off and pressed a button beneath it. A failsafe. Faith filed that bit of information away for future reference, no doubt other panels were constructed in a similar manner.

A dark, damp, earthy smell seeped in even before the doors had opened. They slid back, juddering through damage and disuse. A few lights flickered, casting strange shadows in the looming darkness.

"Why didn't you turn the electric off?" Faith asked.

"It's all linked to the area where the suspension units are held. We couldn't get to the isolation box to separate it and if there was any hope for the others, we wanted to at least give them a chance."

A humanitarian gesture by an inhuman man, it didn't ring true. In a complex of such sophisticated build there had to be ways of isolating a single strand of lights. These lights had been kept on for a purpose.

She stepped forward into the tunnel, taking a torch from Graham, swinging its beam along the walls and ceiling, the pile of rubble, her companions doing likewise.

"Are you satisfied?" asked Howard, as they neared the mass blocking the passage, poking and prodding at it to check its solidity.

Faith was almost ready to say yes but still couldn't throw off the suspicion something else was at play here. She remembered her discovery of the entrance into the Barricade, only a few days ago now, although already that felt as if it belonged in the distant past. Was it possible such a simple subterfuge operated here as well?

She began to run her hands over the surface, this wasn't the jagged rough edges of the metal above, nothing to cut her thumb on…

Malik and the others could see what she was doing, followed suit.

"Hey," said Howard. "There's really nothing to find down here."

His words only served to make them continue. There was something.

"Dad?"

"Son, I think you should go back up. Now."

"Why?"

"Don't ask questions. Just do as you are told."

"Like I did all those years ago when you told me to come with you, that life would be easier and I would get everything I wanted. That if I did as you said, you would help Mum and Josie."

"Well, you got what you wanted didn't you. And I did help Mum and Josie."

"You helped me and Josie?" Faith stopped her search and turned to face Graham. "How in God's name do you reckon you helped us?"

"Faith." Ruth cut into their discussion, pulled her

back to their task. "It'll have to wait."

Faith turned her attention back to the task in hand.

"You had food," continued Graham. "All you could want. Girls falling over themselves because of who you were."

"Bought by you," snarled Callum. "You used people, you had a tariff and if they paid then you would give them what they wanted."

"And you didn't say no."

"Not at first but then…"

She was about to turn back to her son, intervene in the bitter war raging between father and son when Helen called out.

"Faith. Think I've found something," said Helen. She'd slipped through a gap at the far side of the mound. It seemed to be a small crevice but as Helen ran her hand along the curve something had seemed to give.

Faith held the torch up over her shoulder, watched as only a fine film of soil trickled down to the ground and a door swung open.

Then suddenly everything went black apart from their few torch beams as the doors to the warehouse swung shut.

"You really shouldn't have gone poking in there," said Howard.

Faith turned around. Howard had pulled a gun out. As had Graham. To their credit, Lionel and Callum looked shocked, obviously unaware this was to happen, unaware of what lay beyond.

"And now you've opened this particular can of worms, you may as well keep going," said Howard, indicating with the gun the direction they were supposed to go. Further into the tunnels. The darkness awaited.

"Howard? What on earth do you think you're doing?"

Howard waved the gun at Lionel. "Exactly what I've been doing for twenty years," he said. "Keeping us all alive—and in power. Now move, all of you." He waved his gun at the group.

Ruth went first, Faith holding the door open for her, then she followed, reaching for the gun tucked into her waistband. Always present, she often forgot it was there. And now it wasn't. How? She couldn't remember putting it down anywhere. She'd had it when they first came in. The guards had noticed but still waved them through.

"I haven't got mine either," said Ruth. "How did we not notice? How could we be so stupid?"

For so many years they'd lived on edge, always on their guard. Now, in one day, in the one place that they had all agreed to remain on the alert, they had been completely wrong-footed.

"You'll have to forgive me," said Howard. "We took your arms when you slept after dinner. It was easier than I thought."

So they had been drugged. Faith was furious with herself. Seduced by food and comfortable surroundings, she'd completely dropped her guard. The drug though, was a relief, as it occurred to her she could've been at fault, allowed the mind fog— miserable companion to the flushes and mood swings—to jeopardise their safety. Her friends looked as angry as she felt. They'd let each other down.

The passage they'd entered was of solid concrete construction. Howard moved over to the wall by Ruth and tapped a switch. Immediately lights danced along the wall so it was as bright as the complex they'd just left. This was not some abandoned part of the building.

"Keep going," said Howard.

Now Lionel and Callum were walking with Faith and her group, forming a strange new alliance.

"It's not far."

It was hard to tell. As she peered ahead, Faith saw only darkness at its mouth. A solid wall of black. Another camouflage. What would they see when they got there?

The smell of damp and decay grew stronger, overpowering.

"You might want to apply some of this," said Howard, taking out a small tin and smearing its contents beneath his nose. He passed it along to Graham who did likewise and then to the group. Faith recognised it as the common practice when moving amongst the dead or the horribly diseased.

"Don't look so surprised at my consideration,"

said Howard. "I want you to be able to understand everything before you suffer a tragic accident. Of course, we'll tell those above we did everything in our power to save you."

He sought to intimidate her, but despite the guns pointed at them, Faith didn't feel threatened. She felt as if, after all this time, she was finally getting an answer—although she had long ago forgotten the question. No more secrets, no more lies.

Nor would she die down here. If he intended to kill her, she'd bloody well make sure it was above ground, in front of everyone. Then at least they'd all know what he stood for.

CHAPTER EIGHTEEN

Graham took the lead, the smell getting stronger as the lights grew brighter and the tunnel wider before it opened out into a scene she could only describe as from a horror movie—and she'd seen many real horrors as opposed to the celluloid version. Even with the vaseline, she could smell the decaying bodies, saw no corpses.

There were four giant clear-sided tanks in the space. Inside was a swirling vapour which drifted apart every now and then to show bodies packed tightly together like sardines in a can. They stood upright, tubes and wires running from their bodies up to the surface of the tank, other tubes running into the floor. Faith remembered the images she'd seen years ago before the world ended of China's terracotta army, row upon row of soldiers. Here were row upon row of normal everyday people.

The thought made her pause and she looked again. Normal. No, not normal. There was something she couldn't quite put her finger on. Every body was sheathed in what appeared to be a sleeping bag which in turn resembled a cocoon. It made them all look like giant grubs with only the faces exposed. And whilst they appeared to be still, that was the thing she had noticed. They were not motionless. The envelopes rippled, worm-like shapes crawled beneath the material. It was possible it was tubing but she didn't think so, something else was at work beneath that surface. And the faces were contorted in agony. Whatever was going on. They could feel it.

"What are you doing to them?" she asked as she pressed up against the glass, felt its chill beneath her fingers. Eyes followed the movement of her hands in front of them and as she walked along, she could feel those entombed eyes follow her.

A cry from Callum interrupted her thoughts.

"Dad, it's Peter. What's he doing here?"

Faith moved over to the tank where her son stood. He was staring at the face of another man, a horrified expression etched on his features.

"You told me he had died," said Callum.

"He did."

"No, he's alive. Look."

"I'm sorry," said Graham. "This was something we didn't want you to see until you were ready, until everyone was ready to accept what we were doing and why we were doing it. Nobody was supposed to see this yet."

"So, he's alive?" There was hope evident in his voice.

"Yes and no," said Graham. "Locked in you might say."

"What do you mean?" asked Faith.

"There is still some function in the brain, but the body is dead. Take my word for it."

"I don't think that's possible," said Helen, "given your track record."

"They seem aware, sentient," said Malik, "A horrible state for anyone to be in. Not quite the suspension of life these tanks were built for…"

"And the only faces I see are the ones who've disappeared in the past months," said Callum.

"Where are our original inhabitants?" asked Lionel.

He looked as shocked as Callum.

"Those people volunteered in good faith, prepared to suspend their own lives and come back when needed."

"Good faith? They were desperate," said Howard. "They couldn't face a future above ground and the hardship that would entail, and there wasn't room for them initially. This was their opt-out, their *cop-out*."

"Not quite true," mumbled Callum. "A large number were invited. You…"

Faith looked over at him, startled but Ruth

prevented any discussion, still homing in on Howard.

"Regardless of how you viewed them, that still doesn't explain what you've done with them."

Howard lowered his gun. He felt safe in here for some reason, despite there being no obvious backup. Surprisingly, Faith felt no inclination to try and disarm him. Not until she'd learned as much as she could and if he felt he had an advantage, as he obviously did, now was not the right time.

"Twenty years ago, we filled these tanks with two thousand healthy people, each of these eight tanks could hold two hundred and fifty people. Inside their body temperatures were reduced to twelve degrees Celsius and bodies were fed with nutrients and waste removed via tubes. Unfortunately, a glitch in the power supply of four of the tanks, a temporary break which eventually righted itself, went undetected. When our technicians noticed a degradation in the appearance of the occupants and did a back track of data, the power outage was discovered."

"And the final outcome?"

"Final is an apt choice of words," said Howard. "They were to all intents and purposes, dead. There was still some brain activity but analysis of the brainwaves, which were minimal, revealed severe damage due to the interruption of the oxygen feed controlled by the power. They didn't feel a thing."

Faith continued to stare into the tanks, at the

faces gazing out at them. She noticed their expressions were changing, eyes becoming more alert, curiosity giving place to something she could only describe as hunger. It hadn't been Howard or Lionel's guns which had scared her, but this did. She could feel an almost primaeval fear building to what she saw, fought the desire to run.

"So you disposed of the bodies," prompted Lionel.

"In a way," said Howard. "You see when we took the first victims out, and the technicians examined them, we found the presence of an... organism. This creature had taken up residence in each corpse and had merged itself with the different tracts within the body."

"I don't understand."

"Then I'll show you."

Howard led them over to a computer and clicked an icon. A video started to play on the screen.

"An autopsy?"

He nodded.

The video showed the technician slowly cutting open the skin in the traditional Y pattern down the abdomen, pulling the flaps back to reveal digestive and respiratory systems. At first glance it looked as though those still existed but then as the technician prodded the tubing with his scalpel, it moved. And the body's eyes opened. Its mouth moved.

Faith listened as the supposedly dead man talked. Other scientists came in, asked him questions about his life, facts which could be verified against his file. And all the time, he lay on the table with his abdomen carved open and the giant worm writhing around inside.

"Behold the conqueror worm," said Howard. "You wanted to visit the Burrowers' quarters, discover the truth about those elusive creatures. Well, here you are. Here's your other truth."

Faith stared at the body on the screen and then looked across at the giant tanks. These were also Burrowers. The worm? She had expected them to be human, that's what all the rumours had been about, the shadows she had glimpsed in the dark. And that creature didn't look like any worm she remembered, in fact it resembled a giant version of the nematodes she'd once been studying, developing. Tiny creatures which had remarkable resistance to atmospheric pressure, to changes in gas composition. She had admired this adaptive ability. Sought to use it to improve soil quality.

"And there's more. Watch."

The video continued, this time with the abdomen stitched up at which point, the man sat up and looked directly at the doctor making notes at his side, started talking to him. The conversation was mundane, the usual moans and groans about the weather, taxes, work. So normal it made it all the more startling.

"It's a parasite," said Howard, "it burrows its way beneath the skin, eats and replaces the main bodily systems, keeps the nervous system intact so the brain still works and is capable of lucid thought and memory. Two organisms in one skin."

"And you allow it, give it other hosts?" asked Lionel, to his credit he looked as disgusted as Faith felt.

She could not believe Lionel had been kept in the dark about all this. In such a contained environment as the subterranean complex, how was that even possible? It was obvious however, Howard ruled the roost with Lionel as his puppet.

"Yes," continued Howard, "because we've been trying to work out how mankind was going to survive. We need to be in a position where we can survive fire, famine and flood. This way, there is no issue. This creature is going to be the saviour of the human race, provided we welcome it. And we have welcomed it. We will be able to survive in any environment in the future. Nothing will stop us. We have future-proofed humanity."

Faith could see where this was going, but Callum jumped in first.

"This is where everybody's been going isn't it," he was making his way around the tank now, peering as hard as he could into the densely packed bodies. "Mike, Tom, Megan, Evelyn… shit, we've been sending patrols into the tunnels and above looking for them and so many others when they were down here all the time."

"Not all the time," said Graham. "We allow this

particular batch out when they require it, for the most part they need to stay in the tank. There's still an element of adaptation going on, they're not quite ready for complete independence. It's not long now though. Couldn't have come at a better time actually."

"You expect those in the tanks to go above ground and be welcomed back into our community with open arms, don't you? You're going to infect the others so we all become these, these things."

"And you will be leading the way," he said calmly. "Your cooperation would allow the whole thing to go so much more smoothly."

They weren't going to be shot. They were going to be cut open and given over to the mutated nematodes. Where were they though?

"Those shapes you see moving beneath the coverings are the juvenile form. They stay there until we find them a host. When someone's been adapted, no one is able to tell. You, of course, will lead the reassurance. Say it's all for the best."

"You think we will agree to this?" Faith couldn't believe what she was hearing.

"And you," said Helen. "What about you? When do you go through this 'adaptation'.

Howard smiled at her and his eyes seemed to change colour. "I already have," he said. "And so has Graham."

"Oh, my God," cried Callum. "Dad, what the fuck?"

His father went to pull Callum into his arms but the younger man shrank back, looked as if he couldn't bear to be touched by the man who was his father.

"Are all these *nematodes* in the tanks?" asked Ruth. "I mean where did they come from originally? The soil, somewhere deep below here."

"Definitely from the soil," said Graham. "You could say we developed them." He looked directly at Faith and she went cold. "Didn't we?"

Her friends looked at her and she could do nothing but shake her head. "I was working on simple nematodes, microscopic creatures. Not this, this monstrosity."

"But you remember we studied their capacity, projected ratio of adaptation to environment for optimum improvement."

"In the soil," said Faith. "Not in humans, not like this."

"Never could see the bigger picture, could you," said Howard. "Graham though. Oh, he had an eye for the future—as well as for the ladies."

Faith ignored Howard's dig. He was deliberately trying to rile her and she wasn't going to let him.

"Their physiology was the answer to all our prayers," he continued. "The nematodes filter the soil, feed on dead and decaying matter. They don't need the same sort of food as we do. Can you imagine humans being able to live a life without having to grow and process their food as we've had to do? This organism is effectively a backup system, sharing its respiratory function with its host, its nutrient pool. So many things would become automatically easier."

"They look like they are more than nematodes to me," said Faith, studying their shape. The creatures slithered around the tanks, diving in and out of the mist, occasionally finding their way into the shrouds surrounding a human before coming out again. "More like eels or... serpents."

"And once inside their host," said Howard. "They will continue to grow to their full length. At present they are juveniles, their skin is not adapted to their eventual hosts. This is why they swim around in the vapour. It is their way of acclimatising."

"So they are not feeding on them?" She had not wanted to ask the question, the thought already making her sick to her stomach. How could a person move around knowing there was such a creature inside themselves? And then if you didn't know but discovered it, what would you do, how would you react. Such a shock could cause a catastrophic reaction. Faith thought about what she would do, would she rip herself open, tear out her own organs?

Immediately, her mind shot back to Linda. The woman's abdomen had been well and truly mangled, there had been nothing left of her chest cavity, her intestines. No, she couldn't be one of those infected. It would mean she had spent some time below but Linda had always been around. Right from those early days. Unless they had been experimenting before that final severing of societies, turning them into above and below.

No. She couldn't have been. Yes, there had been odd behaviour but the disease, the falling apart of families and society had triggered so much.

"These people, in here," said Callum, "have been put in as part of some sort of conversion programme? How on earth have we not noticed before?"

"You did," said Graham. "You saw the reports of deaths, of criminality, of punishments. We removed those affected for whatever reason and brought them down here. Nobody ever looked any further. Nobody would ever have discovered even this until later when it wouldn't have mattered. But because of recent developments, of those who have not been processed desiring to go above, well, it's all come to light, hasn't it?"

"So, you appearing above ground wasn't your idea?" She couldn't believe it.

"No, not originally. People were getting a bit antsy, demanded a vote. The atmosphere was, shall we say, highly-pressured. Going above at this stage wasn't ideal but took the focus off me for a while."

As Faith continued to look at the tanks, more and more of the serpents swam past, seemingly attracted to their presence for some reason. As they slithered and coiled towards her, she wanted to turn her back, unsee them but something held her, tugged.

"What happens if the power to the tanks is turned off, completely this time?" asked Lionel. "We could stop all this couldn't we?"

"Stop it? We would possibly lose these specimens, but we have come too far."

"Too far?"

"Where do you think they all went?" asked Howard. "Those we have already partnered? They are not here. Not in the tanks."

Helen beat her to it. "The Burrowers. That's who you mean, isn't it? The ones who live within the Barricade."

"No," said Howard. "As I've already said, the Burrowers are those virus-afflicted souls who live in the Barricade. These others do not live there and you might find it hard to accept but they look like everyone else, absolutely normal."

"What do you mean by that?" asked Faith, although she knew the answer, was trying not to think of it.

"Do you think *you* are not affected?"

Faith and Helen looked at each other in horror. Ruth had turned away and started walking, Malik at her side. Faith noticed the gun in Howard's hand remained lowered. He had no intention of shooting them, had never had any inclination to kill them. And if he didn't shoot them, it was because he saw no need.

"How," she choked out, "how do you expect everyone else to react once you go back up. Do you think they'll just accept your word for it?"

"No," said Lionel. "They'll be frightened, become suspicious of each other, maybe kill one or two to look underneath the hood so to speak. Then they'll see and they'll understand and they'll have to try and find a way to come to terms with it because otherwise every little bit of themselves they regard as human is gone, they are gone."

"The human race is gone," said Helen.

"Isn't it already?" said Howard.

Helen and Faith followed the other two out of the chamber and back along the tunnel. Howard made no attempt to follow or to shoot them. That fact alone caused her more anxiety than she cared to mention. Ruth was marching swiftly ahead.

"Ruth! Ruth!" she called. "Where are you going?"

"The labs upstairs," said Ruth. "They have scanners. We can scan ourselves, see if there's anything inside. See if what he said is true."

"You really want to know?" asked Malik. "Could you handle the answer?"

"I don't know," said Ruth. "I just know that I can't live with not knowing, although whether I can live with the answer is another thing."

As they walked along, Faith suddenly stopped. "Callum," she said.

"Callum?"

"Him and Lionel didn't seem to know about this, and they're part of the surviving group. Doesn't that mean they are *not* infected in any way?"

Her son, who had gone below ground now turned out to be one of those who were probably the only original humans left. All her thoughts had been turned on their head. She no longer knew what she should be looking for, or fighting for.

"Faith," said Ruth, as they all caught up. "If you find something like *that* inside you, what will you do?"

"I don't know," said Faith. "I really don't."

"And if it's all of us, do we go back up and tell everyone—"

"There'll be a riot," said Malik. "They won't believe us."

"And it won't matter," said Helen, "because a number of them have already got their human hosts so they're sorted."

"If," reminded Ruth. "If. It's not for certain and he might be pulling a fast one. I mean, it's a crazy idea. We'd have to arrange for a full scan above ground, something people would believe in."

"They won't believe anything except the evidence of their own eyes and that means cutting someone open and then still they might think it's only one or two, that it's not them," said Malik.

She knew he was playing devil's advocate but it didn't reassure her. She wanted to know and she didn't want to know. She wanted to be above ground amongst the people she'd known and survived alongside for years and she didn't want to be with them. She wanted to find Josie. Josie. Could the parasite, for that was what it was, be the cause for her depression and self-loathing. Had she known or suspected something all this time?

As they walked, Faith cast her mind back to all their conversations. The others didn't interrupt her musings, being concerned with the conflicts of their own mind. Josie had never mentioned any physical issues, beyond the usual aches and pains they all complained of. Nor had she described herself as not being 'herself'. There was nothing hinting at a trigger. If she found out, especially accidentally, Josie would not survive. Faith knew her daughter well. These parasitic creatures did not understand the suicidal impulse of the human mind.

"Do you believe any of that shit?" asked Ruth as they eventually emerged into the lobby in front of the lift, pressed the buttons which would transport them back to a nominal civilisation.

"I don't know," said Faith. "I mean we saw those creatures in the tank and in that body but until I see the evidence, feel the evidence inside me, I'm giving it fuck all credence. The guy's just messing with our heads, like he did all those years ago."

What would it do to Ruth? Her daughters had died all those years ago, if they were infected, why did her children die when the organism within could've led to their survival?

And the farmers. Where did they fit into all this? Was that just another screen? Something that appeared normal but wasn't quite?

CHAPTER NINETEEN

"Hello," said Sonia as the lift doors opened. She looked genuinely pleased to see them. Faith could not imagine one of those serpents inside her. Yet she had been everywhere since her arrival. Unless there was no one else and numbers had got really low, in which case the numbers of true humans had reached a critical situation. Did they protect them, without knowing, or did they continue to find the truth for those of their new families above?

"Sonia," said Malik. "We need to carry a quick medical exam out on each of us, make sure we haven't brought any infection with us. Where can we carry out a body scan, check ourselves over?"

Faith expected a confused look but Sonia seemed to understand exactly what they were after.

"I'll take you," she said, without argument.

"They're past the labs, here." She guided them along the passageway and down to the MRI room. "Do you think you're carrying something?" Only now was she backing away from them.

"No, no," said Malik, "It's just been so long we thought it time to give ourselves a complete medical. Peace of mind. You understand?"

"Yes," said Sonia. "I understand only too well. My brother was like you. He thought something was wrong with himself, wanted a proper medical. Managed to get him a scan. Trouble was he never came to me after that, they told him the results and he disappeared, seemed to have been unable to accept whatever was wrong. Sometimes I think there's something wrong with me and then I tell myself not to be so daft."

"How many are there actually living in this complex now?" asked Helen. "Not including anyone in suspension. Just those in the living quarters."

"Not many," admitted Sonia. "And that was what concerned my brother *and* me. Coming down here, my parents had been told we'd be safe. I was only five-years-old back then."

"Where are your parents now?" asked Helen.

"They died and I was brought down here with my brother. Bartholomew and Preeti raised me. They were the best parents we could've wished for."

"Do you have a photo?" asked Malik.

Sonia pulled out a slim wallet and flipped it open. "Here," she said and offered it to them.

Malik looked at it first, nodded as if confirming some thought. Then he passed it to Faith. She looked at the couple. Andrew and Sylvie. Her blood ran cold. These were her friends, the only people, apart from Ruth and Helen, she'd allowed to remain close to her. They'd told her they could never have children when in fact they'd had a son and a daughter and somehow bought her a place below. What had they agreed to do for Howard and Lionel above ground? More lies. If she accepted what Lionel had been telling her, walked through the door he'd opened.

"They look a lovely couple," said Faith.

Sonia sighed. "I think they were. I mean, part of me knows they were. I can't really remember, I was only five back then."

"Do you have a register or database of those who are still here?" asked Helen.

Sonia looked doubtful, not because of not knowing the answer but understanding what her answer might lead to.

"I don't think Howard would mind," said Faith. She was certain now.

"Over here," said Sonia, her shoulders slumping in defeat. She led them back to the reception desk for the floor. Sonia did indeed seem to be the one and only receptionist for the complex. What happened to her compatriots?

A small child hurtled past the group at that point, his shrieks of delight echoed by his parents who were running after him. They paused briefly to look at the visitors and then dismissed them from their minds, running after their escaped son, their joy in their child's delight obvious. You took your pleasures where you could these days, no matter how small.

Sonia pulled up the list of occupants.

"Do you notice anything about these people?" asked Ruth.

"No," said Faith.

"They're all families, apart from Callum here, it's all couples."

"Why was I spared?" asked Callum.

Faith looked at her son. "It's all about connections," she said. "That's always what it's been about."

"Right," said Sonia. "You wanted the scanners. This way." She didn't seem to want to ask any more questions, just deliver them to the lab and leave them. The anxious air had returned seven-fold and Faith knew they made her nervous. She seemed to be expecting trouble.

"Okay," said Faith, looking at the equipment which she had no clue how to operate.

"This is what we want," said Helen, taking charge, moving confidently towards an upright capsule, a clear glass tube standing on a metal disc.

"How can that be a scanner, I thought they were big chunky things…"

"Those were the old ones, standard issue for civilian hospitals. This thing was used by the army, detects all sorts of nerve gases or body compromises."

"Body compromises?"

"I know, it sounds like a date-night gone wrong but it means anything that's invaded the system, bullets, shrapnel, parasites, other organisms and the like."

"And you know how to operate it?" asked Faith, still looking at it doubtfully.

"Slightly older versions but they can't be much different," said Helen. "So, the only question is, who's going to go first?"

They all looked at each other, desperate to know but not sure they'd deal with the findings. Yet there was no room for blissful ignorance. They needed to see how far this had all gone.

Sonia came back in at that point, a sheaf of papers in her hand. "You might want to look at these," she said. "The names for those who were held in the suspension chambers originally and those who went in after."

"You know about the chambers?" asked Callum.

"Not really. I've just been a bit... a bit worried. There seem to have been more secrets lately, more rumours flying around. I decided to do a bit of digging and now I'm my own supervisor – the other admin people have also vanished – I've been pulling information together. It's all here."

She looked at the scanner. "Have any of you been in there yet?"

"No," said Faith. "We were just trying to decide who should go in."

Uncertainty flitted over Sonia's face. Then she appeared to make a decision. "Do you think... do you think I could go in there? I'm not quite sure what's been happening but I want to know I'm... what I think I am."

"And what do you think you are?" asked Faith.

"Human," she said simply.

Faith looked at the others and they shrugged their shoulders.

"Okay then," said Helen. "In you go, just remove any jewellery and your shoes. No need to strip."

Sonia looked relieved at that. Helen pressed a button and the capsule door swung back.

"Stand with your feet in the impressions beneath you," she said.

Footprints were shaped into the metal pad beneath her.

"Sensors feed up through these points," said Helen. "When I start, you'll see chains of lights moving over your body. It's just the sensors taking your readings and these transfer data over to the screen in front of you..."

"So we see what you find straight away?" asked Faith, thinking she'd rather be out of the capsule before she discovered the truth. If you saw something crawl around inside you and you were stuck inside that capsule – which could only be opened from the outside – and the people outside were scared, shocked, refused to let you out until…

She scanned the capsule. What could they do? She went over and peered up inside to the enclosed top, noticed small holes in the covering. If they didn't like what they found, they could fill it with gas, sedate or kill.

Helen saw her looking. "Don't worry," she said. "We won't let you come to any harm."

"But if you find something inside one of us?"

"We'll let you out," said Helen. "I mean, if you were going to do anything, you would have done it by now, wouldn't you? But we are all clueless as to our current physical state."

Helen had pressed the pad by now and Sonia was isolated behind the glass. She suddenly looked even younger, her fear, becoming more manifest by the minute making her appear extremely vulnerable.

"Are you ready?" she asked Sonia.

The young woman nodded and Helen started pressing buttons and adjusting number levels on the monitor next to it. There was a soft glow around Sonia's feet.

"It's warm," she said. "Are you sure…"

"It won't hurt you," said Helen, "it might tickle occasionally but that's all."

Dancing red dots appeared around Sonia's feet and then started to weave up and over her body. Sonia gazing down at them all the time in wide-eyed fascination. As the dots moved, an image started to draw itself on the monitor screen in front of them. Bit-by-bit her body was rebuilt, the computer spinning and turning the image to create the 3D outline. Then it started to fill in the various internal systems, drawing the digestive tract, respiratory system, nervous system so a full view of Sonia— both inside and out—could be seen. There was no sign of the strange organisms they had seen in the Suspension Chamber.

As Sonia looked at the screen, the tension vanished from her and relief took its place. Eventually the image was completed and Sonia was allowed out.

"Thank you," she said to Helen. "You've no idea how relieved I am. I'd better get back now, Howard and Graham will be back soon and I don't want to get in any trouble. If you need me though, just call."

"Someone's happy," said Callum.

"Wouldn't you be if you found out there was nothing wrong with you?"

"S'pose."

"Back to the question then. Which one of us goes first?"

Again, they looked at each other. Wanting to know, not wanting to know. Eventually, Helen started to move forward but Lionel beat her to it, stepping inside and turning round to stare at them defiantly.

"Go on then. I was supposed to be in charge of this mess. Let's see if I'm affected. It's only right."

He stared at her but she could see the fear crouching behind his bravado.

Again the door swung shut and Helen tapped away at the keyboard, triggering the red light beams to spin and whirl around his body, drawing him in 3D to produce a view even he had never seen. Like Sonia, it sketched out his frame, filled in the details. Nothing extra was discovered. No parasite. Nothing to worry about. He too, gave a smile of relief.

"Next," he said, looking cheerfully at his companions.

"Me," said Callum.

Faith had not had time to talk properly with her son, to even begin to get to know him as the man he'd become but she didn't want to see him harmed in any way.

More red lights spun up and around his body. Another image created for them all to view. Nothing more to see.

"So, both Lionel and Callum are clear," said Faith. "Now us, the four from above."

"Me," said Malik.

"No," said Faith. "Me." She stepped past him and into the capsule. Helen closed the door on her and she found herself gazing into the other woman's eyes. Neither could hold the other's look.

"Do it quickly," said Faith, "before I change my mind and disgrace myself!"

Helen laughed, but there was sadness there. Quickly she tapped out the same commands and

Helen felt the heat rise up through the floor, sending its beams of red light dancing over her, twisting and twirling to form the image. She kept her eyes fixed on her feet for some time, aware as the light spread over her that any sound outside the capsule had faded. Nobody was saying anything. She looked up.

Across from her, she could see her outline, the normal external features reassuringly drawn and then... it was as if she was looking at the corpse on the mortician's table again. Her organs and body systems appeared to be drawn normally, but not quite. The tubes and veins pulsed and writhed in place, the creature within her mimicking the structure of the human physiology in order for the host to continue in blissful ignorance, housing it, transporting it, feeding it.

"That's not me," she whispered. "That is not me. Let me out."

She thought for one moment they would leave her trapped inside but Malik came over and released her from the capsule. She expected him to shrink from her but instead he came forward and pulled her into a hug, as did both Ruth and Helen.

"We're all in this together," said Ruth. "Now, my turn."

She gave Faith's hand a squeeze and then stepped into the scanner. Faith watched Helen operate the machine, knowing she would be taking the readings for her friend. When she felt she could, she turned towards the screen and saw the body being formed, the same externals, the slithering mass inside. Two of them.

"My turn," said Malik, as soon as Ruth had exited the capsule and received her own hugs of commiseration. She looked as sick as Faith felt.

Beams ran over Malik, reflected on the plasma screen. Beams of the foreign organism, housed also within his body.

Three of them.

"That leaves me," said Helen, taking her place inside the capsule. "Go on, Faith. Run the test."

Nervously, Faith tapped out the numbers Helen had shown her, the codes which released the light beams from the pressure pads and sent them on their way over the body, pulled by the attraction to the ions floating around the body. How on earth those stayed the same she didn't know. If this was an intelligent parasite, why didn't it deflect the beams or force them to portray the normality of their physiology.

They all stared at the screen.

Four.

Helen retook her place with the group.

"You know, knowing what's inside me, inside all of us, hasn't made me feel any different. I think if I was on my own, I'd go nuts, probably try and rip my insides out..."

"Like Linda," said Faith.

"Oh my God," said Ruth. "Do you think that's what happened to her, somehow she understood there was something inside. Imagine how scared a person would feel if they were on their own, they would be absolutely terrified and terror makes a person do unimaginable and horrific things to themselves."

"Like Linda," agreed Helen.

The whole ghastly business explained why Howard and his cronies had disposed of her body on the Barricade. They didn't want anyone to find out the truth.

"You know the one thing I would like to know above all else is if this thing has any connection to our brains, to our thoughts. Can it guide us, fool us into taking actions and making us believe they're our own?"

That would be the worst thing. To discover you are no longer truly who you think you are. Her eye fell on the papers Sonia had brought in. The list of those from the original Suspension Chamber.

She ran her finger down the list, barely able to contain her shock at the names she saw there. The names of so many people she knew, including her friends with her now and of course, herself. Yet how did she not remember that time, the being put into suspension, the being released, the going above ground? It did not seem possible.

"Our names are all here," she said to the others. "We were the original guinea pigs. Infected and then sent above. We were the ones Howard hinted at."

"Did they drug us? What…"

"They brainwashed us all," said Faith. "They didn't leave us behind. They took us below, we're the invited, the ones Callum mentioned. They did whatever they had to do, then sent us back up. They didn't walk away from us, they kicked us out. We were experiments on another scale while they hid in safety."

"They could really do that?" said Helen. "That's not possible…"

"Like the parasite," said Malik.

None of them could make sense of it and whilst it was worrying, it distracted all of them from the thoughts of what was currently happening inside their bodies.

Faith turned to Lionel. "You were here from the beginning, you must've known what happened. *You* can tell us."

"Me? What makes you think I would know the details. I had no idea this was going on. I let the scientists and the army do their thing. They were the experts. Listen to the science was our motto."

"Did you see us go in though? Who made the selection?"

"I believe your husband volunteered you," said Lionel. "He felt somewhat guilty for what he had done, reckoned at least in stasis you and Josie would be more protected than if left outside. You came in quite willingly. I was told it was purely hibernation. Nothing else. I agreed but I didn't see you before you went in."

Try as she might, Faith could remember nothing of that time. Only the warped and twisted fragments which claimed her in her dreams.

"Was it filmed, recorded in any way?" asked Helen. "Anything like that is treated like an experiment, everything recorded, monitored."

"They didn't do a very good job of it," said Ruth, "allowing the tanks to become compromised."

"And where did those creatures come from in the first place," said Helen. "A mutation from viruses travelling?"

She caught a look between Lionel and Callum. "Or was it something our precious government was messing about with at that time?"

The betraying look between them told her she'd hit the mark. It all came back to FutureProof. Not only had she worked there but her husband had sat as a director on its board. Her work and its value in improving society's access to food, the fight against annual famines in so many countries, had allowed her to suppress her growing concerns over some of the more shadowy aspects of the business and support her husband.

Within the company, there had been other labs, working with living organisms. Graham had said they were at the cutting edge of genetic engineering. He'd never given details of exactly what was being researched in those areas, and she'd never asked, preferring, she had to admit, to not wanting to know. There had once been a laboratory above ground not far from the bunker complex. She'd visited it on more than one occasion although never had a complete tour. When the separation happened, the government sealed the building off and it had, to a certain extent, remained empty.

She continued to think over the shape of the organism, its long length, its cuticle, the mouth. The mouth. Where was the mouth? The stylet? She didn't want to look. She needed to look. There was a small window on the wall behind Malik. She could go over there, *open wide*. For the first time she sensed the nausea rising inside.

CHAPTER TWENTY

"ARE YOU ALRIGHT, Faith?" asked Ruth. A redundant question for all of them except, something in her expression had obviously caused concern.

"Am I? Don't think so," said Faith.

"Genetically modified," said Callum. "Yeah. I got into science, Mum, believe it or not. I wanted to understand more, didn't want to be treated like some ignorant little oik. Lionel has a tendency to patronise. So does Dad."

Faith remembered that. It didn't matter she held a doctorate, was a respected authority in her own field. By virtue of his governmental position, he thought he was above her. But it still rankled he took his secretary. Even if he'd not wanted to be with her, hadn't she earned her place through her knowledge and skill? In light of their discoveries, his action seemed even more petty.

"We need to see what research they've got on these things," said Helen. "Wouldn't they have filmed their first tests? There must be film showing those first infections? And what about when a person died with one of the worms inside them? Did it crawl out, be replaced in the tank?"

Helen was like Faith, she wanted to know so she could deal with it. The trouble was that if there was no way to separate them from their parasites how would they go forward, or would they even want to?

Faith's alarm increased when Howard appeared art the lab door, but this time she sensed no threat from him.

"Come with me," said Howard. "Now you know the truth, I can open up the files for you. It's more comfortable in my office." He was completely unconcerned about their situation. Seemed to think that by knowing, everything he wanted had been agreed.

Faith felt her stomach rumble, her stomach or the worm, she was no longer sure. Was it the nematode protesting its lack of food?

"We can eat whilst we're there," he continued. "At least we can be civilised about all this."

"Can I just get it clear," said Faith. "You knew all about this experimentation?" She was looking at Howard. "But Callum didn't?"

"Yes," said Howard. "We felt it best to keep all those below Level 8 Security Clearance, ignorant of our intentions. We didn't want to start a panic."

"Even though you were going to continue your experiment on them?"

"It wasn't an experiment by that point," said Howard. "It was our last hope. But we knew people would be uncomfortable with the idea, frightened even..."

"You don't say," interrupted Ruth.

Howard glared at her. "You don't realise. It was the only way the human race could survive. This symbiosis was critical."

"The crops in the countryside are returning," said Faith. "So, not as critical as you thought."

"The farmers," said Howard. "Do you think they have been left out of all this? Their cultivation has been carried out in a slightly different way."

"What do you mean?" asked Faith, a cold feeling of dread crawling through her.

"You remember the nematodes were being studied particularly with relation to their ability to enrich the soil in which they lived. The problem was we needed thousands of the things, they were so small. Your particular area of study, Faith, if I recall."

She remembered, disliked the inference she had a hand in this nightmare.

"So you made them bigger," said Ruth.

"How do you mean enrich?" asked Malik.

"We simply allow them to follow their normal biological cycle," said Howard.

"Which is?" asked Ruth.

Faith looked at Howard. She knew exactly how the nematode functioned. The very idea of what it would do was horrific.

"Go on," she said. "Tell them."

"We were running out of fertilisers, running out of burial plots," he said.

"What's one got to do with the other?" interrupted Malik, impatient.

"We came up with a solution. One our green brethren could only accept. It did, after all, fit in with their mantra of 'reuse, recycle, reduce.' Although they were a bit annoyed at the adoption of their tagline."

He paused for a moment as if considering his words. Faith wondered how he would present his facts. It turned out he was going for brutal transparency.

"During the lifecycle of the nematode, it goes through a juvenile stage and finds a host, in our case, a human. At a determined point in time, the nematode releases bacteria. The bacteria kill the host."

"You mean the person," said Ruth. "Never forget you're talking about humans."

"How could I?" said Howard. "I was trying to save the human race."

"That all sounds very noble," said Helen. "But I don't see how."

"No, Howard," said Faith. "I don't see how. So

why don't you finish telling them."

He shrugged his shoulders, completely unconcerned his words would cause any sort of upset, so convinced of his own truth, his reasons for his actions.

"Once the host has died, the nematode feeds on the bacteria and liquefies the body and it is broken down into the soil. Obviously we had to develop a larger form of the nematode to make this latter stage effective. Bodies were interred directly into soil, no coffins, shrouds or other coverings, and they were left to decompose as a result of the parasite's digestive action. The quality of the soil showed a marked improvement."

Faith knew the detail of the nematode's life cycle, had worked out the horrific conclusion to Howard's experimentation, hearing it spoken aloud however, was still a shock. This was all before the final separation, the disappearance below ground. It could only have happened with the collusion of the government.

"We were harvesting organs for transplant," said Howard. "This wasn't so much different. It became even easier after the law was changed and people had to opt out of donating their organs. Didn't realise they'd effectively handed their bodies over to us."

"Not different!" exploded Helen. "Mulching humans back into the soil, planting crops in that earth—I assume you planted crops."

Howard inclined his head.

"We ended up eating other humans by default. You turned us into indirect cannibals. The risk of disease when we eat each other in whatever form, however indirectly. You *know* it."

"You also need to take into account one other factor," said Faith.

They all looked at her.

"Once the nematode has destroyed its host, it leaves eggs behind."

"In the soil, to be digested with the crops and the life cycle begins again," said Malik, taking her comment to its logical conclusion.

Ruth had jumped up and was pacing around. Something more was bothering her.

"You didn't just infect people down here, did you?" she said. "You started the whole business above ground. Those donated rations, the generous bags of flour given out towards the end. They contained the eggs didn't they?"

"Wouldn't people notice?" asked Malik. "I mean the nematodes grow to huge proportions—"

"But the eggs remain the same size," said Faith. "Once inside a human host, the environment triggers their development."

She almost admired the process. It was intelligent, unique and oh, so clever. But it was at the cost of human life.

"If people were infected above ground, why bring *us* below, put us into hibernation?"

"Easy," said Helen. "Military tactic. Husband your resources so to speak. We were to be sent back up when the time was right to start making our world inhabitable again. That was the intention BUT those tanks were compromised and we pretty much went straight back up didn't we?"

Howard nodded. "Yes. That was unfortunate. We'd been hoping to have a longer lead in time but it was still a good chance to see how our plan worked in action. And I must say you and the farmers have done a fine job."

Faith couldn't believe it. Those gatekeepers to the countryside, the very people who'd condemned everyone else for messing about with nature, destroying the planet's ecosystems had been a party to this experiment.

"Is that why the crops have improved?" asked Malik. His face was lined with a mixture of worry and disgust.

"A lot is to do with the re-establishment of the seasons but yes, the bodies have played their part in the replenishment of the soil."

"How did they get them, the bodies?" asked Ruth. "Some have gone missing but not huge numbers."

"The pits," said Malik, coming round to the same conclusion as Faith. "We never really saw the dead, did we? We would wave them off and they would be trundled away to the pit."

"The pit as you call it," said Howard, "is actually

a source of the richest soil around. We made sure we had a number of pits to be filled, an expanse of land to be farmed."

"How could anyone give the go ahead to this work?" asked Ruth. "It's inhuman."

"No," said Lionel, looking at Howard, "merely practical. Government and scientists worked together to create the best chance of survival for our race. The government doesn't always need to know the details."

"Keeping us—and themselves—in blissful ignorance," snapped Helen. "Easier to deny when it all comes out in the wash."

"Well, would you have given permission for any of this," asked Howard. "Honestly? We couldn't afford the time to negotiate. We just had to get on with it."

"And you call that survival? You've made us dependent on another creature. Every human being a host."

"Not every human being," said Howard.

Faith thought of the empty accommodation blocks in the complex, the few remaining families in Block A. All those others had gone. Either in the functioning tanks or up to the farmers to fertilise the soil.

"The families," said Helen, her eyes wide. "They're pretty much the only ones left. You're sparing them!"

"Callum isn't part of that group," said Faith.

"No? There are some yet to become hosts but they will do. The remaining families are effectively our families of the ark. *They* will repopulate the world. *We* will merely feed it. And speaking of food…"

Howard pressed a buzzer and Sonia appeared carrying a tea tray. As she poured out the cups, he told her what they would like to eat.

"You might not feel hungry," said Howard. "But I can assure you, your guests do. And if they don't get fed, well things have a tendency to go awry. It's not a pretty sight." He was laughing, enjoying their fear.

Faith tried to suppress her imagination but she could already see the worm forcing itself out of the body, like an insect moulting, it would shed its skin, find another host or disappear into the soil. She knew Howard was playing mind games. There had been times of hunger, near starvation, and whilst she had suffered, there had been nothing unexpected in her body's responses to its deprivation. *He was lying, wasn't he?*

"We've found a few things out you might want to be aware of," said Howard. "The little buggers have a tendency to secrete an enzyme that affects our brains, disrupts our thoughts, induces hallucinations."

"Like Linda," said Faith.

"Like Linda," echoed Howard.

"That's why you put her on the Barricade," said

Malik. "To stop people looking too closely, getting suspicious."

"I needed to prevent panic. You can understand that, can't you?" Howard was so certain of himself.

Faith however couldn't get the idea of experimentation out of her head. Her experience of science had a tendency to throw up anomalies. Quirks that took her enquiries in different directions. When she considered the nematodes, what would happen there if they deviated? The worms might disappear into the soil or they could perhaps start hoovering up the remaining humans above ground. Nature had a nasty habit of turning round and biting back when messed with. What was supposed to be their saviour might very well turn out to be the final nail in their coffin. A landscape of roiling soil, it sounded like the book *Dune* with its giant worms. From fiction to fact.

"What about other countries, other parts of the planet?" asked Helen.

"Oh, they have their own methods. Weren't too keen on ours although they accepted our food deliveries eagerly enough."

"You've been sending them food, when your own have been starving?"

Food contaminated by the eggs of the parasite, ready to infect other nations. Wipe them out possibly, unless a saviour came to their aid.

"We are a humanitarian nation…"

"You are a self-seeking bastard, you wouldn't do

it unless there was something in it for you."

"Perhaps. But I think we've chosen the best option. I doubt you would prefer any of the alternatives."

"They are not our concern," said Helen.

"Of course they are," said Howard. "Would you want to be the weakest country in this brave new world of ours? Think of our history. All those invasions. The world and his wife dropping in and taking over every few years. Would you want that again? This way it is we who stay in control."

Howard's arguments were scary, even more so because they were practical and he had a valid point.

Faith dismissed it all from her thoughts. She needed to understand the worm's physiology, especially if she was going to work out a way to disentangle it from her organs, expel it from her body. She could see no way forward which did not involve pain and suffering.

"The videos, Howard," she reminded.

"Are you sure you want to watch this? You'll get your meal in a minute. Might put you off your food."

"I don't think anything could be as bad as what we've just seen," said Helen.

She was wrong. Her tea went cold, her biscuits remained untouched, the summons to the meal later, unheard. Her stomach continued to rumble.

"Shouldn't ignore it too much," said Howard.

"Might give you a nasty nip. They have a tendency to bite."

The first video lasted only a few seconds. A man was seen sat next to a doctor, much as a normal consultation might take place. The doctor was telling the man he was having a simple vaccine to prevent him from catching the latest viral mutation of flu. The patient seemed quite happy, accepted the needle without protest. He was also given a small cup of what appeared to be juice. A vitamin boost, they said. Again, he drank it without protest.

As the needle went into the man's arms, his eyes closed and he slumped forward, two nurses running forward to catch him and lift him onto the nearby gurney. As he was wheeled to a bay, a camera focused its lens on the area where the injection had been made. There seemed to be a small movement just beneath the skin, a rippling effect moving up and up the limb and then into the main body of the man.

Figures along the bottom of the screen denoted any time lapses and Faith realised this was a few days compressed into minutes. The rippling beneath the skin had grown bigger, waves of movement sweeping out across the man's body. The patient still didn't wake up. She doubted he would ever wake up again.

Then the rippling stopped. The body placed in a pod, a drip introduced to feed nutrients and tubes to remove waste. It looked as though their experiment, whatever it was meant to achieve, had failed as the guinea pig showed no response to any stimuli introduced into his environment. He stood there, held in place by vices from the wall, like a statue. The timestamps at the bottom of the screen continued to indicate the passing of time, in this case days, until eventually they removed the test subject from the capsule and placed him on an examination table. The monitors showed no response, there appeared to be no brain activity, no heartbeat.

The mortician slid the scalpel into his skin, carved the Y which allowed him to fold back flaps of flesh and reveal inside. Faith stared. She couldn't see the systems so normally representative of the human physiology, at least in its normal state, yes, they were there but they'd taken on a different appearance, as if they'd been drawn in.

A cutaneous covering had wrapped itself around every internal organ, flowed up through the intestines, reformed the windpipe and as she looked, she noticed the tubing was one continuous sheath, feeding up to the mouth. Just beneath that part of the nervous system which led to the reptilian brain and further into the grey matter of the dead man, there was something she recognised. A mouth, the structure of a mouth belonging to a worm of the nematode family, gaped wide. It was as if a worm had hoovered up the insides and taken its place, becoming the missing link between tubes which still retained their normal appearance.

The thing inside was as dead as its host. Other videos showed similar experiments. Each time the worm increased in size, its length weaving in and out of the body, its mouth moving up and beyond the brain stem, sitting gaping at the back of the mouth, ready to receive whatever its host was going to eat, except apart from the nutrients introduced via the drip, it received nothing.

Faith studied the injections, the drinks, read the notes at the bottom which reflected the changed quantities of minerals and vitamins, hormones and other drugs.

"Were they deliberately sedating their subjects whilst they introduced the parasite?" she asked. "At first it looks like they failed but now I don't think they did. I think they deliberately sedated the guinea pigs in order to allow them to develop the parasite inside a living host. The fact that he dies as a result of this is neither here nor there, it is the size of the parasite in these bodies which is important at this stage. What do you reckon?"

Helen was nodding. "I agree. It's the worm that's important here. The subject is incidental."

"Are you sure you want to carry on watching," said Ruth. "There's going to come a point when the subject remains alive. How aware were they of the organism inside them? That must be horrific—I doubt they got it 'right' in those early stages."

Faith nodded. She understood what Ruth meant.

So far, they'd been able to ignore the subject, despite the human deaths, they didn't seem to experience pain or suffering, were simply a shell in which the worm developed. The next subjects however would be the link between those comatose and dying bodies and she and her friends who were walking around with similar creatures inside them as if there was nothing different at all in their apparent physiology.

Yet she needed to know that early cost because humanity was now paying the price. So they watched. It was every nightmare combined. The moment when the subject was roused from his or her comatose state and realised they were no longer what they thought they were. What went through those poor soul's brains? Were they still able to think, to process?

Faith had no idea but it seemed important to discover how the symbiotic relationship had finally been cemented. For the organism to sustain the body whilst allowing the brain to think itself in full control was nothing short of amazing. Focussing on this aspect, she found, allowed her to consider their position in a slightly more detached manner, albeit for the moment. She was fully aware the truth of their predicament would bring them crashing back to reality soon enough.

"Admiring the science?" asked Howard, reading her mind. "It was always impressive work. Cutting-edge in so many ways. You have to admire it."

"Admire? A strange word to use. That was nothing but state-sanctioned murder. Did the guinea pigs know anything about what they were signing up to?" She was fighting to ignore the feeling Howard was actually right in ascribing to her.

"They were people who were facing somewhat long prison sentences," said Lionel. "We were able to offer them a significant reduction in their term in return for their participation."

"And naturally you delivered although not in the sense they would have expected."

"No," said Lionel, "Although as you notice there were some difficulties in those transient stages between the coma stage and full mobility."

She knew areas of FutureProof had been looking at many different ways to improve humanity's survival rate should disaster ever strike—catastrophes of climate or drought and famine. But how the hell had someone made the connection between a parasite and man. What sort of warped mind had jumped to that and proposed it?

"Humans are wasteful creatures," said Howard. "We were looking for ways for man to reduce their pressure on the planet, the government kept urging us to think outside the box. You showed us the way, even if you didn't know it."

Faith turned away from him and back to the screen. A young woman was waking up. She reminded her so much of Josie she had to look away. When she was able to watch again, the girl had sat up and swung her legs over the edge of the bed, attempted to raise herself but fell back again. She opened her mouth as if to say something but nothing came out, then she turned to a nurse. Opened her mouth again. The nurse looked at her and started to back away before a doctor appeared behind her, and placed a reassuring hand on her shoulder. The nurse recovered herself and approached the patient. As the camera closed in on the subject, Faith could see something moving inside her mouth, just to the back of the tongue. It lurked there in the darkness, a void waiting to be filled.

As she watched, the nurse placed a tray of food on a nearby table and started to spoon it into the woman's mouth. It appeared as if the woman was eating and swallowing as normal, except it seemed to excite an extreme response and Faith found herself watching as the worm pushed its way towards the food, attracted by the smell. From the woman's mouth came the creature, weaving in the air momentarily before latching onto the spoon and then the nurse's hand.

The nurse screamed and the doctor and another orderly attempted to pull her away but already Faith could see they were too late. The organism had torn the flesh, ripped open an artery and blood was spraying everywhere, driving the worm into a greater paroxysm of frenzy. The subject had no control, was a rag doll being tossed about by the parasite inside. The worm continued to pull itself out into the room, flesh tearing like paper, the organism appearing as if shedding its chrysalis. This was no butterfly however. It was a monstrous serpent seeking to devour whatever was in its path. As the nurse slumped to the floor, it turned towards the doctor and the technician as if to continue its murder spree but then it too dropped down, slowed, appeared to be dying.

For a few moments more it feebly attempted to continue feeding on the woman until there was a final spasm and it collapsed beside the body. Orderlies wasted no time in removing both the nurse and the organism. Not quite the symbiotic relationship which appeared to go unnoticed around them above ground.

Howard paused the stream at that point.

"As you saw, we hadn't connected the two in such a way that the organism understood its reliance on its host. It was driven by urges and needs buried within its own simple nervous system. These had to be suppressed and we also had to fool the human brain into thinking it was still in full control. To achieve this, we developed a gene-splicing technique which wove the DNA of the worm into a pattern more dependent on the human within which it lived. It had to be recognised as part of the body, had to recognise itself as part of the human. We had to make sure human and worm regarded themselves as two sides of the same coin, they were one."

"And now we have to live with what you've done," said Faith. "The world is righting itself, Nature is coming back. There is no need for all of this."

"No, there isn't," said Howard.

She understood then, exactly what he meant.

CHAPTER TWENTY-ONE

THE SMALL group headed back towards the lift. Nobody made a move to stop them. Graham and Callum had vanished. Faith pondered their father-son conversation. She'd hoped to speak to Callum alone before she left. Events though, continued to conspire against them. This time, it was she who was walking away.

"When you get back," said Howard. "Tell everyone what it's like down here. Tell them we need to come return. For the children's sake. It'll be your turn to make the decision, your turn to play God."

He was wrong there. Nobody would play God. That character had been written out of their script long ago. The last surviving priest in their community had ripped off his dog-collar and jumped from the Barricade.

"Take this," he said, thrusting a folder at her. "It's the names and details of everyone alive down here."

She wanted to push it back at him, knew by seeing names, ages, *photos*, it would be harder to do, must be done. *But.* Decisions had to be made with knowledge. Reluctantly, she took the file, determined not to look at it until she was above. Nor would she keep it to herself. There would be no secrecy. They would be different. Or would they?

She watched the numbers change as the lift returned them to the upper floor. There were the doors to lead them out.

"You're not taking us back through the Barricade?!" Faith could see the doors across the lobby, the small windows which gave on to the ever-decreasing amount of ground between the complex and the construction. Everyone would see them leave the bunker, would start to imagine they'd thrown their lot in with the very people who'd abandoned them.

"Don't worry," said Lionel. "I just wanted you to experience what it's like from our side. You don't have to go out. Just look through those windows. Put yourself in our position."

"Your position! We've thought of nothing else for twenty years. Wondered why you not us."

Even so, she allowed herself to be led towards the doors and found herself looking through the glass. The windows were tinted, could not be seen through by anyone on the other side but even so, she felt exposed. Across the pitted soil, the remnants of grass, she saw the jagged sides of the Barricade. Its angle led her eyes up and up until she found herself focusing on those who stood along its peak.

As she stared at so many familiar faces, the wave of hatred projected in their direction was overwhelming. It was as if she were being crushed by the metallic monstrosity itself. Familiar flares of heat rose up again, adding to her sense of claustrophobia and for one mad moment, she found herself gripping the door handle ready to push it open, escape their confines, breathe.

Helen stopped her. Without a word she pulled her back from the door and sat her on a nearby bench.

"Head down," ordered Ruth. "Deep breaths."

Still the heat came but the panicky feeling wore off and eventually she was able to sit up straight, look her friends in the eye. "Sorry," she said. "Nearly lost it there for a minute."

"We weren't survivors, were we," said Faith, to Howard. "We've simply been your canaries."

Howard nodded but there was a tired look about the man, the air of triumph had evaporated. She'd seen that expression before. It was the one worn by many before they jumped over the barrier.

"But it went wrong. You didn't count on us not accepting you. If the original treatment had gone to plan, we wouldn't be reacting like this, but we are."

"It's almost as if someone sabotaged you," jumped in Helen. "Someone didn't want you to go back above ground."

"We certainly didn't want you back," said Faith.

"I think that might have been Lionel's intention," said Helen. "Wanted to make a stand against Howard at last."

Faith looked around. "Where is he?"

He'd vanished.

"Probably thought it wasn't safe being around us," said Malik. "I'd say he was right."

"Let's get out of here," said Faith, rising to her feet, feeling the heat finally subside.

They followed signs leading to Wing A, found Sonia who directed them to the lift which would take them back to the Barricade. Although she tried to pretend nothing had happened, she kept a clear distance.

"It's not catching, Sonia," said Faith. "The parasite has to be implanted."

Sonia nodded. "I know. And they'll come for me soon, it'll be my turn," she said. "I'm not married and refused to partner up with anyone. As Howard has shown you, only families are valued."

"Callum!" Faith felt a sudden pang for her son. Despite all the ill feeling, she did not want him to go through what had been inflicted on the others. If they took Sonia though, no doubt they would take him too.

"Don't worry about Callum," said Sonia. "He's

got his family, two little girls."

The lift doors opened but Faith couldn't move. "He's got children?! Why didn't he say? Why wasn't I introduced?"

Malik was trying to urge her towards the lift but Faith resisted.

"Faith! We've got to go back up. Speak to people. Tell them…"

"Tell them what? That we're not what we thought. That we came up from below to prepare the way for everyone else. That we volunteered? There is no way in hell they are going to believe any of that."

"We've got the files," said Helen. "Pictures, records. They're letting us take the tablets up with us. We'll be able to show the videos."

"And then what? Can you see the panic, the chaos—assuming they believe us."

"The community will tear itself apart."

"We promised the truth," said Ruth. "No matter what. We can't change that."

"Ruth."

"No," she repeated. "We promised and we owe them the truth no matter what. No more lies, you promised."

The remainder of their return journey was silent. All were still coming to terms with what they'd discovered lay inside themselves, wondering how those above would accept their situation. Faith was also thinking of her newly discovered grandchildren. She flicked open one of the folders Sonia had given her and scanned the list for her surname, her married name. Hamilton, Callum. A thumbnail picture accompanied his details, a basic medical and background. On the same page was a picture of his wife, Nicola. Faith paid no attention to her as two more pictures caught her eye. Janet, aged five and Kelly, aged three. Kelly in particular focussed her attention. She looked so like Josie at that age.

"If the decision remains to keep them below," said Ruth, peering over her shoulder. "What will you do?"

"At least you haven't met them," said Malik. "They could be real brats."

"Brats or not, they're my grandchildren," said Faith.

"And what about the other kids? You said they couldn't come back up. Just because these are related to you suddenly doesn't give you an extra say in things. Or is it going to be one rule for you and another for the rest?"

Faith looked at Helen. Saw the challenge in her eyes. She'd said so much before about not accepting bunker dwellers, she could not change anything now. But these were her grandchildren.

"They are innocent," she said.

"You didn't allow that label for everyone else," said Malik.

They were all looking at her, an unwelcome and

unnerving scrutiny. There was nothing she could do for them. She sighed.

"You're right. Let's get back, tell them, show them everything. Then we'll discuss next steps."

The lift stopped and the group stepped out, walked their way back along the corridor and came out into daylight. There were no guards on the entrance. They walked further out into the deserted area and looked up. There was nobody on the Barricade. Old papers fluttered across the ground, somewhere a loose piece of pipe banged as it was pummelled by the wind. The sky was still a dirty yellow, looking as though it was going to dump a lot more snow on them.

"Looks like a storm coming," said Malik, pulling his coat around him. "Everyone's taken shelter."

"Let's get to Sylvie's," said Faith. "Tell them what we've found."

"Including their daughter?" asked Ruth.

"Including Sonia," said Faith.

They trudged across the lot, still slippery from ice and slush from the previous snowfall. The doors to the containers and warehouses were closed against the cold. No doubt everyone was inside.

Sylvie's door was also shut. Ruth put her hand on the door but Malik stayed her, pulling out the gun reclaimed from Lionel. Slowly he turned the handle and eased the door open. The gap let out a gentle glow of light, a low murmur of voices could be heard and they could smell alcohol, something cooking. The four relaxed and Malik led the way inside.

But the room was empty apart from Andrew, Sylvie and Josie.

Faith moved over to Josie and attempted to hug her but her daughter shrank back, an expression of fear on her face.

"Hey, come on, love. There's nothing to be scared of." A lie on so many levels. Josie still refused to touch her.

"Don't worry," said Andrew. "She's been through a lot lately. She'll come round."

"Come round from what? And where is everybody?"

She caught a look between the two.

"What's going on?"

"Seems people got a bit uncomfortable with you being below ground. There's a rumour going round that anyone who comes out is contaminated. They said when you come back we've got to... got to..."

"Got to what?" Faith looked at both of them.

Sylvie bit her lip.

"Either go back down or leave the community."

"I don't believe it," Ruth exploded. "After everything we've done for them, all the risks we've taken."

"You can't blame them," said Andrew. "It's only human nature to want to protect yourself."

"And what about what we found out?" asked Helen.

"What exactly did you find out?" Andrew's eyes had narrowed and there was an unfriendly look on his face.

"That you have a daughter, Sonia. Lovely girl by the way."

"She's okay? You've seen her?" Sylvie had grabbed Faith's hand and she could feel the desperation in the woman's touch.

"Yes. But I doubt she'll be okay much longer. And I'm sorry, but your son…"

"What do you mean?"

"Sonia told us he'd died, apparently he'd been subjected to the same procedure as the rest of us."

Sylvie turned away from Faith, her look of horror directed at Andrew. "Andy? What's she talking about? They were both to be spared. That was one of my conditions for seeing this through, for staying with you. Sonia and Brendon. You promised, Lionel promised. Tell me it's not true."

Andrew could barely meet his wife's gaze. "I'm sorry," he said. "It was a mistake. A stupid mistake."

"And you knew? All this time, when we would sit and imagine what our children would be like now, you knew Brendon was gone?" Tears trickled down Sylvie's cheeks and despite Faith's anger at yet another betrayal, she understood how Sylvie felt. She was a mother too.

"You knew about us as well, didn't you?" she said to Andrew. She'd always wondered why a leading scientist from FutureProof, so highly regarded, would be allowed to remain above ground simply because of love. He was there to monitor his 'experiment'.

Helen pulled the tablet from her pocket, tapped play and put the video in front of them to watch. They said nothing. Andrew and Sylvie had seen it all before. Josie however, was horrified.

"We show this to everyone," said Faith.

"And then what?"

"That's up to them."

She was washing her hands of the problem, she understood that but there was nothing more she could do for anyone. They all had to make their own decisions.

"They won't believe you," said Sylvie, "unless they see those things in front of them."

Faith understood what she meant. They would never believe their story until they cut someone open.

"So, who's going to volunteer?" asked Malik, directing his question at Andrew and Sylvie.

They looked shocked and for the first time, not a little fearful.

"What's that going to achieve? You need me."

She noticed Andrew said 'me' and not 'us'. Sylvie noticed too, withdrew her hand from his.

"Andy? Malik?"

Faith turned at the mention of his name and saw Malik was training his gun on Andrew as the man reached for his coat.

"Malik?"

"Let's just say trust is now in very short supply," he said, making his way over to Andrew's side and pulling the coat away. He patted the pockets and found a gun tucked inside. He handed it over to Helen, not Faith herself. The lack of trust extending to herself as well as Andrew.

"I think it's time to go to the warehouse and tell everyone," said Malik.

"As I say, they'll want to cut someone open," said Andrew. "They might even insist on it being one of you. I mean, I'm the one who feeds them, gives them drink. You..."

"Are the people who've fixed their electrics, their water and designed the aeroponics system you seem to have claimed for yourself," said Faith. "I think they'll remember that?"

"Maybe when the fuss has died down," said Andrew, "when they're pulling the bodies apart. Depends on who has their ear first. And you can't take me with you gagged, or Sylvie, can you?

Faith was at a loss. This woman had been her friend for so many years and was now a stranger, someone whose marriage appeared a sham. How could anyone pretend for so long? People would always do what they had to, in order to survive. She had.

"We'll tie them up and lock them away somewhere," said Helen. "No problem."

"And the other thing?" asked Faith.

"I'm sure we'll find another body," said Helen. "One always turns up round here, doesn't it?"

A cynical, but true, statement.

Faith stood. She was exhausted, could feel her body betraying her on so many levels and suddenly she no longer cared. She didn't want to be the one responsible for everyone else, she didn't want to carry people any more. No, it was for others to step up to the mark and take responsibility—whether they believed her or not.

She slipped the tablet in her pocket and took the files. Headed out into the compound without even checking if the others were following. She could hear them calling her but did not reply. They could come or they could stay. It didn't matter. Her feeling of antipathy, her nurturing instinct lessened by hormonal changes, was strangely freeing. It would allow her to speak and let the future become what it would.

The warehouse door creaked open. Nobody oiled the doors anymore, such creaks and groans though irritating often served as a warning of intruders. You couldn't sneak about and not be noticed. The open space before the aisles which held supplies and sleeping quarters was filled with benches and makeshift seats. Everybody had gathered and sat themselves in a semi-circle. Only now did she realise how few of them remained. There could be no more than three hundred. Since when had their numbers dropped? Why hadn't she noticed?

The mood was subdued and voices were low. All eyes turned to Faith as she moved to the middle. They looked suspicious, something she'd never experienced from them before.

"You came back then," said one coming over, staring her down, trying to intimidate her. It was the same man who'd spat at her. He looked vicious, mean.

She recalled his name, Ed, someone she'd barely ever paid attention to before. He was one of those who scuttled about the complex, always seemingly busy but never actually doing anything. A man who'd built a reputation in more recent times as a thug, his prejudices and bigotry becoming more vocal in Sylvie's bar. Someone she instinctively avoided.

"Said I would. Take a seat and I'll let you in on Howard's little experiment in human survival, how he turned us all into guinea pigs."

Surprised looks greeted her introduction, giving way to confusion and concern as she started to outline the origins of their community. By now, Helen, Ruth and Malik had joined them and Andrew and Sylvie were just entering. Faces turned towards the new arrivals.

"Is this true? This hibernation shit."

"This is crap. Impossible."

"We wanted the truth, not fairy stories."

The complaints and denials rose to a clamour

and Faith was unable to make herself heard.

In the end, Malik yelled for quiet.

"What she's told you so far is true," he said. "I suggest you let her tell you the rest of it, show you the proof—if you want to hear it, see it. It is hard to accept, beyond possible you might think and it will be hard to come to terms with. I'm still struggling and I know the others are. Some of you may never come to terms with it but you wanted the truth so here it is. Deal with it." The latter remark was directed at Ed who'd jumped up again from his seat as if to launch into another tirade.

The man held himself in check and the hubbub died down, allowing her to continue with her recount. They still looked disbelieving as she finished describing how they'd emerged above. When she got to the part about the parasite however, the creature within their bodies, they erupted once more.

This time, they ignored Malik's shouting, turned on Faith, pushing and shoving her back towards two fiery braziers, lit to give some small semblance of warmth. Ed led them, jabbing his finger into Faith's chest, his face almost touching hers. She was unable to fight back as the pressure from the crowd grew, until someone reached through and grabbed her arm, pulled her out to the side. Helen.

The crowd, frustrated, turned in a tide towards them and Helen pulled out her gun, waved them back.

"You wanted the truth and she is telling you the truth. I would be telling you the same story, as would Ruth and Malik. Now, you might not be able to believe what you hear but what about what you can see? Faith, I suggest you show the videos."

The door creaked again and Faith saw Gary wheeling in a television screen. It was the one from Malik's communal living area in the next container. He held out a cable to Faith and she plugged her tablet to it.

"Please," she said, before the video started. "I didn't make this up. I am as much a victim as you. We are all the same and I don't know what we can do about it, how we live with this knowledge. I think some of you might not want to but I can't take responsibility for that. You must all agree to that. You are all responsible for yourselves. If you feel you cannot watch or listen, that is your choice and you can leave. The rest of you, stay and watch, but do not blame me or anyone else here. When it's done, remember who ultimately caused this issue, remember who is in his pay."

Faith stepped away from the screen and sat down on an old oil drum nearby. She pressed play and soon the videos she'd watched in the complex below were being shown again. Stunned silence greeted the initial clips and then as the experiments progressed, some ran outside where they could be heard retching and groaning. A few fainted. The loud protests she'd experienced earlier did not materialise. Instead everyone sat stunned. Shock and disbelief written across all their faces. Some, including Ed, were gazing down at their stomachs, tentatively poking and prodding themselves.

When it finished, there was silence.

"So, there you have it," she said. "No more secrets. We came from below and we are hosts to a parasite developed to adapt our digestive system to a harsher world, to ensure our own bodies would provide an additional benefit to the soil. The only 'real' humans now are those below and not even all of them, only the families, the ones bringing about a new population. Plus one or two privileged souls."

"Like who?" Ed again.

"Lionel, Howard, Graham, Andrew, Sylvie."

For the first time, Andrew looked uncertain as everyone gazed in his direction. His self-assurance had gone.

"What was your role in all this?" demanded Ed. "You were some sort of high-flying scientist. Why did you stay?"

"We're his precious guinea pigs, that's why, wasn't it?" snapped another. "Has to stay and watch us. Write everything down. Got notes hidden somewhere, have you?"

Andrew's expression told Faith he had.

"But you could go below whenever you wanted to as well," said Ed. "Had the best of both worlds. You and Howard." The man might be a bully, but he had cottoned on to the situation pretty quick.

A low sob caught Faith's attention. Pauline. She remembered seeing her only a few days ago, congratulated her on the imminent arrival of her baby.

"My baby," she said. "What's going to happen to it? What will it look like?"

"We've had births over the years," said Andrew, recovering some of his poise. "I'm sure you'll be fine."

But not many of those babies survived past the first few months, Faith recalled. They'd put it down to the lack of antibiotics, the less sterile environment, all the sorts of things which had affected man in the dark ages. Of course they'd never quite reverted to that stage, started to develop a new civilisation of sorts after the break down of the last one but technological advances—above ground at least—had been limited.

"But this thing inside me, if it's inside me. Will it be in the baby too?"

There'd been reports of babies born with horrific deformities and these too, had been put down to the pollution of the environment, the lack of appropriate diet. Had the parasite caused those? Those born without limbs, a head, had it eaten them? Memories of all these horrors flooded back and she could see those around her were recalling the same thoughts.

"I need to see," said Pauline. "I need to know."

"The only way to do that is to go below," said

Faith. "They have scanners…"

"Then that's what we'll do," said Michael, her partner. "We'll go there, now."

"I don't think they'll just let us in," said Helen. "We've spent all this time telling them they can't come back up. Why should they?"

"We do a deal," said Pauline. "Let them back up if they allow us to be scanned."

"No," said Faith. "What about our law? They went below, they can never come back."

"Things change," said Pauline. "I'm not living in the past, I'm dealing with the present."

"It's not just you and your baby though, Pauline. There's the rest of us to consider."

Pauline turned on Malik. "At least you know. You've all been down there and been scanned. You know what's inside you, even if you wish it weren't. We only know what you've told us. We deserve the truth."

"And we've given you that," said Helen.

"Not completely," said Pauline, her face white, scared. "You can't give us certainty."

"They're right," said Andrew, stepping forward for the first time. "It's best if we get everyone scanned, make sure everything is as it should be."

"As it should be?" Malik had to hold Faith back. "As it should be? If things were as it fucking should be, we wouldn't have these things inside us, we'd be normal. We'd be…"

"Dead," said Andrew.

She stared at him. "We could live without the parasites, we…"

"No," he said. "No, you couldn't. The worm helped you breathe the atmosphere back then. Remember the toxins released into the atmosphere where factories and power plants shut down and weren't maintained. The breathing problems people had? So many died because of the thin atmosphere, the lack of oxygen. The parasite I created, allowed you to breathe, gave your lungs additional support whilst you adapted to the environment. If we had woken you and sent you back up without such support you would've choked to death."

"But what about you? You've not got the creature inside you and you've been living above ground—or have you?"

"I'm sorry," he said. "A little subterfuge was necessary back then, at least until the skies began to clear. You're right, I did go back below to sleep. Nobody knew about those secret entrances then, except Sylvie."

"But you never saw Sonia, did you?"

"No. We decided best not to, let her believe we'd died so she didn't worry. If we went below it would've triggered dangerous questions amongst the lower community. We couldn't risk that. And now? Well, I'm breathing adequately these days. The samples I've been testing have indicated a near match with previous oxygen levels. Respiratory illness shouldn't be a problem."

"So you can take these things out of us," said Ed.

"No," said Andrew. "I'm afraid not. It might've been possible once but we don't have surgeons with the skill these days. The parasite is too closely entwined with your own body. If we attempted it, death would be guaranteed."

"Can't we kill it in some way so it can be extracted?"

"No," said Andrew. "As I said, there is no way to separate the parasite and its host, except on the death of the host that is. I'm afraid you're stuck with each other."

"And when we do die?"

"Nothing happens," said Ruth.

"No," said Andrew. "What you mean is you've seen nothing happen. When people died, you whipped them onto a cart and trotted off to the pits. You did not look or study the bodies."

"Then you can watch me," said a voice from the back.

Faith peered to the rear of the crowd and saw one of their oldest members. Raymond. He'd been ill for some time and they'd watched his skin change colour from pink to almost grey. He could barely move and most days spent his time in bed but today his daughter had bundled him into a wheelchair and brought him with her to the meeting.

"I've not got long left. You could even give me something to speed things up…"

"Dad, no!"

"Come on, love. I can't go on much longer anyway. No one's got anything they can give me for the pain. You can't stand seeing me like this and I don't like you seeing it. Let me go peacefully and serve the community in one final way at least. Let them use me to verify what you've been told."

His daughter buried her face in his shoulder and he was hugging her as she sobbed in his arms, whispering things to her which gradually eased the shaking and she was able to pull herself back and wipe away her tears.

"Good girl," he said. "You've always been the strong one. You'll be fine. When?" he asked, turning to Faith and the others.

"Now," said Ed, moving towards him.

"No," said Malik stepping in his way. "Have some decency."

"Tonight," said his daughter. "Let us have a last afternoon together, a last meal. We can add whatever you need to, to his food."

"Do I get special rations?" Raymond was laughing. "Fancy a steak."

"Can't oblige there, I'm afraid," said Sylvie. "How about my special chilli?"

"Ooh, sounds just the thing," said Raymond.

"And I'll throw in a few bottles as well."

"Can't wait."

It was strange, thought Faith as she watched Raymond being wheeled back to his quarters, how easily he was accepting his death, showed no fear.

"It's okay," he said, as he passed her. "Just make sure you look after my daughter after…"

Faith nodded. How could someone watch their parent die and then see them be carved open in a public autopsy, to become no more than a prize specimen?

"I'd better get on and cook his meal," said Sylvie, turning to follow Raymond.

Nobody else moved. They seemed unmoored, uncertain. Faith understood how that felt. To have all your certainties taken away from you. The future which had slowly appeared to be growing brighter to fall once more into gloom. The latest news was going to need a degree of resilience beyond anything they'd experienced before.

Even in those early days, they'd been able to deal with the situation because their enemies were visible, understandable. When the enemy became internal, invisible, it became difficult.

The enemy. That was how she regarded the parasite. But Howard and Lionel insisted they'd created it for the good of humanity, to aid their survival in a changed, polluted world. It was a mess.

"Penny for them," said Helen.

Faith sighed. "I really don't know what to do anymore. We know what we are. We know there are families below, children, who have been spared the parasite. Do we keep them down there? Do we stay up here? If we do that, then there is no hope for those of this community."

"But what about other communities around the country?"

"Go and join them? No, we can't, knowing what we've become. We can't go near anyone. Those babies born here which survived, if they contain the parasite as well then it shows it can be passed on and that can't be allowed to contaminate another community. We can't be so inhuman as to do that to others."

"A good job we kept separate after all this time."

"Did we though?" asked Malik. "Many disappeared in those early years. Didn't want to stay here, knew there were gangs roaming the countryside. I know a few threw in their lot with those. How do we know they haven't spread the parasite there?"

"You make it sound like something they could catch if you sneezed. It's not a virus or bacteria."

"But we don't know how it reproduces, do we? Aren't worms able to grow again if bits are chopped off? I mean we know about the eggs when external to the host, but what if that too has changed, mutated?"

"I would say you've been watching too many science-fiction programmes if this had been the old days but knowing what we know now, I would say anything is possible."

"So, the decision will be ours," said Helen. "How we deal with the future. If the parasite grows in the womb with a baby, do we stop having families, ban children, force abortions? Do we have the right to force anyone to do anything?"

"If it's for the greater good, perhaps," said Ruth.

"But who decides what the greater good is?" asked Faith. "Lionel and Howard took that decision autonomously, exposed us to an organism without our consent to rebuild the world above ground until those below who were still 'pure' were ready to return."

"Once we have more information about who is affected, then we have to do a full survey, ask everybody. This affects every single one of us, so every single person has a say."

It wouldn't be easy. She looked at Pauline, cradling her belly, whilst her partner rocked her in his arms. They looked lost. A happy event was now tinged with horror. This was not what they had expected of the future. She turned away, it was her fault they were facing this. If she hadn't told them, had been more circumspect, they would still be looking forward to the birth.

"If you hadn't told them," said Helen, as if reading her mind, "what do you think would've happened at the birth? If the baby was deformed in some way? At least with this little knowledge they can prepare themselves for whatever might appear."

And if the child was born perfectly formed, then she had gifted them a life-time of worry, knowing the parasite was growing inside their offspring.

CHAPTER TWENTY-TWO

FAITH DECIDED against being present as Raymond breathed his last. She would attend the autopsy. Everybody would be allowed to view the body in the name of the new transparency but she would not intrude on those precious, final moments.

He'd had his meal in the area which served as a hospital and Malik and Gary had stood guard on the door of the room, giving Raymond and his daughter some privacy. As soon as she'd alerted them to her father's passing, however, Ed and a few of his cronies surged forward.

"Come on, let's be having him then!" shouted Ed.

Malik pushed him back.

"Have some decency, man," he said. "Give her time."

"She can have all the time she wants after we see

what's inside him," said Ed.

"When he's carved open? I don't think so," said Gary. "She can have all the time she needs."

Ed made to push forward again but the door opened and Raymond's daughter emerged.

"Meredith." Faith noticed he kept his eyes down, a typical bully, a coward at heart.

"You can take him now," she said. "But I want to be there when you first open him up."

"Are you sure?" Faith couldn't believe she could watch her own father be examined, cut open and exposed to the gaze of everyone around them, strangers. Scratch that. Not strangers. They had known each other for years, the community had shrunk and although they didn't all spend the time of day together, they were all aware of each other. Knew each other's secrets, and then pretended they didn't know. Privacy was in such short supply it felt only fair to give some semblance of being able to live your own life.

"Yes. I promised him I would. He wasn't just doing this for the community, you know. It was for me."

Two porters appeared with a gurney and entered the room, emerging a few minutes later with Raymond's body strapped to it. The corpse was covered with a sheet to preserve some dignity as he was wheeled past the community which had gathered in the waiting rooms and in the corridors.

They took him to what was officially called the

operating theatre but which in reality was no different to any other room. It was no more sterile or clean than the bays, despite all their attempts to maintain the elements of hygiene necessary to ensure survival should you be unlucky enough to enter its doors. Most who went in ensured they had said the necessary goodbyes to those closest to them, they did not expect to come out alive.

"A pity Donald is no longer with us," said Malik. "He would've been able to carry out a proper autopsy."

There were no other doctors of any note. A few of the nurses had started learning the rudiments but there was no one who was sufficiently skilled to carry out the examination.

"Let me," said Andrew, stepping forward.

"Why you?" said Ed. "After all the lies and what you've done, you're going to get your hands dirty now?"

"I've had some autopsy experience. When, when we were testing our earlier... subjects, I was involved in those examinations. Now if you'll let me prep..."

"I'm staying," said Ed. "I don't want to find you hiding anything."

"Still suspicious. Of course, you can stay. If you can stomach it. I can't have everyone in here at first though, and of course there's Meredith to consider." He was looking at Faith and Helen as he said this.

She nodded and moved the crowds back a little.

"You'll all get a chance to look," said Malik. "Just be patient."

There was murmuring but nobody pushed themselves forward. Faith understood how they felt. They wanted to know but they didn't want to know. Having seen the scans, she was a little more prepared, but to see that *thing* in broad daylight, she was having a hard time coming to terms with what she might see. She was happy to wait a bit longer.

The doors closed behind her, leaving Andrew and the porters, who were doubling up as reluctant assistants, Meredith, Ed, Sylvie and Ruth. Ruth had taken up position by Meredith, ready to support her if needed.

They stood in silence outside the closed doors to the operating theatre. Nor did anyone else speak. Pauline sat with her husband, gripping his hand tightly, as did other couples. Most spent their time looking down, jiggling legs or twisting hands. Anxiety and fear filled the air.

Eventually, the doors opened and Ed stumbled out. He ignored the comments and questions of others as he pushed his way outdoors, hand clamped firmly over his mouth, his face pale and shocked.

Then came Meredith and Ruth. They too were pale, but more composed. Sylvie remained inside. They nodded at Faith and she, Helen, Malik, Pauline and her husband went in.

Raymond lay there, a cloth placed over his face

to make the viewing more anonymous, even though everybody knew him. The touch made it a little more impersonal, a little easier to cope with, although not by much.

The skin of the abdomen had been peeled back, his ribcage split to better show the organs beneath. At first sight, it looked normal.

The digestive tract appeared to be laid out with textbook precision. Andrew stood to the side and merely watched as they moved in to study the body more closely. The organs glistened in the light, slick and grey, shades of pink, patches of crimson.

The oesophagus ran cleanly down to the stomach and she could see the coils of the intestine. It looked so normal and oh, so, strange. She moved closer. Where was this monstrous creature they had seen projected on the scans down below? Had it been faked?

She continued to stare at the still, dead body. Smelt flesh and blood, the meat of Raymond. Andrew hadn't washed the body down before he'd opened it, not disinfected it. As well as the smell of exposed tissue and organs, she could smell the lingering body odour of the old man, his unwashed skin, the staleness so many of them emanated. It reminded her that in front of them lay a human, someone who'd, until recently, been as alive as any of them.

"What's that?"

"Huh?"

Helen had nudged her arm, was directing her gaze towards the lower coils of the intestine. They were rippling, seemed to be lifting up and out of the body cavity leaving tubing grey and deflated behind. Faith stared and then quickly looked at her companions. All of them were transfixed by the sight in front of them. Pauline was stepping back as the tubing moved and writhed, separated itself from its framework of the stomach. More and more began to peel away until Andrew stepped forward and lightly ran a piece of plastic over it to nudge it back down. A slight hiss, as if a sigh, was expelled and the worm collapsed once more to shroud the organs.

"I can't let it separate completely, just yet," he said. "There's too many who need to see it in situ. Once everyone's had a look, come back and you can see what'll happen once it completely separates."

"Can it last that long?" asked Helen.

"Yes," said Andrew. "It's quite a resilient little organism. But we do need to get the viewing moving along, in case…"

"In case what?" Faith continued to stare at the rippling mass.

"It can, I mean it has been reported as, well, it can find a new host. Latch on so to speak."

"But aren't we all occupied?" asked Helen.

"Most of us," said Faith, looking at Andrew. "Some still have a 'Vacancy' sign hanging over them. I don't think it's us who's in danger. More like him and Sylvie."

"Perhaps we should just let it free itself then," said Malik, a glint in his eye.

Much as she would've loved to have followed through on that, Faith knew those beyond the doors deserved to see what was going on inside the room.

"I'll get the crowd moving," she said, opening the door and directing those nearest inside.

In they trooped, one after the other. Sometimes they would stand silently, others would sob, a number ran outside where they could be heard retching. Pauline had to be helped out and Faith wondered what she was thinking, how she felt towards the baby in her belly. Apart from these reactions, of choking, sobbing, retching, no words were exchanged. The silence continued and that in its way was as frightening as anything else.

Then came Corinne.

"I don't think she should see this," said Sylvie. "She's been pretty unstable lately."

Faith looked across at Corinne, she stood behind those currently looking at Raymond's body. The woman was the same age as her daughter and had her own demons. These became public when Helen and Malik found herself carving her arms open one night at the top of the Barricade. She had told them not to worry, she wasn't going to jump. She just wanted to give them her blood.

On further examination that night, Helen reported back there were many older scars on

Corinne. Her self-harm had been taking place over many months. They all found different ways of coping, Faith knew. Alcohol, drugs, infidelity, but to be in the position where you deliberately inflicted pain on yourself to numb your mental anguish was one she found particularly hard to deal with. You couldn't judge however, only offer what little help you could. Corinne's reaction was not what she expected. Rather than fear and shock, she seemed almost jubilant.

"See, see," she cried. "I told you there was a monster inside me. I told you it needed to be cut out. But you wouldn't listen." She was smiling at them as she spoke. "I wasn't mad, I'm not mad, am I? A frantic look gleamed in her eye, her cheeks flushed.

They'd dismissed the monster she referred to as merely being a reference towards herself.

A look of relief passed over the faces of those around them as Corinne calmly gazed down at the dead body, nodding her head in complete acceptance of what she saw. Her brother Craig, nodded at them as he guided her out and others took her place. Craig did not look as comfortable as his sister but he'd suppressed his feelings in order to get his sister through the ordeal.

The people continued to come. Even the few children. Their parents wanted them to see things as they really were. To survive you couldn't believe in fairy tales and you couldn't be protected. You needed the truth, no matter how hard. Circumstances couldn't leave people any more traumatised than they already were so this was, in a way, nothing.

A scream outside made the queue pause.

"Keep them going," said Malik, to Gary who'd been at the door. "Make sure everyone sees this. We'll investigate."

Malik ran outside, closely followed by Faith, Helen and Ruth. Recent events had disrupted community life so much there were no patrols or guards checking on the site, on its inhabitants.

"Malik, Faith!" It was Craig, Corinne's brother. They could see him by a stack of crates, his head dipping down and then reappearing. Dipping down again, accompanied by shouts of "No, no."

Then they heard a scream of such pain it tore right through them.

The two ran towards Craig, bystanders followed and as they rounded the pile of boxes, they found Craig stood over his sister. She was still alive, barely, was smiling as she waved her knife at her brother to keep him back. It was not meant as an attempt to harm him. Instead the harm had been directed at herself. Corinne had sliced through her clothes, her skin, pulled back loose flaps, was scrabbling and tearing at herself even as her life began to slip away from her.

"There's still a chance," said Malik, getting close to look. "She's cut deep but not too deep."

In response to his words, Corinne turned the knife back on herself. Where she got the strength from, Faith could not imagine. The blade cut further this time and Corinne was able to insert her fingers into her abdominal cavity.

"She's trying to get it out," said Craig.

"But if she does that, she'll die," said Malik.

"Maybe she wants to," said Craig, his voice low, sad. He'd dropped back from his sister and watched as she took hold of the writhing mass which had masqueraded as her digestive system for so long.

"Shit, Corinne, stop!" Faith plunged forward but suddenly found the knife waved in her direction.

"No," said Craig. "It's too late now. Even if we stop her, she'll die from those injuries. You know our medical care is more limited these days.

"We could get her below," said Faith.

"And put ourselves in Howard's hands. He'd use her situation to bargain with us. And who's to say she'll survive anyway?"

"We can't just..."

"No," said Craig. "You're right. We can't 'just' but I can."

Before she could stop him, he'd pulled out a gun and pointed it at his sister. He pulled the trigger.

"I just want to rip that thing out of her," he said, anger building up as he approached Corinne.

"No," said Malik. "Keep back. Remember what Andrew said about the possibility of transferral? You don't want that thing on the loose."

"What do you mean? I'm already occupied, I doubt it would find any room inside me."

"Makes you wonder how many a human could sustain, doesn't it?" said Malik. "I wonder if they've experimented with that."

Faith couldn't bear to think of such a possibility. It was bad enough to be host to one parasite but to discover you had a whole ecosystem in your body was beyond anything she could ever come to terms with. She didn't think Howard and Andrew had gone that far and yet she wouldn't put anything past him.

Gary had disappeared and now returned with a body bag and thick gloves.

"Sorry, Craig," said Malik, as he threw an old sheet over her so they could roll her up in a shroud, keep a barrier between themselves and the organism before they lifted her up and put her in the body bag.

"She won't be the only one," said Helen. "People are too stunned at the moment to do much but that will subside. More will attack themselves."

"We need to see Howard and Lionel," said Faith. "We need to go back below."

"Not yet," said Gary. "Didn't we say we would have a vote about what we would do first. Get everybody's opinion."

"But that's going to take time."

"It doesn't matter how much time it takes," said Ed, coming up behind them. "We all get a say.

Personally, I'd like to stick a bomb under the whole shebang but that won't get us anywhere."

Faith was surprised. Ed always acted or reacted first and thought later. Now though, they had to find a new way forward or there would be nothing left for anyone.

"Has everyone seen Ray's body?" asked Malik.

"Yes," said Gary. "That's why I came out after you. They've all gone back to their homes for the moment."

"Give them time to talk," said Faith. "Then I suggest we gather again this evening. Talk over our next steps."

Gary nodded. "I'll get the word out. What about Corinne?"

"She goes on the Barricade," said Craig. "It's what she would've wanted."

"I hope she'll be the last," said Faith, but something told her there would be others joining the woman on the structure before their gathering that evening. It felt as if the community was facing its dying days. The hoped-for future was dwindling, despite the clouds above thinning enough to let a weak sunlight, not normally seen at this time of year, peep through.

"Where are you going?" asked Ed as she turned away.

"Back to my house, to think," she said. "Anyone who wants to talk, can join me."

He said nothing, his earlier bullying tone had

gone.

"We'll come," said Helen, looking at Ruth and Malik who all nodded their heads.

The small group of friends left the community zone and walked beyond its gate which stood wide open. Nobody was on duty. The familiar streets were as deserted as always and for once she did not experience the feeling of being watched. Were they now regarded as contaminated by those who had stayed separate from their society all this time, no longer worth stealing from?

"Why, why, why did we stay?" asked Faith, kicking at an old can as they turned into her street. "Why did we go with Howard?"

"I keep trying to think back to those early days," said Malik. "Howard said we went below and were then sent back up. How could we have allowed ourselves to be put in that position?"

"We would've been desperate," said Ruth. "That much I know. Our families had gone in. We all knew that. It was probably a promise made that we could go in for a while and then be reunited in the future."

"And the promise of an easier life than those who didn't have our contacts," said Helen. "You can't deny a number would've given their right arm for something which would've guaranteed them a future."

"Well we certainly gave them a part of our body," said Malik. "I think I would've preferred the arm though, it would have been a lot simpler."

Faith shook her head. "I want to remember. I need to remember more."

They passed Linda's house.

"I should've listened," said Faith. "The poor woman knew and none of us would listen."

"You can't blame yourself," said Ruth. "The whole thing is so fantastical, no one would be able to believe it without evidence, without seeing the videos and the scans like we have."

"But to feel so isolated. To watch us all and guess we were the same and to try and warn us and us not listening, treating her as disturbed. I feel terrible. If only..."

"No," said Ruth. "You can't feel guilty for any of that. You might not have believed her but you looked after her, got her food, let her talk. You showed her friendship and that was more than many people did. There's *nothing* to feel guilty about."

Faith gave Ruth a grateful smile. They were words she'd needed to hear. They were at her door now and it swung open even before she'd had a chance to put the key in the lock. Josie stood in front of her. She was holding a mug of tea and smiling. Behind her, Faith could see the glow of a fire. This was a normality she had forgotten about.

"Don't just stand there with your mouths open," said Josie. "Come on in. We'll lose the heat otherwise."

The four entered and followed Josie into the

front room. "Sit down, make yourselves at home," she said, seeming to forget Faith's ownership of the house. "I'll be back in a minute."

They struggled to remove their boots, lining them up near the fire so they could dry out, then they all leaned in to the fire themselves, allowed its warmth to touch their skin.

"You said we need to talk," said Helen. "How can we with Josie here? I don't think she knows…"

"Don't worry about me," said a voice, behind them. They jumped as Josie reappeared with a tray. "I know everything about what's been going on, our suspension, the parasite, those below."

Faith looked at her daughter. She did not look fazed or scared by their comments. If anything she appeared more confident and collected than she had done in a long time.

"How?"

"I didn't see Raymond," she said, as handed out mugs of tea. "But I glimpsed the parasite when… when I saw Linda being killed. I always thought it was my eyes playing tricks on me, shock or something like that. But Andrew explained it to me when you went with Howard. Told me how she came from the complex. You didn't know that, did you? Remember how she just appeared all those years ago. We thought she was a wanderer but she wasn't. She burrowed her way out, she said. Needed to breathe air."

Burrowed her way out. They had let her go?

That didn't seem likely.

"Trouble was, once she was above ground she couldn't adapt. Her agoraphobia was genuine after all those years below. She went a bit nuts. Well, you saw that, didn't you? We all did."

Faith was surprised at Josie's calmness, her almost detached manner as she related what Andrew had told her. It was a standard coping mechanism though. Close down your emotions, and you just might make it through.

"Faith," said Helen. "I know you want to sort this but we don't have time. We have to decide what we're going to say, what we want to do, for when we go to the meeting this afternoon."

"I know, I know," said Faith. Helen was right. There would be time to talk to Josie later. It wouldn't change anything that had happened whereas the question they were going to pose later to themselves as a community was going to change their lives. "What do we do then? What do you want to do?"

Ruth stared into the fire and began to speak. "I accused my mother of leaving us behind, of killing my children when it seems we weren't left behind and it was me who made the choice to live above ground. I brought my children with me and I condemned them. I think we need to reconsider how we treat those below, especially those who haven't been infected by the parasite."

"Are you so sure you brought them back up?"

asked Helen.

"You heard what Howard said, you saw the videos, the machines, the empty containers and our records."

"How can we be sure that wasn't him manipulating us?" asked Malik.

"I think we all need to just clear our heads a bit, try and remember those early days. See if there's anything, anything in our minds we can recall of back then."

They fell silent and Faith did her best to push Josie's revelations to the back of her mind. Compartmentalise. It was a trick she'd learned over the years. A coping mechanism. It took all of her will power however to do so now.

She leaned back in her chair and closed her eyes, sent her mind drifting back to those hazy moments at the founding of their community. Images of crowds pushed forward, sounds of shouts and screams, crying children. Josie? Where was Josie? Her daughter's hand in hers as they were swept along by the crowd. Out into the light.

Out? Where had they been? She pushed back again. Felt darkness enfold her, smelt something, it choked. She couldn't breathe, felt herself falling. Faith came to with a start, she'd been dozing, old nightmares infiltrating her mind.

"You okay, Mum?" asked Josie.

At least her daughter was concerned about her, still regarded her with some attachment.

"Yeah," said Faith. "Think I've finally realised those nightmares I used to have weren't bad dreams but memories."

"What did you remember?"

Faith described the scene, felt annoyed at the gaps which prevented her building a constructive image from the scenario.

Helen nodded her head. "Mine was like that too but I do remember something before. A meeting with the FutureProof HR. They were talking about families, how best to support them. Said they could help the whole family and not just a couple of members but we had to do something for them. I can't remember anything more than that though. Sorry. It just goes dark."

Faith pushed back against the wall of her memory, searched for the meeting Helen described but came up blank.

"I don't remember that either," said Malik. "I do remember being in a huge space though, there were hundreds of us there, names were being called out and we were being moved along. I went into a tunnel, it felt like it anyway. I could make out shapes of people ahead of me, like ghosts they drifted. I felt dizzy, then nothing. It's all a blank."

"We need to move back from the gathering. More to the time Helen describes. The meeting. What had we agreed to? Why did we agree to it?"

"Whichever way you look at it, the gaps don't matter too much. We know now we are partly responsible for our own situation. We can't blame everything on those below. We are culpable."

Faith didn't like to think that. It had been so much easier when she had been able to fixate on an idea, use it as a focus for all her pain and suffering, everything the community had gone through.

"We have to speak to Howard and Andrew again," said Malik. "And we have to let people go below to be scanned. We know the ways in, it shouldn't be difficult if he denies us but I doubt he will. After all, they want to come up."

"We swap places you mean?"

To do such a thing would've been beyond imagining. Now it seemed as though the impossible was becoming possible.

"We can't carry on as we have been doing," said Ruth.

"Or we could just move out," said Josie. "Find other communities."

"No," said Faith. "Not while we carry this thing inside us. We cannot risk harming anyone else."

"Why tell them?" asked Josie.

Her coldness shocked Faith.

They spent the remainder of their time trying in vain to dredge up earlier memories, covering the same ground again and again. It all pointed to the same answer. One way or another Howard would get his way and those who lived below would be able to return to the surface.

CHAPTER TWENTY-THREE

THE GATHERING place was crowded. A table had been set up near the front and Ed had taken a seat there, a ledger in front of him, slips of paper in a pile by Sylvie who sat at his side. Andrew had taken on the role of co-ordinator. It should've annoyed her, but Faith felt the old antipathy wash over her, the tiredness and heat assaulting her body in equal measure and she just wanted it to be over, to sleep. Let the others make the decision, she thought. She'd had enough.

It felt wrong to have such thoughts. What was going to be discussed would have far-reaching effects on people for the rest of their lives but she didn't care. Was this nature's way of ensuring the old gave way to the young, stripped them of their energy, the zest for life so others could carry the torch? She pushed herself forward suddenly, away from the back of the chair as a volcano ignited her back. She pulled her layers away from her skin and a chill crept over her, thankfully cooled her down a little and allowed her to relax once more. The heat in her face also subsided and she was able to refocus on proceedings.

"Welcome, everyone," began Andrew. "I understand how difficult today has been for you all. To finally discover at least a part of the truth of your survival. Although why it had to happen this way is still something you have yet to understand."

There was an interruption as a guard came in and handed a paper to Andrew. He in turn passed it to Ed who scanned what appeared to be a list and began to copy it into the book in front of him.

"Some of you, it seems," continued Andrew, "felt unable to wait for this afternoon's discussion to become aware of the possibility of hope for your own futures as well as those below. They have decided it would be better to opt out of this world altogether. They have given themselves to the Barricade."

Faith caught Ed's frown as he glanced up at Andrew. A look of suspicion that didn't bode well.

"Let us take a minute," said Andrew, "to remember all who have lost their lives. Those in the initial days of chaos, those above and below, and those in more recent times."

Everybody bowed their heads and silence washed through the building, broken only by the rustle and flap of loose coverings, the noise of the wind echoing through pipes as if crying with them. It was enough to quell the unsettled murmurings of the crowd which had greeted Faith on arrival. Josie sat to her left but looked straight ahead, did not react to Faith reaching out to squeeze her hand.

Then there was a stirring and a rise of the hubbub again. Some of Howard's men had reappeared carrying a small battery pack. Another fixed up a projector.

"Before we proceed with any discussion," said Andrew. "We felt it right to remind you of those early days, of what you agreed to do for the community. I think you will find it useful to make a fully informed decision about your own fate and the fate of those below."

"What's he playing at?" asked Ruth.

Faith shrugged her shoulders. She didn't know. Couldn't work up any of the old anger or indignation. Ruth looked at her curiously, evidently surprised by her once volatile friend's new lack of concern.

A video started to play across the screen. It was of a gathering, much like the one they were holding now, she even recognised a few of the people there. It looked like a mirror image of the crowd, albeit from an earlier time, they all looked a lot younger— and there were more of them.

A younger version of Andrew was speaking on the screen

"By now you will all know those who have been chosen to go below. We understand how those who have not been selected feel. If we could take everyone we would. But we know you understand that isn't physically possible. We do however have an option which we offer only another select few, those of you who now stand in front of me. Your partners, relatives and friends requested you be chosen if such a circumstance arose. They did not want to leave you behind, please be aware of that. You were not abandoned or betrayed. We, the government, had to draw the line but we did not pull up the drawbridge completely."

Not abandoned. Had not been betrayed? Yet neither Graham or Callum had said anything about that when she'd met them below.

"Well, we do have a circumstance which can help you but we must tell you the technology is in its infancy and it is not without risk."

The camera shook and people screamed as the sound of a blast erupted outside, accompanied by the rattle of gunfire. And Faith remembered. She remembered sitting in that earlier audience clutching Josie's hand, promising her it was going to be alright, that they hadn't been left behind after all. Graham had given their names to Andrew hadn't he?

"We have developed a facility which will allow humans to enter a state of hibernation. We can take all of you here if you wish and then, when conditions in the world around us have settled, we can wake you up and you can return to the world and rebuild your lives. At that point, I am hoping those families we have given rooms to in our underground ark will also be ready to return. You will be reunited with your loved ones."

"How will you do this?" asked someone at the front. Faith recognised the voice, it was Ed.

Another clip was shown, video within video. It showed a dark cavern lined with capsules and tanks. The camera zoomed over capsules, showed people, bodies inside. The tank was multiple occupancy. She wondered at this segregation. Their take on first class and economy class?

A capsule was wheeled in. It was attached to gas canisters, cables and wires tentacled behind. It was occupied. As technicians fiddled with valves, a timer was displayed on the door panel, counting down. As soon as it hit zero, a technician opened the door. At first the occupant didn't move, but then their eyes gradually opened. The person looked shocked as he took in those in front of him but visibly relaxed on seeing Andrew.

The technicians helped him out and he made his way slightly unsteadily to Andrew's side. They shook hands.

"It worked," said the man, his voice betraying surprise.

"Of course," said Andrew. "I said it would, didn't I?"

"So I get the money?"

"Already in your bank account."

A few laughed in the audience. Faith understood. The poor sod didn't realise money had lost its value. He'd been played. The technicians led him away.

"This subject has been in hibernation for one year. As you can see, he came out unharmed."

Andrew paused the video. "You all agreed," he said. "I didn't force you, no one did. You went into those tanks of your own volition."

He fast-forwarded the tape to show queues of people lining up to the entrance of the underground chamber. He zoomed in to pick out Faith and she watched as she led Josie by the hand into the capsule, relief and determination written over her face. She did not seem at all uncertain.

"Okay," said Faith, as Andrew stopped the video at last. "It seems we agreed to that bit. But what about how we ended up above ground. The parasite?"

"The support mechanisms to your chamber were compromised and we could not maintain you any longer. An unfortunate circumstance you will agree. We could not allow you to come into the main zone of the bunker, there were insufficient resources to maintain so many extra mouths. You had to go back up and so we released you."

"Together with our little friend."

"Yes," said Andrew. "We took a risk. We knew the air was barely breathable, nuclear and volcanic activity across the planet had destroyed the atmosphere's balance in many places. Remember you had been working on the nematodes, Faith? There was one whose genome could be engineered so it developed a harmless symbiosis with its host whilst supporting respiratory function?"

"Yes," she remembered. Tiny little worms beneath the microscope able to filter atmospheric gases and survive the most extreme environments. She had injected mice with these microscopic creatures and they had been able to survive in even the most polluted of atmospheres. "But they were tiny."

Andrew nodded. "Yes. What happened to you is an unfortunate example of adaptation and mutation. Seems the atmosphere causes them to become more than they originally were."

"But you introduced the worm to those below as well!"

Andrew turned to Helen. "We wanted to give everyone the best chance. The families would also have gone through the same treatment but we had discovered how the worm grew by that point and stopped."

"And yourselves?" Helen asked Andrew. "There are a number of you who weren't 'families'."

"Mere luck," said Andrew. "We were due to be conditioned, as we call it, but… well, let's just say the truth revealed itself in a rather gruesome fashion and we stopped it."

"Yeah, right," said Ed.

Andrew looked embarrassed. "I assure you, that's all it was."

Faith thought back to the numbers below. Not many were left. "What happened to the rest of them. All those empty rooms?"

"We let them go," said Andrew. "Some went a bit stir crazy and we thought it safer we let them above ground…"

"But we never saw them." Ruth.

Andrew shrugged. "It seems they stayed within the Barricade. They became the origins of your Burrower legend."

"But the numbers!"

"Those who came up first needed to… eat."

"Fuck."

"The stories were correct with regard to what happened to those who jumped. It seems such offerings were not enough however, so when others were released through the tunnels to return, they never found their way beyond the Barricade."

"Again," insisted Malik. "The numbers."

"Humans cannot eat their own kind without eventually succumbing to diseases of the brain. They went mad, would kill anything and anyone within reach, before the disease took them completely and they died."

Faith heard people sobbing behind her, fearful young voices asking their parents if they would go mad, parents reassuring their children with a fake confidence everyone could see through. They had not been abandoned. They had not been betrayed, at least not intentionally. The old adage 'They chose to go below, they cannot return', no longer applied.

She looked up at Andrew. "And with the planet apparently in recovery mode, those families who have been untouched by the parasite would be able to survive above ground now?"

"Yes."

Her grandchildren could live beneath the sky.

"Then we need to make things ready for them," she said.

Some voices murmured agreement, others reacted angrily, their fury at the recent revelations blinding them to consider any other alternative but punishing someone, anyone, for what they had gone through.

"You should be fucking strung up," said Ed, rising and turning on Andrew. Ed's cronies moved forward and stood behind him.

"Put me on trial? Of course you could do that," said Andrew. "But what would it achieve? We've all got to put our own personal feelings aside and consider what to do for our future's sake. Think of those of you who've still got relatives below. Don't you think you owe them that chance?"

"They deserve a chance," said Malik. "But I don't think you do. You may not be infected, but if we agree to go below, to switch places, which is what I think you have been aiming at, then you come with us. Infected or not. Howard can stay below as well. If you're really thinking of everyone else and not your own survival, let's see how much of a sacrifice you are prepared to make."

For the first time Andrew appeared lost for words. Malik had come forward with an idea Faith hadn't considered. It was a perfect revenge to sweeten what they would have to do. Murmurs of agreement backed Malik's comment.

"I think it's time we heard from everyone else," continued Malik. "It'll take a while I daresay but we've got our voice back and I think everyone deserves to be heard. We'll put down the proposals once everyone's spoken and take a vote. Everyone, man, woman and child, gets a say in this. It's only fair."

The sun, which had made so many welcome reappearances in the past few days, despite the cold, failed to show as they spoke, deepening the gloom. It was hiding its face, not wanting to be part of the horrific decisions being made below.

Every family, every person took to the stage and spoke. Nobody shouted or heckled, they all listened quietly even if they shook their heads to show disagreement. Some parents allowed their children to speak for them, small voices wobbling as they announced what they wished to do. Faith however, felt it a cynical ploy to use innocence and force those who held opposing views to feel guilty for doing so. When she was offered her turn to speak, she declined to do so.

"I've already made my decision regardless of what everyone else decides," she said. "I don't want to influence anyone else."

"But we might not agree with your decision, if you want to stay above ground—"

"Who says I'm staying?" she replied, taking the slip of paper Sylvie had handed to her. It was time to vote. She ignored Josie. Her daughter could make her own decision. She would not let herself be influenced by anyone else. She ticked the box for 'Go below/Let them return' then went to stand at the Barricade gate. She did not look behind her.

She looked through the small dirty windows and made out movement on the other side. The doors were opening and the bunker inhabitants came out into the clearing. They were carrying belongings, weapons. She could see Graham and Callum. A woman and two small children stood by her son. Her grandchildren. She recognised them all from the photo.

A cold wind started up, sent a shiver down her spine but she didn't wrap herself up against it, instead embraced its cold touch, its sharp purity now reclaimed in these reborn days. It would be the last time she felt it.

As the minutes passed, she heard footsteps behind her, felt a presence build up but didn't turn round, kept her face on the group seen through the glass. They were the true survivors and it had all been down to luck. She couldn't condemn them for that.

The press of bodies shifted and Malik came to stand one side of her, Josie the other.

"They counted the vote," he said, "but it wasn't necessary. Everyone's voted with their feet. Even Andrew's here, although not quite willingly. And we'll have to grab Howard and his cronies when we go in."

Faith nodded and the gate opened. They walked towards the small gathering in the compound, kept a space between them, so wary of contaminating each other, even now.

Callum stepped forward, there were tears in his eyes. "Mum, I..."

"Ssh," she said, as she had done when he was a child. "This time it's my decision. I choose this."

"Yeah, but..."

"No," said Faith. "We've been messing with our bodies, with nature, with the environment for long enough. It's time to start again but humanity needs a clean slate and unfortunately, at the moment, we can't offer that."

"You might find a way," said Graham.

She smiled. "I dare say Andrew will get to work on that straight away and I'll do everything I can to help. At least give the children here a fighting chance." This time she looked back at the children behind her and was rewarded with hopeful smiles. She had to give them something.

"We'll keep in proper contact, arrange meetings, help with food..."

"Go on," she urged her son, "take them out. My house is waiting for you. Perhaps one day we might even come and visit. And the farmers, don't go near them. Not until we can do something about the soil, eradicate the parasite."

Graham nodded and began to walk towards the gate now standing open for them. The rest of the bunker occupants followed him, faces pale, staring at the floor, unable to meet the eyes of those they passed. Until the sun suddenly burst through the clouds, a late afternoon blaze which shone upon the two groups. As one they all looked up and this time, Faith saw them release their burden of guilt and allow themselves a moment at least, of hope. They all had a future, they just had to find it.

Stephanie Ellis writes dark speculative prose and poetry. Her novels include The Five Turns of the Wheel, Reborn, and The Woodcutter, and the novellas, Bottled and Paused. Her short stories appear in the collections The Reckoning and Devil Kin. She is a Rhysling and Elgin Award nominated poet and has written the collection Foundlings (with Cindy O'Quinn), Lilith Rising (with Shane Douglas Keene) and a solo collection, Metallurgy, as well as appearing in the HWA Poetry Showcase. She can be found supporting indie authors at HorrorTree.com via the weekly Indie Bookshelf Releases.

Website: https: https://stephanieellis.org
bsky: stephellis.bsky.social

9 781645 620228